By George C. Chesbro

~~~ THE FEAR IN ~~~
YESTERDAY'S RINGS

GEORGE C. CHESBRO

THE MYSTERIOUS PRESS

New York · Tokyo · Sweden

Published by Warner Books

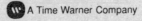 A Time Warner Company

MYSTERIOUS PRESS EDITION

Cover design and illustration by Tom McKeveney

The Mysterious Press name and logo are trademarks of Warner Books, Inc.

 Mysterious Press books are published by

Warner Books, Inc.
1271 Avenue of the Americas
New York, N.Y. 10020

 A Time Warner Company

Printed in the United States of America

Originally published in hardcover by The Mysterious Press.
First Mysterious Press Paperback Printing: April, 1992

10 9 8 7 6 5 4 3 2

For:

Mel Berger

Marsha Higgins

William Malloy

Lawrence McIntyre

Neil Nyren

Otto Penzler

Joan Sanger

Steven M. Weiss

and all the rest of Mongo's friends who've given him a leg up along the way . . .

CHAPTER ONE

Memories, some truly happy and others merely wearing the false grimaces of tired clowns, tumbled like acrobats in my mind as I stared at the old, crumbling circus posters laid out on the hospital gurney in a curtained-off cubicle at the rear of the emergency room in the Bellevue Medical Center. The posters' original garish colors had all faded to mud shades of brown, yellow, and green, but considering the fact that they were more than twenty years old, they were reasonably well preserved as a result of having been sealed in the plastic bag draped over one steel rail of the gurney. I doubted there were many posters of their vintage left in existence outside of a few art museums with specialized collections.

All of the posters advertised the Statler Brothers Circus. The largest was dominated by an illustration of a rather diminutive fellow riding triumphantly between roaring columns of fire on the back of a trumpeting elephant. Ringing this central illustration were smaller pictures, framed in ovals, featuring other performers and freaks, including a giant, a "crocodile man" with green, scaly skin, and a "snake woman" who was depicted unconcernedly chucking the chin of a monstrous, nasty-looking snake that was coiled around her body—which was only slightly less buxom in reality than it had been in the artist's fevered imagination.

The giant's name was Hugo Fasolt, and some years before he had died saving my life, using his great tree trunk of a body to absorb a hail of bullets meant for me. The "crocodile man" was now a real estate mogul and the best poker player I'd ever met, and the "snake woman" was someone I'd once loved. The elephant's name was Mabel, and she was one of the few African elephants ever to be successfully domesticated, if that was the word, and coaxed into circus performing; even on her best days, Mabel could be considerably more cranky and dangerously unpredictable than her mellower Asian cousins.

The little guy on top of the elephant, a star performer the poster identified in bold, black lettering as Mongo the Magnificent, was me.

"That's you, Mongo, right?"

I turned toward the intern who had spoken, a midnight-skinned Haitian by the name of Jacques Lauture, who also happened to be the third baseman on Frederickson and Frederickson's championship softball team. I grinned and nodded somewhat shamefacedly. "Right. It's none other than yours truly, in his callow youth."

"*Damn,*" Jacques said, shaking his head as he stared at the poster, obviously impressed. "Did you really ride an elephant, jump through rings of fire, and all that?"

"Jumping through rings of fire was the easy part; riding that damn elephant was something else again. In fact, I was the only person who could ride her. Her name's Mabel, and she's African. See the big ears? Most of the elephants you see in circuses are Asian. African elephants are bigger and meaner, and they don't take kindly to either captivity or people. She was a baby and sick when we got her; my boss had taken her off the hands of a sleazeball carnival owner who'd been mistreating her. For some reason, she took a shine to me."

"Wild," Jacques said, still shaking his head. "Everybody knows you used to be in the circus, but I never realized you rode elephants and did all that other stuff. Jesus, you were a star from the looks of this poster. I always figured . . ." His voice trailed off as he stepped closer to the gurney. He placed his index finger on the face of the crocodile man and shrugged. "You know what I mean," he finished weakly.

"You thought I worked as a freak?"

"No offense, Mongo," Jacques said quickly, looking at me strangely.

"No offense taken, Jacques. It would be a natural assumption. Sideshows used to be known as 'dwarf heaven.'"

"Hey, I'd never call anybody a freak."

"As a matter of fact, the people in the sideshows prefer to be called freaks; it's what they call themselves, and they don't consider the term derogatory. They think of themselves as business people, entrepreneurs exploiting the only assets they have. Some of them are pretty shrewd. The last I heard, that guy with the green skin and scales you just had your finger on was married to a former Miss Georgia and owned a string of upscale motels across the South. He's worth millions."

Jacques grunted softly. "How'd you manage to, uh, get where you got?"

"On top of Mabel, in the center of the poster?" I paused and laughed at the memories, which were beginning to lose some of their sharp edges under the gentle buffing of Jacques's open, honest curiosity and naive awe. I felt a twinge of nostalgia and found myself more willing than usual to talk about my circus days.

"Garth and I grew up on a farm in Nebraska," I continued somewhat distantly as I gently stroked one of the fragile posters with the back of my hand and smiled grimly. "Nebraska's a whole different planet, my friend, and I was the resident alien. In your small farming communities in the Midwest, ninety percent of the social activity and talk centers on high school sports, especially football and basketball. Garth was a star in both sports. I desperately wanted to belong, to be able to compete at something, but it's hard to find a football or basketball team that has much use for a sixty-eight-pound dwarf. So I had to find something else to do.

"I'd always had excellent coordination and above-average upper-body strength. I'm an achondroplastic dwarf, and those

3

skills sometimes go with the territory. I'd been doing somersaults and cartwheels just about from the time I could walk. I was a pretty good gymnast even in elementary school—I'd taught myself by watching sports programs on television. Hell, tumbling was something *I* could do better than anyone else in school, and I worked at it every chance I got.

"Anyway, our high school had a gymnastics team—of sorts; it worked out on prehistoric equipment in a storage area next to the boiler room, since the gym was always being used by the basketball team." I paused to execute the obligatory self-deprecating mock bow, continued, "Well, yours truly made the varsity team when I was in seventh grade, and by the time I graduated from high school our team was nationally ranked. People came from all over to see our meets—actually, to see me, if I may dispense with false modesty. I was a three-time High School All-American, and our team won the high school nationals when I was a senior. It damn well should have gotten me a scholarship to a school with a world-class gymnastics program, but it didn't. Representatives from all the schools with top gymnastics programs came to see me, admitted I did things no other high school student could do, but then said they didn't think I'd be able to compete successfully at a college level. Of course, that was bullshit. What they really meant was that they were afraid people would laugh at them if they had a dwarf on their team; to *them* I was a freak, and they were afraid their meets would be seen as freak shows if I was on the team. Well, the fact that I'd been born a dwarf in the first place tended to make me feel just a bit disgruntled from the time when I first realized I was different from other kids, and now the fact that all of my athletic accomplishments were being written off and I was being denied a scholarship because I was a dwarf *really* pissed me off.

"Big brother Garth had graduated two years ahead of me. He was in an excellent college, and I knew it was costing my parents a pot of money to send him there. Now my folks wanted me to go on to school. There was never any mention of money, but I knew they'd have to take a heavy mortgage on the old homestead to do it. I didn't want that, especially since I was still plenty pissed about being the best high school gymnast in the country and being denied a scholarship.

"That summer the Statler Brothers Circus rolled into Peru County, Nebraska, for the first time. It gave me a perverse notion. I hung out there from dawn to dusk for days in a row, checking out their aerialists and gymnasts. I'd never been on a trapeze, swing pole or teeterboard, but I knew that I could control my body in the air. They had routines, glitzy costumes, and acting flair, and they were all good, of course, but I judged that my basic acrobatic skills were as good as or better than those of the people I saw earning their livings under that circus tent. That's where I wanted to work—but if I wanted a job with the circus, I was damn well going to have to find a dramatic way to show whoever owned or managed that circus that I had the goods, and I didn't have a lot of time to do it. The circus was leaving town the next day.

"I went home and took one of my father's old straight razors. I sharpened it up, then lashed it to the end of a clothes pole that was about twice as tall as I was that I'd sharpened to a point at the other end. Then I went to see the owner of the circus. His name was Phil Statler, and his 'office' was the cab of one of the flatbed semis they used to haul the circus around the country. Phil Statler was a tough man, Jacques, with a whiskey voice like a buzz saw, but at the same time he was one of the kindest men I've ever known. Here he was faced with a smart-ass seventeen-year-old dwarf who said he wanted to be a circus acrobat, and the man never blinked an eye, never even smiled. He just told me to show him what I could do. I'm sure he thought he was only humoring me, but he had the courtesy and sensitivity not to show it. The man took me *seriously*, which was what I needed most at that time in my life, and it was enough to make me love him on the spot.

"We went out to a patch of dirt behind where they'd pitched the main tent, and I stuck my clothes pole in the ground with the straight razor at the other end three or four feet above my head. Then I asked him to tie my hands in front of me. By this time I could see that I was making him a bit nervous, but he went ahead and did as I asked.

"I hadn't practiced the trick I intended to do, because I couldn't afford a mistake. If I slashed a wrist practicing, the circus would be long gone by the time it healed, and I didn't even want

5

to think about what my father would have to say. So this was the first time I'd tried a stunt I'd only *thought* of the day before; it was one all-or-nothing performance. I paced off about twenty-five yards, then went into a running and tumbling routine, gaining as much speed and momentum as I could as I approached the pole and the razor. At the last moment I threw what I knew had to be the highest backflip I'd ever done, straightened out in the air as I passed over the pole so that I could scrape the rope around my wrists against the razor." I paused, shrugged. "It took me three passes, but damned if I didn't finally manage to cut through the rope around my wrists with no more damage than a nick on my left thumb that a Band-Aid took care of. Phil offered me a contract on the spot—provided I agreed to let the pros in the circus help me work up a safer routine, and that my parents gave their permission. It was the last point that worried me.

"My folks were not exactly pleased when they found out about my little performance with my dad's straight razor, and they were shocked and more than a little disappointed when they found out I wanted to join the circus. But they also realized that, considering the fact that I'd risked my life to make my point, it was important to me. Phil promised to look after me as if I were his own son, I promised to continue my education during the off-season, and my folks checked off on the deal. Phil did treat me like his own son, and I did use my earnings to go to college during the off-season. I went on to improve my acrobatic skills, and I eventually became a headliner. Phil considered me somewhat otherworldly, so I was given the performance name 'Mongo' after a small planet in the Flash Gordon series." I paused, smiled wryly, shrugged again. "I was billed as 'Mongo the Magnificent' because I was, after all, absolutely magnificent. End of story."

Jacques stared at me for a few moments. He seemed mildly disappointed. "Yeah, Mongo," he said at last, "but what about the elephant? The story about you and the razor is pretty cool, but how did you learn to ride the elephant?"

I resisted the impulse to roll my eyes toward the ceiling, breathed a small sigh. "Jacques, you really want to hear about the elephant, don't you?"

The Haitian nodded eagerly. "Yeah. I like elephants."

"Well, my friend, how I learned to ride that elephant is another long story, and I'll tell it to you some other time. Where on earth did you get these posters? Statler Brothers Circus isn't exactly Ringling Brothers, Barnum & Bailey, and I wouldn't think there are too many of these old handbills left around."

Jacques frowned slightly. "Didn't I tell you over the phone?"

"No. You just asked if I could drop around for a few minutes because there was something you wanted to show me."

"They're not mine, Mongo," the intern said in a low voice. "These are the only things we found on this old derelict they brought in off the street last night; he didn't have a penny in his pockets, not even a rag to blow his nose in. There were just these old posters. He kept them in that plastic refrigerator bag you see there, taped to his belly; whatever happened to everything else he owned, he managed to hang on to these. They must be very important to him. I figured maybe he had something to do with that circus, and when I saw your name all over them I figured maybe you knew him. From the looks of the old guy, he could sure use a friend."

•   •   •

At first I didn't recognize the emaciated old man lying asleep or unconscious on the hospital gurney with tubes up his nose and needles in his arms. The ward to which he had been assigned was already filled to overflowing, and his rolling bed had been pushed back against a wall in the corridor. Even in the noisy, crowded hallway, his raspy breathing was clearly audible, and it sounded all too much to me like a death rattle. When I did recognize him, I groaned, then felt tears come to my eyes. When I reached out and touched his arm, his loose, liver-spotted skin felt like cold parchment.

"Mongo?" Jacques said in alarm as he stepped up beside me. "What's the matter?"

"It's Phil Statler," I replied, choking back a sob.

"Oh, Jesus. The guy you were telling me about, the guy who hired you for his circus."

I wiped tears from my eyes, nodded. I hadn't seen Phil Statler in more than a decade, when he'd appeared in my office to hire me to find a strongman who'd skipped out on his contract with the circus. It was a case that had eventually involved me with the Iranian Shah's secret police, almost cost me the love of my brother, and then nearly cost both Garth and me our lives. I estimated that Phil would be in his mid-sixties now, but he looked closer to eighty lying between hospital sheets that were only a shade or two whiter than his flesh. His eyes were a very pale blue, watery, his face mottled and florid, marbled with alcohol-ruptured veins, his rotting teeth uneven and tobacco-stained. His hair, still black when I had last seen him, was now all gray, the color of his grizzled beard.

He looked terribly out of place away from his circus.

"What's wrong with him, Jacques?" I asked quietly.

"Oh, man, he's got a bagful of health problems—but he's not as bad as some I've seen. He's a derelict; we get a lot of them in here, especially during the winter."

"This is July, Jacques."

The intern shrugged. "When they're found unconscious on the street, dying like this one is, the cops bring them here no matter what the season. There are always guys like your friend here who just won't go to a shelter or accept any other kind of help."

"How do you know he wasn't in a shelter?"

Jacques looked at me, sadness swimming in his ebon eyes. "He's missing a few fingers and toes: gangrene brought on by frostbite. It's what happens when they won't go inside when it drops below freezing. The amputation scars aren't that fresh. He didn't lose the digits this last winter, so it means he's been living on the streets through at least one winter before the last. Right now he's suffering from heat exhaustion, pneumonia from the sound of him, and a host of parasitic infections. That's just for openers; he hasn't had a complete examination yet. He could have tuberculosis; a lot of them do."

"Where was he found?" I asked in a voice that had suddenly grown hoarse.

Again, Jacques shrugged. "I don't know; just on some street, or in some alley, or maybe Central Park. A couple of young cops brought him in."

"I don't understand how he could have . . ." I paused when my voice broke, swallowed hard, continued, "God, we haven't

8

been in touch for years, but he knows I live in New York. He could have looked up my number in the phone directory. I don't understand why he didn't call me if he needed help."

"It's a waste of time blaming yourself in any way for what's happened to this man, Mongo," Jacques said evenly, watching my face. "A lot of the hard-core homeless refuse any kind of help, and I'd put your friend in that category from the looks of him. They get crazy on the streets, or maybe they ended up on the streets because they were crazy in the first place. Maybe he didn't call you because of pride, or maybe he didn't—doesn't—even remember who you are."

I wondered. Phil Statler might not remember me in his present condition, but he certainly had at some point during the hellish roller-coaster ride that had left him living on the streets of New York City, a simple phone call away from food, a bed, shelter, medical attention. Love. The fact that he hadn't called on me for help somehow made me feel ashamed, as if—despite Jacques's assurance—this lack of action was somehow my fault. And maybe it was, at least in some small way. Phil Statler had always been an intensely proud man, fiercely independent. And beneath his gruff exterior had been a man of unparalleled generosity and compassion. It had been his pleasure to help other people, particularly "freaks"—yes, like me—for whom the Statler Brothers Circus was a home where we could earn a living and live and love with dignity. But something had happened to Phil Statler or his circus, really the same thing. He'd lost his circus, and with it his livelihood, his dignity, and finally his health. This man who had helped so many others had been unable, unwilling, to ask for help himself. He had been like a father to me, and I knew I had been wrong to lose touch with him.

"Jacques," I said, drawing myself up and taking a deep breath, "I want this man transferred to the first private or semiprivate room that becomes available; I want him out of this corridor, off this ward. I also want the best specialists available to take care of him. I'll cover all the expenses. Who do I see to make the arrangements?"

Jacques grunted. "The cashier downstairs, man. What you want is going to cost you some shekels."

"It doesn't matter. When he's well enough to leave here, I want him moved to my place. With Garth married and living up in Cairn, his apartment in the brownstone is empty. When it's time to move him, I'd appreciate a recommendation from you for a private nursing service."

"You got it, Mongo," the Haitian said quietly. "You really love this man, don't you?"

I nodded. "I guess I never realized just how much until I saw him lying here."

"You make the financial arrangements downstairs, and as soon as I get the okay I'll take care of things up here. I'll keep an eye on your friend, man. Leave it to me. Don't worry. And I'll get word to you as soon as he comes around."

"Thanks, Jacques," I mumbled, then turned and headed back down the corridor as tears once again began streaming from my eyes.

CHAPTER TWO

Phil regained consciousness a day later, but he wasn't talking—not to his doctors, not to Jacques, and not to me. The first time I walked into his room his recognition of me was clearly reflected in his pale blue, watery eyes, but then he quickly averted his gaze and wouldn't look at me again. It was the same the next day, and the day after that.

They released him from the hospital on the sixth day, into my care. The doctors had cleared up his pneumonia and a half dozen other infections on and inside his body with antibiotics, but he was still very weak. They estimated he would need a minimum of two or three weeks of rest before he would be strong enough to be on his own—presumably to return to his life on the streets. I was strongly advised to keep him away from booze. I'd contracted with a private nursing service for Phil's at-home care, and I had him transported by private ambulance from the hospital to my brownstone on West Fifty-sixth Street, where I put him to bed in Garth's apartment on the third floor.

He still hadn't spoken, and he still wouldn't meet my gaze.

Fearing that brain damage, Alzheimer's, or some other condition had robbed him of reason or speech, I checked once again

11

with the doctors and was told once again what I had been told before—brain scans had indicated no organic damage, and there was nothing to indicate his mental faculties and vocal cords were not intact. Their suspicion was that Phil's muteness was caused by the same bone-deep depression that might have prompted him to take to the streets in the first place. Antidepressant drugs were contraindicated for the present time because of the other medications which had been administered to him.

And so I was just going to have to wait. Each day I popped up at frequent intervals from the offices downstairs to check with the nurse on duty to see how Phil was doing. I'd sit next to his bed and talk about anything that came to mind, but he would always turn his head away and remain silent. The plastic bag containing the circus posters I'd returned to him lay unopened on the night table next to his bed. I'd anticipated—dreaded—having him ask for a drink, but he didn't even do that.

On Thursday, four days after I'd brought my former boss home, I was in my office working on a report for a corporate client when the day nurse stuck his head in the door.

"Dr. Frederickson, I think you'd better go upstairs to see Mr. Statler. He just told me I was fired."

I paid the nurse for the rest of his shift, then bounded up the stairs to the third floor, fearing that the reason for Phil's sudden burst of animation was that he'd caught a glimpse of the well-stocked bar in the living room of the apartment. But Phil wasn't at the bar. I found him sitting up on the edge of the bed; he'd found the clothes I'd bought for him. He'd managed to pull on a pair of corduroy pants and was trying, with badly trembling fingers, to take the pins from a new shirt.

"I can't afford nurses," he said in a low, hoarse voice as I entered the room and approached the bed. He didn't look up but simply kept talking very rapidly, occasionally shaking his head from side to side for emphasis. "I can't afford that private room you put me in at the hospital, and I can't afford those fancy doctors you sent around. I wanted to walk out of there, but I was just too goddamned weak. If you think Phil Statler needs the goddamned dwarf he plucked off a farm in Nebraska to take care of him in his dotage, you've got another think coming. I don't know how right now, but I'm going to pay you back every goddamned cent you've spent on me."

It was the terribly injured pride of a terribly proud man speaking. I just let it go on. When he paused for breath, I stepped close to him, wrapped my arms around his neck, and hugged him to me.

"Oh, God, Mongo," he sobbed into my chest, encircling my waist with his arms. "I'm so ashamed to have you see me like this."

"Be quiet, Phil," I said softly, rocking him back and forth like a child. "Finish putting your clothes on, and I'll show you around the offices of Frederickson and Frederickson. Even though my brother's my partner, I insisted on having my name listed first."

•   •   •

"Where's your big brother?" Phil asked in a slightly less hoarse voice as he sipped his third cup of coffee.

We were sitting at Garth's kitchen table, close to a window where the sound of heavy rain splattering against the glass almost drowned out his weak voice. I judged that Phil was at least forty pounds lighter than when I'd last seen him, and Garth's bathrobe hung around his now-frail body like a shroud. My former boss was going to need a lot of tender loving care, some fattening up, and something else I had no idea how to give him.

"He got married, and he's happy as a clam in a mud bank. He married a woman by the name of Mary Tree. They're living in her place, in a town called Cairn; it's about fifty miles north of here, on the Hudson. He quit the force a few years back and came into partnership with me."

"Mary Tree the folk singer?"

"That's her."

"Antiwar activist? Pacifist?"

"Ex-pacifist."

"Good-looking woman."

"You've got that right."

Phil sipped at his coffee, holding the cup with two trembling hands. Then he set the cup down, stared into its depths. "I lost the circus about two and a half years ago, Mongo," he said to the cup. "After that I lost myself; things just kind of got out of control. Now it's all sort of an alcohol blur to me."

"You don't have to talk about it, Phil," I said quietly. "You don't owe me any explanations."

"I want to explain."

"If it'll make you feel better, go ahead. But, like I said, you don't owe me anything."

Now he glanced up from his coffee cup, and his pale blue eyes glinted with what might have been anger. It was the strongest hint of any feeling but depression I'd seen in him yet, and I decided it was a healthy sign. "I appreciate what you've done—what you're doing—for me, Mongo. The kindness you've shown to me is the kind of debt a man can't repay, but I'm telling you that I'm going to find a way to pay back every penny you've spent on me."

"Sure," I said evenly.

He stiffened. "You don't think I mean it? You don't think I can work and pay you back?"

"Of course you can."

"Then don't 'sure' me like that. I'm no welfare case. I may have lived on the streets and eaten out of garbage cans, but nobody ever had to support me. There's no way you could know this, but this is the longest I've been sober in a lot of years. I don't even want a drink. The reason I don't want a drink is that the minute I woke up in the hospital and saw you, I knew you'd been taking care of me. I'm too used to having people depend on me, Mongo, and I can't stand to be dependent on anyone; I'd rather starve or freeze to death. When I realized what you'd done, I knew I was going to have to find a way to earn enough money to pay you back. That's more important to me than booze."

Phil Statler, I could see, was going to be a problem; there's nothing more difficult to nurse than someone else's wounded pride. "Phil, you mentioned kindness, and how difficult it can be to repay. Well, think of all the kindness you showed to me, the skills you nurtured in me, and then the fame and fortune that those skills brought me. But the greatest gift you gave a certain defiant, defensive, and decidedly self-conscious young dwarf was an opportunity to live with dignity and self-respect. I wouldn't be where I am now, Phil, and I certainly wouldn't be anywhere near as comfortable with myself as I am, if not for you. As far as I'm concerned, this is at most simply payback time."

Phil sighed, once again looked down at his coffee cup. "I appreciate it more than I can ever say, Mongo," he murmured.

"I'm well aware of that, Phil. No problem."

"And I'm going to find a way to pay you back."

"Whatever you say, Phil. In the meantime, I'd take it as a personal favor if you'd think of this place as your home. It's a big house, as you can see, and I've been kind of clanking around in it since Garth moved out. I'd like you to keep me company, at least until you get your strength back and your plans in order. When it comes time to reimburse me for medical expenses, or whatever, I'll give you an itemized bill, if it'll make you happy. I'll always think of you not only as my mentor but as a second father. Now I'm asking you to let me be your friend. Please accept my help, Phil, until you're back on your feet."

He looked up, opened his mouth to speak, then closed it again when tears welled in his eyes. He nodded, then rose and retrieved the coffee pot from the warmer on the stove. He refilled both of our cups, then sat down again. "What do you know about the circus business these days, Mongo?"

"Well, there's the Big Apple Circus, and Ringling Brothers, Barnum and Bailey still comes into Madison Square Garden for a few weeks every year. Aside from that, I don't know much. To tell you the truth, I always had mixed feelings about being in the circus. Despite the fact that you'd made me a headliner, I still felt that being in a circus was somehow just too *common* for a dwarf."

Phil shook his head impatiently. "I don't understand what the hell you're talking about."

"People *expect* to find dwarfs in a circus; it's like going to see *The Wizard of Oz*."

"I still don't understand what the hell you're talking about."

"It doesn't matter."

"It's the same as I could never understand why you quit the circus to take a job as a college professor after you got that doctor's degree. You were at the top when you quit, and I know you were making a hell of a lot more money than you were ever going to make as a professor. Hell, the world has college professors up the ass, but there aren't a whole hell of a lot of circus performers who could do the stuff you did."

"There weren't—aren't—that many dwarf college professors. There are a hell of a lot fewer dwarf college professors than there are circus performers."

He stared at me for some time, and I could see pale shadows move in his pale eyes as he struggled to understand. "Ah," he said at last, raising his gray eyebrows slightly. "You mean it's the same thing as saying there aren't a whole hell of a lot of dwarf private investigators?"

"Now you've got it."

He shook his head slightly, brushed a strand of gray hair back from his eyes. "You're a pisser, Mongo. Always were."

I grinned. "Garth always says I have a tendency to overcompensate. But it all started with you."

"Yeah, well, I guess maybe you got out at the right time—even if you did just about break poor Mabel's heart and leave me with an elephant nearly nobody else could handle. The days of the real Big Top were about over, and everybody knew it but me. Ringling had already started developing into the mechanized arena show it is now, and it wasn't long before the Cole and Clyde Beatty people started going down the same road, booking up all the largest indoor arenas along their routes and cutting back on everything that wouldn't fit into one ring inside some goddamn armory.

"At first I was delighted to see Cole and Clyde Beatty going that way. Hell, our circuits had always overlapped, and we'd always been fighting tooth and claw to be at the top of the second-tier circuses, behind Ringling. Now, the way I had it figured, my competition had written themselves off by going into the indoor arenas. Statler Brothers Circus was the only genuine Big Top left in the whole goddamn country, not counting the little mud shows, and I couldn't imagine that parents and their kids would be content to sit inside some air-conditioned warehouse for two or three hours to watch what amounted to a vaudeville show when they could spend a day at a real circus, in real tents pitched in a field where they could wander around the midway or through the sideshows as long as they wanted, and then go inside a *real* Big Top to watch a *real* circus."

"And you were wrong," I said quietly.

The old man grunted, took another sip of coffee, said: "Yeah, I was wrong. I still don't understand it, Mongo. I kept doing everything the way I had been doing it, the way I'd been taught by my father and uncles. I got the best performers I could find and paid them well, kept a large stable of good animals and kept them in peak condition. I had the most interesting freaks, I made sure that the food at all the concessions was quality stuff, and I made damn sure that none of the carny barkers ripped off the rubes. But attendance just kept dropping off. Each year it got worse. I tried upping the advertising budget, but that was like pouring money down a rat hole. Toward the end we'd be playing matinees outside some town and we'd get maybe fifty people inside the tent. And damned if the other shows weren't packing people into the indoor arenas."

"There may be no place left in this country for real circuses anymore, Phil," I said evenly. "People just don't have the time, or maybe the patience, to spend walking around circus grounds. They're not interested in watching animals being fed. They want packaging, shows they know will start and end at a certain time; they want to be able to get reserved seats, and they want to be comfortable. Once you saw that you weren't getting the people to come out anymore, why didn't you follow along after the other big players and book indoor arenas?"

He shrugged. "Even if I'd wanted to, by that time it was too late. The other shows were already in place in the arenas, and they had exclusive contracts—as far as circuses were concerned—with all the best sites. Besides, it would have meant cutting loose the freaks and getting rid of more than half the animals."

"And you wouldn't cut back on operations."

Phil glanced at me sharply, smiled without humor. "Cut back on operations? Is that what you'd call it, Mongo?"

"Phil, I know—"

"What was I supposed to do with people like Roger, Harry, and Lisa? Give them a pink slip? Where were they going to find work? Some of those freaks had been with me since they were teenagers, just like you; they weren't just employees, they were family. You know freaks can't just go out and find some other job. I wouldn't go on welfare myself, and I wasn't going to put any of my family on welfare; cutting them loose would have meant just that for a lot of them. And what about the animals? Zoos don't like circus animals, even when they have room for them, because circus animals don't do well in zoos. Hell, put Mabel in a zoo, and she'd end up killing some keeper. Sell them off cheap to some mud show or carny operator? I'd rather shoot them myself and save them the misery. We took in Mabel from a carny man, Mongo, remember? You remember what kind of shape she was in?"

"I remember, Phil. So the bottom line was that you couldn't bring yourself to lay off anyone, or cut loose a single animal, if you weren't sure they'd be well taken care of. But there was no other place for them, as you saw it, so you had no choice but to try and keep going."

"That's right; I had to try and keep going. It was a bust, but I don't regret it even now. I'm a *circus* man, Mongo. I don't know anything else—and, to me, those shows you see sitting in a steel shed in the middle of some goddamn city aren't really circuses. I sank everything I'd saved over the years into the circus to try to keep it together. It took everything I had. Then I started losing my best acts, because I no longer had the money to pay them what they could get elsewhere—with Cole, Clyde Beatty, or Ringling. Finally, in the last couple of years, we became just another mud show, although I hated to admit it."

"Some mud show," I said, and sighed. "It had to be the only mud show with a full complement of freaks, a herd of animals no other show would take, and enough acts to fill three rings."

He spent a few minutes idly stirring the ounce or so of coffee left in his cup, finally said: "I'd always been a pretty hard driver, Mongo, as I'm sure you recall, and a heavy drinker. Now, when the troubles began coming down, I really started hitting the sauce. It was the only way I could find to fight the worry and the pain. I couldn't stand to see what was happening to the circus, or think about what was going to happen to my people and animals if it folded. I ended up drunk most of the time. Toward the end I got an offer from somebody to buy it. It was a good offer—more, really, than the circus was worth. But the buyer wouldn't agree to keep all the freaks. I was told they had no interest in sideshows and that they'd bring in all their own acts.

All they wanted from me was the equipment, the animals, and the rights to our permits around the circuit we did."

"Who made the offer?"

"The guy I talked to was some tight-ass lawyer type in a pinstripe suit who wouldn't tell me the name of the buyer. I was drunk at the time. I think I cursed him out when he said the freaks and performers couldn't be part of the deal. I told him I wouldn't help kill my own circus, and I threw him out.

"By then, I'd run out of operating expenses. We were just outside of Chicago, so I drove in and managed to get a bank loan, with the semis and all the rigging as collateral. That was a stupid play, I suppose, but I didn't know what else to do. I was hoping it could still be like it used to be and that there'd be throngs of people waiting for us in the next town. What I got instead was a notice from the bank that I was in default on the loan and that the circus had been auctioned off. Christ, I can't blame them; I was so drunk all the time that I'd missed five payments and hadn't even known it. The next thing I knew there were marshals on the grounds ordering everyone off. I think whoever had wanted to buy it in the first place had managed to pick it up at the auction, because the only things the new owner or owners wanted were the semis, the rigging, and the animals."

"Did you ever find out who bought it?"

"No."

"Didn't you ask the bank?"

"They wouldn't tell me; they said it was confidential information. I was too drunk to argue."

"Maybe it was Cole, or Clyde Beatty, or even Ringling; one of the big boys trying to gobble up the competition."

Phil shook his head. "No. I checked. I swear I'd have killed somebody if I'd found it was circus people I knew who'd taken my show away from me." He paused, swallowed hard, continued, "After the marshals threw me out of my own circus, I just walked away. Right now I don't even recall where I walked to. As far as I was concerned, my life was over; I'd lost everything. I had no money, no place to go, and I just wanted to die. I can't even remember how I eventually ended up here, in New York. I ate at soup kitchens as long as they'd let me wash dishes to pay for it, and I collected soda cans off the street and out of garbage cans to pay for my booze. I was busy drinking myself to death, and I guess I was pretty close to succeeding until you had to come along and butt your nose into my business. Now I owe you, and I always do my best to pay my debts. I don't even dare take a drink until I manage to pay you back."

"Well, if you only plan to stay alive and off the booze long enough to pay me back, you're going to find from my itemized bill that private hospital rooms and private nursing care in New York City are very expensive commodities. So you'd better plan on staying around a long time. But let's stop talking nonsense. There's something else I want to ask you, because something about this business strikes me as curious. By your own account, you were running an operation that couldn't even pay its way as a mud show. And even if you had dropped the sideshows and cut back on everything else, you'd still have been left out in the cold because the other shows had exclusive contracts with all the big indoor arenas on the circuit. Right?"

"Right."

"Even at the bargain-basement price the circus must have gone for at the bank auction, who would want it?"

"Beats me, Mongo."

"And then the new owner gets rid of all the performers and only keeps the animals. Christ, Mabel alone eats nearly a ton of hay a day, and that can get expensive. Buying that circus in the first place, and then keeping only the animals, doesn't seem to make any business sense at all. If people aren't going to come out to see a full-rigged circus, I doubt they'd come in any numbers to see a traveling zoo."

Phil merely shrugged and shook his head sadly.

"What's the name of the bank in Chicago that gave you the loan on the semis and rigging?"

"Hell, I don't remember. Why?"

"Just curious. Think, Phil. What's the name of the bank?"

He cocked his head to one side as he pondered the question, idly drumming his fingers on the tabletop. "I think it was an outfit called United States Savings and Loan," he said at last.

"Are you sure?"

"Yeah. Why the curiosity about the bank?"

"Let's just say that I want to know what bank not to do business with in Chicago."

•   •   •

"Now, my friends, I've got good news, and I've got bad news."

Garth froze with his brandy halfway to his mouth, then slowly set the snifter back down on the linen tablecloth. He brushed a heavily muscled hand back through his thinning, shoulder-length, wheat-colored hair, then turned to his wife. "What did I tell you, Mary? There's no way Mongo was going to invite us into the city and spring for dinner at Café des Artistes unless he wanted something from us. I've seen some very nasty situations spring up from Mongo's 'good news, bad news' crap."

Our table had been attracting attention all evening, and for once it wasn't the dwarf that people were staring at. Mrs. Garth Frederickson was Mary Tree, and she came complete with a stunning figure and presence, piercing blue eyes, sculpted features, and a magnificent, flowing crown of thick, white-streaked blond hair. Mary had first burst onto the music scene and into the national conscience and consciousness in the sixties, when she was a teenage, barefoot, flowers-in-her-hair folk singer and antiwar activist. And she had always been Garth's dream-lover, his idea of the perfect woman. I'd met her the year before, while I was investigating the death of a friend, and Garth had met her through me. Mary's career had declined in the seventies and been virtually eclipsed by the early eighties. But a small record company in New York had released a new album of hers at just about the time she and Garth were getting married, and it had turned out to be a crossover success, revitalizing her career. The album had put her back on top, and she was once again the "queen of folk." And so people stared. It tended to annoy my brother, but Mary had the grace to pretend that she didn't notice. Now she laughed lightly, touched Garth's arm.

"Now, now, darling, be nice to your brother. Remember that if it wasn't for him, we never would have met."

Garth heaved a mock, heavy sigh, looked back at me. "My wife says I should be nice to you, Mongo, despite my distinct sense of foreboding." He paused to lift his crystal snifter and drain off his

21

brandy, smacked his lips. "Give us the bad news first so we can get it out of the way."

"I've got a problem. You remember Phil Statler?"

"Sure; the circus owner, your ex-boss." He turned again to Mary, smiled thinly, continued, "Phil Statler is the man who transformed grungy, plain old Robert Frederickson into Mongo the Magnificent."

"He's sick, Garth. As a matter of fact, I'm putting him up in your apartment in the brownstone. Right now, I've got Jacques baby-sitting him."

Garth frowned slightly. "What's the matter with him?"

"The doctors would cite alcoholism and the effects of living on the streets and eating garbage for a couple of years, but I'd say he's dying of a broken heart. He lost the circus because he couldn't bear to put people, freaks especially, out of work, and he went right down the tubes. The cops picked him up off the streets and took him to Bellevue, which is where I found him; Jacques found some circus posters with my name on them, and he called me."

Mary made a small, sad sound in her throat, shook her head, and looked away.

Garth said, "That's heavy, Mongo. The man must be close to seventy now. Can't Social Services do something for him?"

"He's too proud to accept any kind of help. Besides, I believe the real problem is that he's lost the will to live; he *wants* to die. He as much as told me that the only reason he's not back out on the streets right now boozing it up is that he feels an obligation to stay sober and get well long enough so that he can get a job and earn enough money to pay me back for his hospital bills. I'm not sure how much longer I can keep him around the brownstone."

Mary reached across the table, took my hand in hers, and squeezed it. "That's terrible, Mongo," she said softly. "How can Garth and I help?"

"I'm getting to that, Mary. But first Garth has to ask me about the good news."

"I don't feel much like joking around anymore, Mongo," Garth said evenly. "I know something about how the street people suffer, and I know how much you love that man. Just tell us how we can help."

"Not so fast. I insist you ask me about the good news."

Mary started to say something, but Garth silenced her by putting a finger to his lips. Without change of expression or tone, he asked, "What's the good news, Mongo?"

I glanced back and forth between my brother and Mary, smiled wryly. "If Phil's basic problem is that he's lost the will to live, I think I have a solution to the problem."

Garth leaned forward on the table, peered at me suspiciously. "Which is?"

"I'm going to try to buy a circus for him to run."

"Great, Mongo," Garth said, rubbing the bridge of his nose. "A circus is just what you need. And what will you—?"

"Hear him out, Garth," Mary said, wrapping her long, tapering fingers around my brother's thick wrist. "Go ahead, Mongo."

"Thank you, my dear," I said, nodding to the woman with the sky-blue eyes before turning my attention back to Garth. "Now, listen; Phil lost the circus when the bank holding a lien on it sold it off at auction, but there was something decidedly funny about the deal, judging from the way Phil described it. Assuming he was sober enough at the time to know what was happening, it sounds to me like the Statler Brothers Circus may have been some accountant's bright idea of a tax write-off; for all we know, that circus may now be owned by Gulf and Western. At the least, I hope to find out just who does own it. The bank that auctioned it off is a Chicago outfit called United States Savings and Loan. If it is a tax write-off, a lot of depreciation has already been claimed by now; the owner may be tired of the whole thing and just might be receptive to an offer that would now give him a fair return on his original investment."

Garth grunted, shrugged. "No matter what deal you may be able to make, buying a circus is still going to take a lot of cash. If you're asking if it's all right with me to take a second mortgage on the brownstone to finance the deal, of course it is."

"Whoa, hoss; let's not get ahead of ourselves. I'm thinking it would be a good idea to look for partners in the venture in order to spread the risk around, and I'm pretty sure I know where to find them. Phil kept his entire stable of freaks on the payroll right up to the bitter end, long after just about every other circus in the country had packed their freaks off to whatever fate awaits people like a three-legged man and a pig-faced lady. Even freaks who never worked for Phil Statler have heard of him and respect him; freaks who worked for him love the man. Well, there are a whole lot of retired freaks living in a small town in Florida, just outside Sarasota. Naturally, there's a large percentage on welfare, but others made good investments over the years and are well enough off so that they might not mind using a circus themselves as a tax write-off if it couldn't turn a profit. What I'll propose to them is a corporation, a limited partnership where individuals will own shares, and where actual operations will be turned over to Phil Statler, who'll be compensated on a profit-sharing basis after his expenses are covered. He may need some outside help to advise him on how to best manage and compete with the other big shows, but that's a step or two down the road. The first thing I have to do is go to Florida and see if I can line up backers. If I can, I then head to Chicago to pry the name of the owner out of United States Saving and Loan."

Mary asked, "Why not just find out where the circus is now, go there, and make your inquiries?"

"Oh, I plan to check out the circus itself, but before I do that I want to find out who I'm dealing with. If it is just one of hundreds of entities owned by some huge corporation or holding company, I have to know who I can approach to talk business; the circus manager wouldn't necessarily give me that information or take me seriously.

"Anyway, that's my plan; I may be able to put it all together, or I may not, but I feel I have to try. I figure it will take me a week, maybe two, to take care of business. Garth, that means I have to ask you to handle our entire caseload while I'm gone. We've got those two big things hanging fire—Bechtel's offer of a permanent retainer, and possible work for the Belgian consulate."

"I'll take care of it, Mongo," Garth said absently. He was looking at me, but his brown eyes were slightly out of focus, and I knew that my empathic brother was thinking of Phil Statler's plight and pain, and the suffering of all the homeless people on the streets of the nation's cities and towns. "Put us down for a piece of the action if you can put a deal together."

"And make it a big piece of the action, Mongo," Mary said, her eyes misting with tears. "The album sales are going well, so we'll have money to invest. If it all ends up a bust and we have to write it off, that's all right too."

"We'll talk figures if and when I can structure some kind of deal in the first place. In the meantime, I was wondering if the two of you can keep Phil company while I'm out of town—either at the brownstone or taking him back to Cairn with you."

Garth asked, "Which do you think is better, brother?"

"Take him back up to Cairn with you, if you've got the room. I think the change of scenery might do him good."

"Will he agree to come?"

"I don't know. We'll have to make up some story; it's important that he doesn't know what I'm up to."

Mary smiled coyly, batted her long, pale eyelashes. "We'll all go back to the brownstone now, and I'll work my feminine wiles on him."

"You're a good man, Mongo," Garth said in a low, husky voice, "and I love you."

"Harrumph," I intoned as I signaled our waiter for the check. "You'd never know it from the way you talk to me sometimes."

CHAPTER THREE

Palmetto Grove is a small town of a few thousand people located an hour's drive northeast of Sarasota. One of the most unusual towns in America, it isn't listed in any tourist brochure, and few people have even heard of it; the residents prefer it that way. For decades, before the decline of the Big Tops and their accompanying sideshows, Palmetto Grove was where circus freaks, refugees from ultimate birth-marks like mine, owned homes where they went to live in the off-season, or to retire when their "performing" days were over. Although most of the freaks prefer, even here, to stay out of the public eye, the mayor of Palmetto Grove was—the last I'd heard—a "dog-faced man" by the name of Charles Harris. It was not at all unusual to see a half dozen or so "bearded ladies" chatting together in the municipal park or pushing their children in strollers. The state trooper unit with jurisdiction over Palmetto Grove often pressed the town sheriff—an eight-foot giant who came complete with his own customized van—into service when they thought the situation demanded. There was no rowdyism, no Saturday night bar fights, in Palmetto Grove.

Neither Hertz nor Avis counters at the airport had any models

I would feel comfortable driving, or they would feel comfortable renting to me, but I finally found a local car rental agency that handled Isuzus. I rented a Trooper and drove out to Palmetto Grove. I stopped in a motel-restaurant on the highway just outside of town, ordered coffee in a container, and took it out to a pay phone in the fern-lined lobby. I took out a pad and pen, then began thumbing through the local directory, looking for names of people I might know, and who would remember me. By the time I'd finished scanning the C's I already had four names, but I kept going out of curiosity. It was when I reached the R's that I saw a name that made my breath catch in my throat and my mouth go dry. I stared at the name, feeling bittersweet memories swell in my mind, and wondered what this particular woman was doing in a town filled with freaks.

Harper Rhys-Whitney was no freak—not unless you held her accountable for the freakish effect she had on the glands and good judgment of virtually every man who had, at least in the past, laid eyes on her. Including me. Especially me. When, as a teenager, I'd first met her, I had instantly decided that this other teenager was the most beautiful and desirable woman I would ever meet in my lifetime. I'd only been half right. I'd since met a number of beautiful women, had affairs with a few, and loved one—a gorgeous and compassionate witch from upstate New York, a woman by the name of April Marlowe. April had not only saved my life and mind but had also given me the courage, for the first time in my life, to overcome the insecurities and feeling of emotional vulnerability that go with being a dwarf and loving someone freely in return. However, my deep love for April notwithstanding, no woman had ever had the same instantaneous, raw, and lasting impact on my libido as Harper Rhys-Whitney, with her aura of primal, animal energy and sexuality.

And all of this thinly veiled promise of sensual paradise radiating from a woman who, while almost perfectly proportioned, couldn't have weighed much more than a hundred pounds and stood only five feet tall—not that many inches taller than I am.

I'd been with the circus a year and a half when Harper had descended upon our company with her scaled menagerie like a bolt of heat lightning out of a clear summer day. Although she was nineteen, certainly of age, she was still, in effect, a runaway. And what she was running away from was influential wealth and power that others would have killed for.

Her family, I was to discover, was blue-blood, Mainline Philadelphia society, seriously rich, their fortune made in textiles in an industrial empire founded by her grandfather. As Harper had told it, she and her family never got along; they considered her a juvenile delinquent, primarily because of her defiance of virtually all authority, but also because of her obsession with dangerous reptiles and her propensity, from the time she was thirteen, to run with motorcycle gangs. Over the course of her childhood and adolescence she was frequently punished by having her snake collection taken away, and she was shipped off to more than a half dozen ultra-expensive boarding schools specializing in educating and smoothing the jagged edges off the troubled sons and daughters of the rich. She was thrown out of all the boarding schools and somehow always managed to start a new snake collection no matter where she was. Finally, upon turning eighteen, she invested a not inconsiderable sum of money into a large, and most impressive, collection of exotic reptiles—including not only many species of poisonous snakes but giant constrictors and a full-grown Komodo dragon with a taste for Big Macs and sauerkraut. She put her collection in cages, packed them all up in a truck, and went off looking for a circus. She worked for a few carny shows, didn't like them, set off again. Finally, she found Statler Brothers Circus. Phil hired her on the spot, with only a cursory glance at her menagerie in her truck. Sex, he'd patiently explained to his dwarf tumbler, sells tickets; if Harper Rhys-Whitney couldn't really handle snakes, then he'd simply teach her to do something else. Anything else. She had that much presence, was that magnetic.

And yet this wild thing with flowing black hair, full breasts, and maroon, gold-flecked eyes had turned out to be a consummate professional.

I hadn't known much about reptiles, their care or handling, myself, but I'd been assured by experts who did know about such things that this fiery girl with the pouting mouth and eerie eyes was one of the best snake handlers they'd ever seen—a talent, apparently, one either had or didn't have, and one which couldn't be taught. The caged Komodo dragon sitting outside the tent, munching on his burgers and kraut, served to very effectively draw the rubes inside; once there, what they saw was sufficient to keep them coming back for more and then spread the word to their friends and neighbors who hadn't yet trekked out to the county fairgrounds to see the circus. Flanked by giant constrictors in cages on either side of her, Harper, dressed in a skintight jumpsuit, sat cross-legged in the center of a huge glass enclosure with only the hypnotic aura of her swaying body and the musical vibrations of an E harmonica to keep four huge king cobras at bay. When I'd asked her why a harmonica and not the snake charmer's traditional wooden flute, she'd replied that it made no difference whatsoever to the snakes, who couldn't hear the music but only responded to the vibrations, which they picked up with their flicking tongues. Her cobras, she explained, liked E harmonica vibrations. A jazzed-up rendition of "Nearer, My God, to Thee" seemed to be especially pleasing to them, and on occasion she would actually manage to get all four of the cobras swaying back and forth in front of her, together and in time to the music—a weaving, scaled chorus line of death.

She was bitten once, three months after she joined the circus, and barely survived with the help of an antitoxin flown in by helicopter from Dallas. Phil was apoplectic, insisting that she give up her snake-charming act with the cobras altogether, or at least substitute rat snakes. She offered to compromise by going with only two cobras, and Phil reluctantly agreed. He had to; like me, Harper could have had a job for the asking with any of the other big shows, including Ringling Brothers.

She also had virtually every male in the circus constantly in heat, a tension-inducing situation Phil tolerated only because Harper was so exceptionally good at what she did. I'd always considered her only slightly less dangerous to a man's well-being than the poisonous snakes she handled with such grace, invention, and courage. Indeed, she displayed far less grace handling the procession of men who were constantly vying to share her bed. Nobody had ever been killed over her, but over the course of our mutual tenure with the circus there were innumerable fistfights and one stabbing that cost a high-wire artist his spleen and his career. Of course, not a few of her rejected conquests dearly wanted to stab Harper; at least once a week, or so it seemed, Harper ended up "hiding out" with me, usually near the animal pens where I would be keeping Mabel and the other circus animals company. *Femme fatale* is a term that might have been coined especially in Harper Rhys-Whitney's honor.

I, of course, had lusted after her just like all the rest of the men, most of whom would have killed to spend as much time with her as I did. But I was a dwarf, and extremely self-conscious about it. I didn't make plays for women, and I always went out of my way to avoid any emotional entanglement that could be construed as anything but purely platonic friendship. Harper and I had become good friends, and it was me she sought out in her increasingly frequent times of emotional need.

In the Palmetto Grove directory her name had *Ph.D.* printed after it. Since the Harper Rhys-Whitney I'd known had never graduated from high school, I wondered what the Ph.D. could be all about. There was really only one way to find out, I thought, as I rummaged in my pockets for a quarter. As I dropped it in the coin slot, I noticed that my hand was trembling slightly. I suddenly imagined I could hear the haunting music of her harmonica in my mind, and I thought I had a pretty good idea of how her captive snakes might have felt.

•   •   •

Harper's home on the outskirts of Palmetto Grove was a three-story Gothic affair, slightly spooky and not a little amusing, totally unlike any of the single-frame houses in the area. It had cost her some money to build. The huge lawn in front of the house was carefully manicured, and there was an abundance of bright flowers in a number of beds and flanking the walk leading up to the front door. Just visible behind the house were two long, low buildings that might have been greenhouses except for the fact that they appeared to be all wood, with no windows in them at all.

I parked the Isuzu at the curb across the street from the house, turned off the ignition. Harper had obviously been watching for me out the window, because I had just stepped down out of the car and was closing the door when she burst out of the front door, bounded down the steps, and came running toward me.

The sight of her, with the bouncing of her full breasts only slightly restrained by the fabric of her form-fitting jumpsuit, took my breath away, and I just stood, dumbfounded by my own feelings, as she approached. Her hair, once jet-black, was now a smoky gray, and she wore it pulled back from her oval face and tied into a pony tail with a bright red calico ribbon. It didn't surprise me that she did not dye her hair, but its grayness seemed to be her only concession to age. Her strange, gold-flecked maroon eyes had lost none of their shine, and her trim, lithe body was exactly as I remembered it from when we were both teenagers. For me, at least, she had lost none of the aura of sensuality that seemed to radiate from her like some light beyond the visible spectrum, a glow that worked directly on the other senses.

The woman's effect on me was absolutely ridiculous, I thought. Virtually paralyzed, I was still harboring that thought when she finally reached me, draped her arms around my neck, and hugged me to her. The result was to crush my left cheek against the ample, soft mound of her left breast; I could feel her heart beating, and her hard nipple, through the fabric of her clothing.

Outrageous.

"Mmmph," I said.

She finally relaxed her grip—but that was all; she kept her hands locked behind my neck as she slowly forced me to turn with her in a full circle, her eerie maroon eyes locked on mine, her face with its slightly pouty mouth only inches away. I didn't think she was wearing perfume, but she had a pleasing, clean smell about her, like that of finely milled soap.

"Robby, Robby, Robby," she intoned in the voice, still so familiar in my mind, that had always seemed impossibly low and sultry to be coming from such a small body. "Mongo the Magnificent. How I've missed you over the years. You look absolutely *scrumptious*."

"Yeah, me too. I mean, uh, I've also thought a lot about you over the years. And you look scrumptious."

The best lines of a red-hot lover. Talk about feeling foolish and tongue-tied . . .

"Robby, your face is red."

"Jesus, Harper, you do look absolutely magnificent."

"Come on," she commanded, grabbing my left hand and half leading, half hauling me across the street toward the sidewalk to her house. "Did they feed you on the plane?"

"Yeah. Lunch."

"I know what airline food is like. I'll make you something to eat."

"I'm, uh, really not hungry."

"Then I'll make us drinks."

"*That* I could use," I said feebly as she hauled me up the steps, across the porch, and through the open front door into an oak-paneled foyer made bright and airy by a skylight. Two Edward Hopper originals hung on the walls flanking the entrance to the living room.

Something heavy suddenly came to rest on my right shoulder as something else flicked against my right cheek and ear; the something else tickled. I shied away, half turned, and found myself face-to-face with a thick, triangular snake's head that was as big as my fist. The head was attached to a sinuous neck that tapered down to a huge, tubular body coiled like the hawser of an ocean liner in a pool of sunlight directly beneath the skylight; the snake's body was easily as big around as me.

"*Jeesus!*" I shrieked at the top of my lungs as I shot backward and landed hard on my backside.

Undeterred by what could have been interpreted as a rejection, the snake slithered through my splayed legs, came up over my groin and stomach and onto my chest until its head was once again in my face, its fleshy, forked tongue flicking out at my eyes. I couldn't decide whether it was hungry or wanted to make love, and neither prospect particularly appealed to me.

"*JEEEsus!*" I shrieked again, even louder, and abruptly raised myself on my hands and feet and crabbed backward until my head collided hard and painfully with the wall behind me.

"You silly goose," Harper said to me as she peremptorily grabbed the snake about a foot behind its head and draped it over her left shoulder. The triangular head disappeared from sight behind her back, then reappeared a moment later on her other shoulder. It nosed its way around her neck, up through her hair, peeked at me over the top of her head. "Frank won't hurt you; he was just being friendly. Reticulated pythons usually have a lot of personality. Sometimes they can be downright playful, like a dog. Frank is my watchsnake. He's harmless, but I like to think that the sight of him might deter burglars."

I glanced at Frank, who had now closed his eyes. He looked as if he might be purring. "Yeah," I said, rubbing the bump that had already begun to form on the back of my head. "I can see why you might think that."

"I'm surprised you didn't recognize him; he may have recognized you. Frank used to be with me in the circus."

"Do tell. He looks bigger now."

"He is bigger now," Harper said approvingly in a tone of voice that most definitely had the ring of maternal pride. "Twenty-five feet. That's pretty close to a record for a reticulated python in captivity, *or* in the wild."

"Yeah? What do they do in this neighborhood, count the dogs and kids every night?"

Harper laughed—obviously assuming that I'd been trying to be funny. "I've also got an anaconda, two rock pythons, and a fair-size boa, but I keep them out in the garage. The anaconda's downright nasty, and the others don't have Frank's predictable toilet habits. But Frank is a pussycat. That's why I let him have the run of the house." She paused, frowned slightly. "I really am sorry, Robby. I guess I should have warned you. The truth of the matter is that my friends and I are so used to having him around, I forget he might come as a shock to someone not expecting to see him."

"Think nothing of it, Harper. My nervous and adrenal systems have been in need of a major overhaul like this for years. I feel like a new man."

She laughed again, said, "Actually, Robby, I'm a little surprised at you. As I recall, you used to have an almost mystical bond with animals. I envied it a lot."

"My mystical bonding techniques tend to break down when a giant constrictor sneaks up behind me and pecks me on the cheek. Are you sure Frank doesn't eat dwarfs—or wouldn't like to?"

Harper smiled, shook her head, then reached up and chucked her giant, cold-blooded companion under its broad jaw before casually undraping its head and neck from her shoulders and dropping them on top of the rest of its massive, coiled body resting in the pool of sunlight. Then she abruptly reached down, grabbed my right hand, and hauled me to my feet. This little girl was strong.

"You really are a scream, Robby. But then, you were always funny."

Frank was resting his head on one of his hawser coils and eyeing me. I eyed him back. "Who's being funny? Considering Frank's size, he might not consider me much more than an appetizer."

"Frank eats chickens. I buy them frozen, wholesale, by the crate. I used to raise them myself, but chickens are really a pain—messy like you wouldn't believe—and I found out it wasn't all that much more expensive to just buy them. But I still breed my own mice and rats."

"That's because Frank requires a balanced diet, right?"

She shook her head again, smiled cryptically, led me toward the archway at the end of the foyer. "Come on, Robby; let's get you that drink."

"Well, in honor of my reunion with dear old Frank, now you can make it a double—or even triple—Scotch, with a couple of ice cubes."

Harper's large living room had leather sofas at either end, lots of glass, and original Picasso charcoal sketches of circus clowns and dancers. In the middle of the room was a circular bar. She motioned for me to sit down on one of the sofas, but I followed her to the bar and stood beside her as she made us both drinks. Her Scotch on the rocks was as overstuffed as mine, and mine was big.

"I'm not just a snake charmer anymore, Robby," she said in her low, husky voice as we clicked glasses. "Now I'm a herpetologist—and quite a noted one, I might add without even an attempt at false modesty."

"I noticed the Ph.D. after your name in the phone directory, Dr. Rhys-Whitney."

"Indeed, *Dr.* Frederickson."

"I have to admit I was more than a little surprised to find you in Palmetto Grove—almost as surprised as I was to find you listed under your maiden name."

"Oh, I've been married, Robby. Four times, as a matter of fact. After my last divorce, I decided that either my husbands had lied when they told me they didn't mind my snakes, or I just wasn't cut out to be somebody's wife. It's probably both. As far as my living here is concerned, I finally realized that the only people who had ever truly cared about me for something besides my looks or money were my friends from the circus. That's why I moved here and built this house. It was eight years ago."

"I'm sorry, Harper. I didn't mean to be so personal."

She raised her eyebrows. "Oh, you didn't? I was kind of hoping you had meant to be so personal. I certainly did. You know who inspired me to go back to school? You. You were my role model. Every winter, while the rest of us were kicking back and sunning ourselves down here in Florida, you were off to school in New York to pick up more credits. I missed you during the winter, Robby. Everybody missed you. And then one day you were off for good, to be a college professor, of all things. That's when I *really* started to miss you. A year later, I decided to follow your example. I picked up a GED around here and then talked my way into a community college. I got straight A's on my way to an associate's degree, and that got me into a four-year school. Then I went on to graduate school." She paused, gestured around her, continued: "Obviously, I couldn't afford all this on savings from a circus career and income as a herpetologist. My parents were overjoyed when I went back to school, and that's an understatement. It turned out they didn't mind me playing with snakes, just as long as some school was going to give me a degree for doing it. All was forgiven. I was reinstated in the family's good graces and will, and when my folks died a few years back I inherited the family fortune."

"I'm sorry to hear about your parents, Harper. I never met them, but they must have been very special to have cooked you up."

Her lips curled back in a bittersweet smile, and she again clicked her glass against mine. "Thank you. You're right; they were certainly pissers. I'm glad we finally became friends before they died. I do believe they were even proud of me. I certainly gave them more than their share of grief while I was growing up. Anyway, back to the first subject, I wasn't the only one who missed you, Robby. For a dwarf, my friend, you filled up a whole lot of space. Everybody missed you—animals as well as people. With the possible exception of Mabel, though, I think I'm the one who missed you most, and I'm so glad that I finally have the chance to see you and tell you that."

The stiffness of Harper's nipples was clearly visible through the fabric of her form-fitting jumpsuit. I looked down into my glass of whiskey as I raised it to my lips.

"I've embarrassed you, haven't I, Robby?"

"No," I mumbled, forcing myself to look back up into her maroon eyes. "But you do flatter me. Thank you."

We both studied each other as we sipped at our drinks. Then she abruptly grabbed my left elbow, steered me around the bar and toward a set of double doors at the far end of the room. "Now it's time to continue the tour," she said brightly. "I want to show you my office."

Her "office" turned out to be one of the long, low buildings I had glimpsed from the road. There were four rows of glass cages running the length of the building, separated by two aisles. Inside each case was something deadly. In the case directly in front of me was a black mamba. In this snake there was none of the tubular sleekness one often sees in reptiles like Frank, the reticulated python, or in rattlesnakes. The mamba was a dull black, and puffy, as if it had no skeleton to hold in its guts. It looked like what it was, an ugly, black bag of death.

"I milk venomous snakes for pharmaceutical companies, other private researchers, and a number of universities," Harper said. "I also conduct research on hemo- and neurotoxins myself. My labs are in the other building. I have a full-time staff of lab assistants and keepers, but I sent them all home after I received your call." She paused, smiled broadly. "I wanted you all to myself."

She paused, turned toward me, set down her drink on top of one of the glass cases, and pulled up the sleeves of her pale blue jumpsuit. There were a number of tiny scars on both forearms and on the backs of her hands.

"I've been bitten more than forty times," she continued matter-of-factly. "The trick is in surviving the first two or three bites. After that, it gets easier. You develop antibodies. Now I'm virtually immune to most kinds of snake venom, and my blood is almost as good as any antitoxin serum. Once, when a kid in Idaho was bitten by a rattlesnake and they couldn't get the right serum, they gave him a pint of my blood. He lived."

"I'm impressed, Harper," I said evenly.

"Good," she said brightly as she picked up her drink again. "I want you to be, because I'm certainly impressed by you. I've been reading and hearing stories about you for years. You're quite a famous man, you know."

"It's not something I give a lot of thought to, Harper."

"I have a thick file of clippings about you somewhere in the house. Its seems dwarf private investigators who get involved in the kinds of bizarre cases you handle get a lot of press coverage. I know you live in New York City. I've thought of calling you a number of times over the years."

Somehow we had become separated as we continued to talk; I had veered off and gone down the aisle on the right while Harper had continued on down the other aisle. I was about three quarters of the way through my drink. It had been a big one, but I'd drunk a good deal more on other occasions without feeling any ill effects. Now, however, I felt positively giddy as I looked across the tops of the glass cases filled with very dangerous creatures into the maroon eyes of another very dangerous creature.

"Why didn't you?" I asked quietly. I felt slightly short of breath.

"I'm not sure," she replied thoughtfully, cocking her head slightly and studying me through narrowed lids. "I think I was afraid of you."

Of all the possible answers, or excuses, she might have offered, that was absolutely the last one I'd have expected to hear. "You were afraid of *me*?"

"You tame wild things, Robby," she said softly. "You do it whether you mean to or not."

Feeling as light-headed as I did, I reacted naturally—by taking another long pull on my drink. Then I looked down. The glass case in front of me looked empty except for some leaves, a few bare branches, and sand with tiny crawl marks in it. "What's supposed to be in here?" I asked.

"Oh, it's there; it's very small, and it's probably hiding behind some leaves. It's a krait. In Africa, they call it the 'hundred-foot snake.' Obviously, it's not called that because of its length. It gets its name from the fact that a hundred feet is about as far as a man can stagger or crawl after he's been bitten by one. Ounce for ounce, it's probably the most poisonous snake in the world."

"Charming."

"Venomous snakes are of enormous medical benefit, Robby. Medicines made from venom are responsible for saving thousands of lives each year. Observing how venom acts on the mammalian nervous system has taught researchers an enormous amount about the nervous system itself. I try to spend a few weeks each year in Brazil with an international research team looking for new species, trying to keep ahead of the people who are cutting down the trees. At the rate the rain forests are being destroyed, it's conceivable that dozens of unknown species could vanish before we're even aware of their existence. It's also conceivable that the venom from any one of those unknown species could provide us with a cure for multiple sclerosis, muscular dystrophy, maybe even cancer."

"I loved you, you know," I blurted out, looking up across the rows of cases into the woman's eyes.

"I know, Robby," she replied evenly. "I believe I loved you too, but I just didn't realize it. I was such a child. I mean, I had all those big, burly things after me, and you were just a dwarf. How could I be in love with a dwarf? At that time, you were something I needed far more than just another lover; you were a *friend*, probably the only real friend I had during that period of my life, or at least the best one. You truly cared for me as a person, and you always did your best to look out for my interests."

"You never needed anyone to look out for you, Harper."

She shook her head impatiently, sipped at her drink, said, "It never occurred to me at the time that I might love you. You were just the person who related well to *all* the wild things in the circus."

I looked away, drained off the rest of my Scotch. Now I was feeling *really* giddy. Softheaded.

"I never saw the man then," Harper continued.

"Mmm."

"You were always there when I needed you—or when anyone or anything else needed you."

"Mmm."

"Are you married, Robby?"

"No."

"In all those years, Robby, who was there for you when *you* needed a friend?"

"The wild things."

"You were always cheerful and even-tempered; you always had a kind word or a joke to cheer up someone who was sad. It was only after you left that it occurred to me how lonely you must have been all those years you were with the circus."

I walked to the end of the aisle, around the cages, back up the second aisle toward Harper. My gait, like my speech, was steady enough, so I decided it wasn't the Scotch I had consumed that was responsible for my light-headedness. Harper had once again set her drink down on top of one of the snake cages and was waiting for me, arms at her sides. I knew she was waiting to be kissed.

I stopped a pace away from her and held my empty tumbler in front of me like a shield. "Phil Statler's in trouble," I said. "It's the reason I flew down here."

If she was surprised at my reluctance to take her in my arms, she didn't show it—and I decided that my notion about her waiting for me to kiss her had only been a fantasy. Her brows knitted, and shadows moved in her expressive eyes. "What's the matter with him, Robby?"

I told her how I had come across Phil Statler, homeless, missing fingers and toes, waiting to die in a welfare ward at Bellevue Medical Center.

"God, Robby," she said in a small voice. "I had no idea; *nobody* had any idea. I left the circus almost eight years ago. A while back I heard that the circus had changed hands, but we all just assumed that Phil had sold at a good price and was off lazing around on the beach of some Caribbean island."

"No. Phil's circus was his body and soul; he would have died working it, and now he'll surely die a lot sooner if he doesn't get a circus to work. I want to make a stab at buying his old one back for him, maybe through some sort of limited partnership deal, a consortium with Phil actually running the show like he always did. I'm here to see who might have some money to invest in a venture that, even if we could keep it going, might never show any real profits. If I can get a promise of financial backing, then I'll approach whoever owns the circus now and make an offer. At this point, quite frankly, the idea is all I have. For all I know, the circus may no longer even exist."

"It exists," Harper said with an abrupt nod of her head. "I'll tell you what I know about it—which isn't much. We don't get the kind of scuttlebutt on that show that we do on all the others. All the performers now appear to be foreigners; if they speak English, they don't let on. Nobody around here knows anybody who works it. It's been renamed 'World Circus.' The only things the new owner kept were the hardware, the rigging, the tractor-trailers, and the animals. They brought in a whole new stable of performers—people none of us had ever heard of. I don't know where all those people came from, but people around here who've caught the show say they're damn good. Every act. In fact, they've got an animal trainer named Luther who's supposed to be as good as Gunther Goebbel-Williams, which means that it's a small miracle that Ringling Brothers hasn't hired him away by now. Believe it or not, this Luther rides Mabel the way you used to—and he's even managed, from what I hear, to teach the old girl some new tricks. I'd have bet a lot of money that nobody but you would ever get Mabel to do anything but rigging work."

"Are you sure nobody around here knows who those performers are?"

"I'm sure. Whoever they are, they didn't come from the usual places, American or European. What's more, World Circus doesn't do a whole lot of advertising or any other kind of promotion. They don't feature headliners, the way most circuses do. Everybody's a star—and nobody is."

"You mentioned how good this Luther is."

"Word of mouth, not promotion. It's a different way of doing circus business, almost as if they're attracting attention without even trying. I can't see how it works. You remember Henry Catlander?"

"Yes."

"He caught the show last year in Illinois, and he said there were barely a hundred and fifty people at the matinee. But he also said that all the acts were top quality; not a filler in the bunch. It just seems odd to have that kind of talent and then not do any major promotion. They *must* be losing money."

"I certainly hope so. You hear any rumors about what individual or corporation owns it?"

Harper shook her head. "I've told you all I know—except for the fact that everybody connected with the circus seems to be very unfriendly. Henry wanted to go back to the pens and dressing area after the show to say hello—you know, as an ex-colleague—but they wouldn't let him. Nobody knows where they go in the off-season. They all keep pretty much to themselves."

"Where do they winter the livestock, store the rigging and the trucks?"

"Beats me. They don't come anywhere around here."

"Well, with a little luck I'll be able to change World Circus back to Statler Brothers Circus. A lot depends on my getting a name and financial figures from the bank that auctioned off the circus in the first place. If I can do that, then I can prepare to make an offer—assuming I can get the financial backing I need. Do you suppose there's anyone living around here willing to take a flyer on owning a piece of a circus that would be run by Phil Statler?"

"Considering the circumstances, I think you'll find a number of enthusiastic backers—especially me. But it's easy enough to find out. I'll arrange a little get-together for tonight, and then you can make your pitch yourself."

"Harper, I didn't call you because I wanted to put you to any trouble."

"Don't be silly. Just about all the entertainment in Palmetto Grove takes place in people's homes, and everybody's ready to party on short notice. I won't go to any trouble. I'll have a batch of pizzas delivered, and you can make your pitch after we eat. Let me take care of it. Why don't you go upstairs and take a nap? You look tired."

"What? Oh, I don't think—"

"Go on," she said, pushing me ahead of her in the aisle between the glass cases, back toward the main house. "I want you to make yourself at home. You can take a nap in my bed. It's very comfortable. You'll like it."

Outrageous.

•   •   •

A "batch of pizzas" turned out to be an exquisite fondue smorgasbord that Harper had shopped for and prepared while I slept. Twenty people, all of them ex-circus performers with money, had been invited. I knew about half the guests, having worked with them at one time or another; the other half had heard of me, and knew Phil Statler.

After dessert of fruit compote and angel cake, I made what amounted to a sales pitch without financial figures. All of the successful businessmen and women at the gathering were eager to take part in the venture. A woman by the name of Florence Woolsey—one of the three former fat ladies at the party who had participated in a weight-loss program after retirement and who was now, if not exactly svelte, at least no more than *zaftig*—was a lawyer, and she volunteered her legal services if and when the time came to draw up agreements and corporate papers. Everyone agreed that the new owner must have picked up the circus at a bargain price, and I was authorized to make an offer that would guarantee the owner up to a hundred percent profit; if he was willing to sell but wanted more money, I was to bring back his counteroffer for the group's consideration.

All in all, I decided, it had been a most remarkable day and evening. Now I was in the kitchen with Harper, helping her empty the dishwasher and put the dishes away. Screwing up my courage, I sidled over to her as she stacked dishes, pecked her on the cheek. I said, "Thank you, Harper. You did real good."

Her response was to turn and press her lips against mine. "The pleasure was all mine, sir," she murmured in her husky voice. "You're quite a public speaker; that was some speech you gave."

Suddenly I felt flushed, and I dropped my gaze. "The project sold itself. Everybody wants to help Phil."

"What do you think of the werewolf killings?"

"Huh?" I was still very conscious of the feel and taste of her lips on mine, and more than a bit distracted by the sudden physiological change she had effected in me, in my groin.

"The werewolf killings. Jesus, don't you remember? That's what everyone was talking about by the end of the evening. Henry had just come back from Kansas, and he was telling us about them. It's all they talk about in that part of the country. I would think a werewolf would be right up your alley. I have a file on you, remember? I know the kinds of strange cases you get involved in."

"Well, it sounds to me like your file is out of date. I don't get involved in that kind of stuff anymore." It wasn't quite true, but the more bizarre cases Garth and I had become entangled in over the past few years were not matters I wished to discuss with Harper. "My brother and I are partners now, and mostly what we do are cut-and-dried investigations for corporations, congressional committees, and lawyers. It's a lot more boring than working with poisonous snakes, I assure you."

"But don't the killings interest you? There have been seven of them so far—all men, disemboweled and with their throats torn out, and partially eaten. Ugh."

"Sure, they interest me, but not because of the werewolf angle. That's just a tag the supermarket tabloids came up with to sell papers; I see the stupid headlines every time I go shopping. The only good story I've seen on the matter was in the *New York Times;* they ran a piece after the fourth killing on the growing hysteria in the Midwest. It's interesting, yes, but werewolves don't exist."

"I know, but what kind of animal kills like *that?*"

"My guess is that the culprit is that most dangerous and savage beast on the face of the earth—one of us, a human being. Those killings have all the earmarks of the work of a serial killer."

"A subject on which Dr. Robert Frederickson is an acknowledged expert."

"You flatter me. I told you I don't do that stuff any longer."

"But even the *eating* of the flesh . . ."

"Sure—assuming the flesh really was eaten and not simply made to look that way. What else could it be but a human? There aren't any wolves or bears left in that part of the country; even if there were, no single rogue individual or pack would operate over the range indicated by the killings, sometimes hundreds of miles apart, across the Midwest. The same holds true for feral dogs, and a rabid animal would have died by now. No, it's a man. He could be using special instruments for all the rip-work, but it's not inconceivable that he's using only his own teeth and fingernails. When you're dealing with serial killers, no degree of savagery or kind of behavior is too bizarre to be discounted."

"But they're supposed to have found tracks, hair, and saliva—and they can't identify the animal that left them."

"That sounds like tabloid headlines. My sources may not be all that much better, but from what I've read, the FBI isn't talking about what they've found. But even if it is true, it just means the killer is having fun at the expense of the media while he thinks he's being clever. Footprints are easily faked, as any Bigfoot aficionado will tell you, and the DNA of hair and saliva can be altered by irradiation or chemicals. The man gets his jollies by killing, and then by ratcheting the terror up a notch by having people believe there's some kind of savage, maybe even super-natural, animal loose."

"Robby, what if a tiger escaped from the circus—I mean our old circus, World Circus? If you look at a map, you'll see that all the killings have taken place roughly along, around, the route the circus takes—or used to take."

I shook my head. "The circus had to be the first place the police, state troopers, and finally the FBI checked. The World Circus people may be unfriendly, but I have to believe they'd feel sufficient civic responsibility to report to the authorities if a tiger was missing. A tiger might have the natural equipment to kill like that, but it would be far more likely to go after cattle and sheep than people—especially a circus tiger. Besides, where—and for how long—could a Bengal or Siberian tiger hide out in the Great Plains? No, this werewolf is a man, a heavy-duty psychotic, and you can bet there are almost as many FBI agents in the field in the Great Plains states right now as there are farmers. I'll let them hunt the werewolf; I'm going out there to hunt a circus."

Harper thought about it, nodded. "I guess you're right," she said. She paused, then—as if the thought had only just occurred to her—grinned and snapped her fingers. "Oh, by the way, did I mention that I was going with you?"

I stared into her face, slowly blinked. "Actually, I don't believe you did mention it."

"Well, I am. I owe myself some time off, and I can't think of a better way to use it than to help Phil—and to spend some days with you. It just so happens that I have a Lear jet parked at an airport a twenty-minute drive away; she'll go eight hundred twenty miles an hour, no sweat. I'm a hell of a pilot, if I do say so myself, with instrument rating. You want to find a circus that could be anywhere along a fifteen-hundred-mile circuitous route between northern Texas and the Dakotas. Unless you enjoy driving and have a lot of time to kill, I figure a small plane can't hurt. What about it, Robby?"

"What about it? Are you kidding me? I hope you didn't make that very generous offer as a kind of gesture, hoping I'd turn it down, because I definitely accept."

"Good. It'll be fun. We'll drop your car off first thing in the morning and take a taxi to the airport. I'll file a flight plan, and we'll be off."

"Outstanding."

Harper nodded again. "Now that you've got your own personal pilot, sir, I'd say you have more options. Do you still want to start off at the bank in Chicago, or do you want to try to get a fix on the circus itself first?"

"Let's find the circus first. I'd intended to start off at the bank, but it might be a good idea to eyeball the show first to see just what it is we intend to buy, and I may be able to pick up some information."

"Check. Want a brandy?"

I shook my head. "No, thanks. Because of you, I've had more than enough . . . stimulation for one day. If we're leaving first thing in the morning, I'd better get some sleep. I saw a motel out on the—"

"Robby, you really *are* a silly goose. Now that we have our traveling plans settled, we have to get the other thing out of the way."

"Uh . . . what other thing is that?"

"Sex, of course. We're going to be spending a lot of time

together. I certainly think we both have a real itch for each other, and if we don't scratch it we're just going to be distracted. In a way, you and I have been lusting after each other for close to twenty years. Don't you agree that we should do something about it?"

"Uh, I—"

"Don't you *want* to sleep with me, Robby?"

"Uh, I—"

"That's exactly what I thought," she said as she pushed me ahead of her out of the kitchen, toward other quarters.

•   •   •

Harper shuddered, sighed deeply, then rolled away from me in the warm sea of darkness that was her bed. "My God, Robby, that was good," she murmured.

Good? It had been . . . outrageous.

"Mmm."

"You've been practicing."

"Mmm."

After a few moments she rolled back toward me, settling her naked body against mine. Her full breasts pressed against my ribs. "Good night, Robby," she whispered.

"Mmm," I replied as I put my arms around her and held her tight. I could feel the beating of her heart, almost indistinguishable from my own.

I couldn't recall a time in my life when I had been happier, more at peace. More *satisfied*. And yet, in the back of my mind, always, there was a dark place where an inextinguishable fear flickered like an eternal black flame. I was a dwarf; I was different. All my life I had expended a great amount of energy competing, trying to make up in daring, wit, and sheer skill, not to mention stubbornness, for what I lacked in physical size. It was something I could do myself, and did not require anyone else's cooperation. I had been in love with April Marlowe, but the gentle witch from upstate New York had been quite different from Harper Rhys-Whitney, snake charmer *extraordinaire* and legendary crusher of strong men's egos. *Loving,* desperately wanting a woman, was not an adventure I was certain I had sufficient courage to try again.

And it might already be too late to turn away.

I'd come to hunt and bag a circus, but, lying in the darkness still redolent with the odors of our lovemaking, I couldn't help but wonder if I hadn't been the one hunted, already trapped, by an exotic creature from the circus in my past.

CHAPTER FOUR

It was now almost midsummer. In the past, Statler Brothers Circus had started the season in March, in northern Texas, then worked its way north in a zigzag pattern through the Midwest to the Dakotas, then south to end the season in Louisiana in November. It was a fifteen-thousand-mile route, a lot of territory to cover. However, there seemed no reason not to assume that World Circus was not following the established route and schedule Phil Statler had originally traced across the heartland of America. If so, the circus would now be somewhere beyond the Ozark Plateau, in Missouri or Kansas.

It was midafternoon when Harper landed her Lear jet at a small airfield a hundred or so miles west of Springfield, close to the town of Lambeaux, which was our goal. Getting to Lambeaux turned out to be a good deal more difficult than our journey from Florida; there were no taxis, and no places to rent a car. However, we were able to flag down a Greyhound bus that took us to a highway stop on the edge of town. Greeting us when we got off the bus was a faded, rain-soaked poster stapled to a telephone pole; according to the schedule listed on the poster, we had missed the local appearance of World Circus by ten days. If the information was accurate, the circus was now playing just south of Topeka, on county fairgrounds near the town of Dolbin, and would be there for four more days. The thing to do, we decided, was to fly to Topeka, rent a car, then drive the hundred and ten miles to Dolbin.

Inquiries in town informed us that there was no bus heading back in the direction of the airport until nine-thirty. We decided to spend the night at a bed-and-board in town and start off again in the morning.

The dwarf in the company of the beautiful woman attracted a good deal of attention, but the people of Lambeaux turned out to be open and friendly. We were told that World Circus had attracted decent crowds from towns within a hundred-mile radius for the week that it had been there. Considering the fact that the eighth "werewolf killing" had taken place only forty-five miles west of town while the circus was playing, townspeople thought it quite remarkable that so many people had been willing to leave the safety of their homes to drive any distance out in the open, especially at night. I tended to agree, and I wasn't pleased at all to hear that World Circus seemed to be solving its attendance problems.

There wasn't much to see in Lambeaux, and we saw it all in half an hour. Then, holding hands, we walked a ways out on the prairie, toward the setting sun. I could feel my sexual hunger for Harper growing in me, and I looked forward to returning to our room after dinner in order to continue our exploration of one another. As we reached the border of a wheat field, Harper abruptly kissed me long and hard to show that she shared my hunger and need.

The town's only restaurant was really nothing more than a coffee shop that, in the evening, traded plastic tablecloths for linen, turned down the lights, and set candles on the tables. That was fine with us. In fact, the atmosphere was quite nice, and although it was a Thursday night, the restaurant was almost filled to capacity with farmers and their families, all scrubbed and dressed up for what was to them obviously an important occasion. I'd expected to feel the disorientation and sense of alienation I always felt when I returned to this part of America, where I had been born and raised, but in fact I felt quite comfortable. I suspected Harper had more than a little to do with this newfound sense of well-being. The Midwest was still, of course, no place for a dwarf to escape constantly being stared at, but I'd partially solved that problem by having us seated at a table at the back of the restaurant where I could sit with my back to the wall and hide, as it were, behind the flickering nimbus of our candle.

The house specialty was roast chicken, and it was good. We'd polished off a bottle of wine and were working on our brandies, talking softly, occasionally touching hands or brushing knees and generally getting ourselves worked up, when Harper abruptly looked to my right, at a spot just above my shoulder. I turned in my seat, found myself looking up at a tall, lean man with long, gray-streaked black hair and sharp, angular features in a rather long face that his hair tended to accentuate. His eyes were black, bright, and he had a slight cast in the right one. His hair was definitely not heartland, nor was the soiled khaki safari jacket he wore. He had New York City written all over him, what with his almost studiedly unkempt appearance and his slightly frenetic air. He was staring down at me, breathing with his mouth open as if he might be suffering from asthma or some allergy.

"Can I help you?" I asked in a tone that was perhaps a bit more terse than was necessary. I didn't like being stared at from such close range, and I particularly didn't like having my little tête-à-tête with Harper disrupted.

"Oh, I—uh, I just wanted to make sure it was you, Dr. Frederickson," he said in a high-pitched, nasal voice. "I've been out in the field for some time. One of my graduate students working with me came into town for supplies. He spotted you and drove right back out to tell me. I was afraid I'd missed you, but then I asked around and was told there was a dwarf eating in here, and—"

"Who the hell are you?"

"Oh, I, uh, excuse me." He took a deep breath through his open mouth, and I could hear the air rasping in his lungs. If he wasn't asthmatic, he had a pretty heavy summer cold. "I'm Nate Button, Dr. Frederickson. Dr. Nate Button. I apologize for interrupting your dinner, but I think I may be able to help you. I think we can help each other. I, uh—"

He wasn't going to go away, but I got him to stop talking by abruptly standing up and nodding toward Harper. "This is Harper Rhys-Whitney, Dr. Button. Why don't you sit down— for a few moments?"

The man with the long hair and face nodded gratefully with a quick, nervous bob of his head. He pulled an empty chair up to our table, sat down.

Harper asked, "Would you like a drink, Dr. Button?"

The man smiled nervously and shook his head, then turned his attention back to me. "If you'd waited a few more months before resigning from the university faculty, Dr. Frederickson, we'd have been colleagues. I'm there now. I've heard a great deal about you, to say the least. You made a lot of friends at the university, and everybody's sorry you left. In fact, nobody seems to be quite sure just why you—"

"What department are you in, Dr. Button?" I interrupted. I had no desire to talk about the incident that had led to my resignation. I had considered myself betrayed by the university administration while I had been searching for a friend whose life was endangered by the very people who had been pressuring the university to pressure me to cease and desist. Besides, I was once again sharply aware of the light-headedness that had nothing to do with alcohol, everything to do with the woman sitting across the table from me. As far as I was concerned, our intense, nervous visitor couldn't have picked a worse time to pop around; I'd been just about ready to suggest to Harper that we retire to our room for the evening.

"Zoology," he said. He paused to sniff, and clear his throat, then added, "Actually, my specialty is cryptozoology. In fact, I founded and edit what's considered to be the foremost journal in the field. I've been doing everything I can to make my particular area of study a bit more . . . uh, respectable."

Harper looked at me, raised her eyebrows. "What's cryptozoology?"

"The search for so-called hidden animals," I replied, suppressing an impatient sigh. "Cryptozoologists spend their time hunting for things like the Loch Ness monster, yeti, and Sasquatch. And maybe unicorns."

I'd tried to keep my tone even, but Nate Button might have

picked up just a trace of sarcasm in my voice. A flush, visible even in the candlelight, spread up and over his prominent cheekbones, and he leaned forward in his seat.

"We're not all fools, Dr. Frederickson," he said, an edge to his voice.

"I never intended to imply—"

"We don't all traipse around the Northwest going gaga over phony plaster casts of footprints by Bigfoot. No *serious* crypto-zoologist believes that Sasquatch exists, although the jury is still out on the yeti. There *are* 'hidden' animals, Dr. Frederickson, and the best example I can give you is the coelacanth—a fish thought to be extinct for a hundred million years, until a fisherman in the Mediterranean caught one in his net some years back."

"I can certainly attest to the fact that there are hidden animals, Robby," Harper said thoughtfully as she leaned forward and rested her elbows on the table, "not to mention 'hidden' plants and insects. It's why I go to the rain forests each year, to search for them. My interest is poisonous reptiles, but I've seen an estimate that only a fifth to a third of all the insects on the planet have been discovered and classified."

Great, I thought. For our unexpected visitor to have found a conversational ally in Harper was just what I needed.

Nate Button suddenly produced a worn leather briefcase I hadn't noticed before. He pulled his chair back, placed the briefcase on his lap, and started to open it. "Here, let me show you what I have."

"Maybe I can save you some time, Dr. Button," I said quickly. "You said you thought you might be able to help me, or that we could help each other. What makes you figure that?"

Button rested his large hands on top of the briefcase and leaned toward me in a conspiratorial manner. His black eyes now seemed very bright as they reflected the light of the flickering candle. "I know what I'm about to tell you will sound incredible, and there are still a number of questions I don't have answers for. Nevertheless, I'm sure I know what's been killing those people."

In the silence that followed his announcement, I glanced at Harper, then back at Button. Off to the right, somewhere in the kitchen, somebody dropped a tray of glasses. "Would you be talking about those werewolf killings?"

"Why, yes," the cryptozoologist replied, looking surprised and somewhat taken aback. "Of course. However, needless to say, it's not a werewolf."

"Needless to say. Just what makes you th—"

"I'm virtually certain it's a lobox."

"A who?"

"A lobox," he repeated, opening the flap of the briefcase and putting his right hand inside. "I have some—"

"Dr. Button, just what makes you think I'm interested in those killings?"

He stopped with his hand halfway out of the briefcase, stared at me, and slowly blinked. He seemed almost startled by my question. "But aren't you investigating them?"

"No. What on earth gave you that idea?"

He flushed again, obviously embarrassed, then turned to Harper, as if she might have the answer. When she merely cocked her head to one side and smiled sweetly at him, he turned back to me, shook his head slightly. "I just assumed . . . an investigator of your stature in this little town out here in the middle of nowhere, only a few miles from where the last killing took place . . ."

"You assumed wrong, Button. My reason for being here has nothing to do with the killings. I'm engaged in personal business."

"Oh, I see," the man said in a small voice, clearly disappointed and embarrassed. Much to my relief, he slid his hand out of his briefcase, closed the flap. "Well," he said, addressing the candle in the middle of the table, "now I'm afraid I feel a little foolish."

"Think nothing of it," I said, raising my hand to signal for the check. "Now, if you'll excuse us, we have to—"

"What's a lobox?" Harper asked.

Button looked hopefully at Harper, uncertainly at me. "If you have to go . . ."

"We have time," Harper said sweetly.

Button eagerly reached back into his briefcase, drew out what appeared to be an eight-by-ten photograph. Whatever it showed, I was going to have to wait my turn to see it; he handed the picture to Harper. "*That's* a lobox."

I watched Harper's face in the candlelight as she studied the photograph Button had given her. Her eyes widened, and she absently nodded her head in what seemed to be appreciation. Finally, she handed the photograph across the table to me.

It was a photo of what seemed to be one of the eerie and hauntingly beautiful cave paintings from Lascaux, in France, but I couldn't be certain; I owned a book on the paintings and had leafed through it on a number of occasions when contemplating my own mortality, but the painting I was looking at was unfamiliar to me. The light from the camera's flash had wiped out the ochers and blacks at the edges of the painting, but in the center was a stylized drawing of the head of a beast. Except for the eyes, which seemed almost human, and the great fangs, which had certainly been exaggerated, it might have been the head of a wolf. All about the fierce head, puny stick figures representing men ran in terror.

Button produced more photographs, more prehistoric depictions of the wolflike beast he had called a lobox. In one, a lobox had a stick figure by the throat. Another depicted its great claws, with one protruding from the rear of the black leather pad on its paw, making the full set of claws appear almost like a raptor's talons. Clearly, the Cro-Magnon who were responsible for the cave paintings had not hunted this creature; it had hunted them. Except for one painting, which had a quite different feel from the others, almost comical, and which looked like a lobox trying to stand on its head, what projected from the paintings was the experience of sheer terror our ancestors had felt before this creature. I handed the photographs back to Button as I felt the hairs rise on the back of my neck.

"*Canis lobox,*" Button said in a low, tense voice.

"I'll take the one trying to stand on its head."

"Obviously done by a lesser artist," Button replied, looking slightly pained at what he might have considered my irreverence. "Until now, *Canis lobox* was considered only a mythical—'speculative' is the word I prefer—creature. These photographs are recent, because the drawings were only recently discovered at Lascaux, very deep down in the network of caves, far below the level where most of the other paintings are found. Because of their location, some scientists are speculating that the paintings of *Canis lobox* may have had religious significance to the Cro-

Magnon who produced them sixteen thousand years ago. These are the only known depictions of this creature, unique among mammals for the claw at the rear of its footpad. There's a very sparse fossil record that hints at the prior existence of such an animal, but that record is far from conclusive. Many of us now feel that these paintings confirm that it lived. Because of the special placement of the paintings in the cave, it could mean that prehistoric man viewed the creature as some kind of terrible god.

"The lobox flourished across North America in the Quaternary period, beginning forty thousand years ago. It was the age of the great mammals. Lobox coexisted with mastodons, mammoths, saber-toothed cats, and other creatures that we're much more familiar with. Lobox was a cousin to the great dire wolves, and descended from the same ancestor—*Tomarctus*—as present-day wolves and dogs. Its closest modern-day relative, besides the wolf, is a breed of dog called the kuvasz, which was originally bred hundreds of years ago, in Europe, to protect sheep herds from wolves. But the lobox was very special; no other creature in any of the Lascaux cave paintings is depicted in this much detail, or evokes such a feeling of sheer terror on the part of the artist. Using a little imagination to extrapolate from the small fossil record, it may be easy to see why this animal was so feared."

Button once again reached into his briefcase, withdrew two pieces of paper, handed one to Harper and one to me. It was an artist's rendition of how a lobox might have appeared, drawn from a variety of angles. The animal certainly looked fierce enough to me. It resembled something that could have been a cross between a wolf and a Great Dane, with the wolf's spindly legs and large paws, and the Great Dane's huge rib cage and muscular withers. But no wolf or dog possessed this creature's broad snout and gaping nostrils. Obviously enhanced by the artist's imagination, the yellow eyes of the beast were very bright, shining with a distinctly humanlike quality that was very much like that in the photograph of the painting that was sixteen thousand years old.

"The reason for the lack of an extensive fossil record," Button continued, excitement building in his voice, "is that they didn't get caught in tar pits, like the one at La Brea, for example, even though they were probably larger than dire wolves. The speculation is that they were simply a lot smarter than the animals that did get trapped in fossil-producing places like tar pits. If a fossil fragment of a lobox skull is any indication, its brain pan was relatively large in proportion to its body weight—approximately the same ratio as the porpoise. The lobox was probably second in intelligence only to Cro-Magnon, and may have been smarter than Neanderthal; in fact, there are a few scientists who believe that the lobox may have played a very large role in wiping out Neanderthal. It certainly had the keenest sense of smell of any creature that's ever lived. Elephants are believed to detect specific odors from as far as four or five miles away; the lobox may have had an olfactory range twice that. It must have been like a kind of ultimate bloodhound, and it apparently had a taste for human flesh."

I grunted, handed the sketch back to Button. "You're saying you think one of these is responsible for the killings?"

"Yes," the cryptozoologist replied tersely. He raised his sharp chin slightly, in an almost defiant gesture. "I do."

"Uh . . . where do you suppose this critter came from?"

Now he lowered his chin as well as his gaze. "That's something I haven't quite worked out yet," he said quietly.

"Well, it's certainly an interesting theory," I said evenly, trying to be polite. Nate Button seemed to me to be an obvious world-class crackpot, and I wondered how he'd lasted as long as he had in the highly critical academic community, where even lesser fools are not suffered with much good humor.

"Interesting, but highly unlikely," Harper—who, at least in the past, had not herself displayed much fondness for fools—said with disarming sweetness. "Now, let me get this straight, Dr. Button. You believe that a creature called a lobox, which if it actually did exist at all has been extinct for more than ten thousand years, has been running around ripping up people all across the Midwest? Even assuming that a few members of the species did survive, where have they been keeping themselves all these millennia? You certainly can't believe they've been hiding out in the wheat and corn fields. I can see how a Sasquatch or yeti might remain hidden in the Pacific Northwest or the Himalayas, but where could something like the lobox hide out in Kansas? And why has it only recently started to eat people? And, of course, there would have to be more than one, unless you also believe in spontaneous regeneration. There would be mommy loboxes, and daddy loboxes, and little baby loboxes running around. Why hasn't anybody spotted even one? Really, Dr. Button. Do forgive me if I seem to belabor the obvious."

To my considerable surprise, Button began to nod almost enthusiastically; he actually seemed to prefer Harper's scathing critique of what passed for his thinking to my polite, if somewhat condescending, attempt to simply brush him off. He abruptly swiveled around to face her, offering me his back.

"I completely understand your reservations, Miss Rhys-Whitney," Button said in his odd, piping, nasal tone. "Believe me, I'm well aware of the problems inherent in my theory. I know it may sound preposterous, and I can't really answer any of your excellent questions; all I'm left with is evidence that the thing doing the killings *is* a lobox."

"The killer's human," I said in a flat tone to the man's back.

Button turned around, once more reached into his briefcase, took out more photographs, and laid them out over the table-cloth. They were Polaroids, or copies of Polaroids, that had apparently been taken at one of the killing sites, and were gruesome. They showed a victim, a man, whose throat had been torn away, almost decapitating him. In addition, there was a crater in his belly from which his torn innards were spilling, almost as if a grenade had exploded in the man's stomach, blowing out his guts. I thought it was rather tactless to show the photos to two people who'd just finished dinner, but I'd grown accustomed over the years to such unpretty sights, and when I glanced up at the woman on the other side of the table, her face displayed no shock or horror, only interest.

"These are photos taken at the site of the first killing, in Missouri," he said tersely. "As you can see, there are some faint tracks next to the body."

"Where did you get them?"

Button sniffed loudly. "I took them myself, Dr. Frederickson, as part of my initial investigation. You may be surprised to learn that I'm a highly respected zoologist, and I do what might be termed forensic zoology. Despite what I know to be your initial reaction to me, I'm not a crackpot. Police departments around the country—indeed, around the world—think enough of my talents to call me in to consult when there appears to have been a death caused by some animal which they can't identify. I was first called in by the Missouri state police because, understandably, they couldn't figure out what kind of an animal had done this. You'll observe that the flesh and intestines in the stomach wound appear to have been pulled *out,* rather than slashed or shredded, almost as if the stomach had been cored. There are claw marks around the periphery of the wound, although you can't see them well in the photographs. In order to pull flesh *out* in that manner, a kind of opposable, or posterior, talon or claw is required in order to grip—think of the talons of an eagle or a hawk. However, this man obviously wasn't killed by any bird. Then what was it that killed him? No *known* large mammal has this kind of claw configuration. The only large creature that ever lived that is thought to have had an opposable claw on its footpads is the one I have described to you. The tracks you see in the photograph show an elevated area at the rear of the paw that could contain a retractable claw. Add to that the hair and saliva samples that can't be matched to any known, living animal. What you end up with is what I think killed this man, as well as the seven others killed in a similar fashion: a lobox. Given the background and information I've just supplied to you, Dr. Frederickson, what would you have said?"

"You have my attention, Dr. Button. By now the FBI is seriously at work on the matter. What do they think killed these people?"

The cryptozoologist pursed his lips, slowly shook his head. "The FBI came in after the second killing—and they cut me out; they wouldn't allow me to visit that killing site, and they've banned me from the other killing sites as well. By the time I'm able to get on a site, it's already been completely worked over, evidence gathered and taken away, or obliterated. I've been searching for tracks and other signs around the peripheries of the killing sites, but that kind of work is almost impossibly difficult— like searching for needles in a corn field, if you will. In addition, the FBI refuses to share with me their lab analyses of the later hair and saliva samples they must have found. Frankly, I'm at a loss to understand their refusal to cooperate with me. It's almost as if they're trying to cover up the fact that there could be a lobox loose, and which is a danger to every man, woman, and child living in this area."

"Is the FBI aware of your theory about this creature?"

"Of course. I told them what I thought it was."

"In that case, Dr. Button, I think I can explain the FBI's attitude and behavior. The FBI doesn't have much time or patience for tracking 'hidden animals,' especially those that have been extinct for fifteen thousand years."

"But to actually bar me from the other sites—"

"The bureau isn't going to want it known that they've accepted advice from a cryptozoologist—even if they consider what you've told them vital, and I'm pretty sure that's the case. They took what you had to offer them and then cut you out because they don't want to be associated with you in any stories that appear in the press. That's one reason."

Button shook his head. "They wouldn't listen to anything I had to say."

"I think you're wrong. My bet is that they consider what you told them *extremely* important. In fact, it told them what *not* to look for—in this case, they can rule out the possibility that any of those people could have been killed by an animal. They're hunting a serial killer, Button. Count on it."

Nate Button stared at me for some time, breathing noisily through his mouth. He looked thoroughly bewildered. "That's insane," he said at last. "You're telling me the FBI is searching for a human killer precisely because I told them all the evidence points to a lobox?"

"You've got it."

"Are you mocking me, Frederickson?"

"No. You have to understand that the bureau people aren't for a moment going to take seriously the possibility that the men were killed by an extinct animal from prehistoric times, and you helped them rule out the possibility of any other animal—boars, bears, rabid dogs, what have you. What that leaves is a human— but a human with very specialized knowledge of paleontology and zoology. How many people would even know about a lobox, much less leave a corpse that could make another specialist like yourself believe a lobox had done the killing? Do you see?"

The cryptozoologist slowly shook his head, but I couldn't tell whether he was indicating that he didn't understand what I was getting at, or simply rejected it.

"They questioned you very closely about your colleagues, didn't they?"

He looked surprised. He licked his lips, closed his mouth, swallowed. "As a matter of fact, they did. They even demanded the subscription list for the journal I edit. At the time, I thought they wanted it just so that they could consult other experts . . . Oh, my God."

"Now you're beginning to get the picture, Dr. Button. Their first and foremost suspect would have been *you* after you laid all this business about the lobox on them, but you must have had an airtight alibi at the time of the Missouri killing and when the second victim was found. Still, you can bet they know what you've had for breakfast, lunch, and dinner on every day since then when a victim has been found. So you're no longer a suspect, but they are hunting someone else with your same interests and expertise. They bar you from the sites because they don't want to be associated with you, but also because they now want to keep as many details secret as possible; it helps them screen out false confessions."

"I hadn't thought of that," Button said distantly. "Perhaps you're right. It's just that. . . . Why would a killer go to the considerable trouble of making his murders look like the work of an extinct prehistoric creature virtually nobody outside a small field of specialists has ever heard of?"

"Well," I said with a shrug, "that's certainly a good question, and a debating point for your side. I do know that you can never tell what's really going on inside the mind of a serial killer. This one's apparently an academic, scholarly type who's using his deep grounding in paleontology to amuse himself while he thinks he's baffling the experts."

"Frankly, your theory doesn't sound any more plausible than mine," Button said tersely, and sniffed. "In order to create paw prints, fang marks, and body wounds like those I observed at the Missouri site, a man *would* have to go to considerable trouble; even then, he would have no guarantee that an expert like myself would come along, recognize the signs, and say that the killing was the work of a lobox."

Harper brushed a strand of gray hair back from her eyes, said to Button: "You don't think that Robby's scenario is more credible than the notion of an extinct creature suddenly coming back to life, popping up out of nowhere in the middle of the United States?"

The cryptozoologist took a handkerchief out of one of the pockets in his safari jacket, blew his nose loudly, carefully wiped it, put the handkerchief back in his pocket. Then he looked at Harper. "Maybe it didn't 'pop up out of nowhere,' Miss Rhys-Whitney."

"Then where did it come from, Dr. Button?"

"Perhaps from the north—Canada, Minnesota, perhaps even down from Alaska. It could be a throwback, a single mutant. There is a phenomenon known as 'reverse breeding.' It's a practice usually indulged in by scientists or specialist breeders, but it's possible that it could have happened naturally, in the wild. In upstate New York, at a place called the Catskill Game Farm, there's a large herd of small, striped horses. They're members of a species that was extinct for close to a hundred thousand years before some scientists began a reverse breeding program with a selected group of modern-day horses. They bred for hidden, submerged genetic traits; when there were offspring that showed even a partial trace of the traits they were looking for, they matched those offspring. The result is a herd of 'prehistoric' horses, which you can see with your own eyes.

"It's just possible that a lobox was created in this manner by accident, a wolf breeding with a dog—perhaps a kuvasz. One offspring in the resulting litter was this animal, a freak of nature; it may not be a purebred lobox, but the genetic inheritance was strong enough for it to have developed the lobox's distinctive claw at the rear of the footpad. It was born far to the north, then migrated south, away from the cold, and only recently settled into this pattern of hunting and killing its . . . natural prey."

Harper shook her head, rested her elbows on the table, placed her fingertips together to form an arch. "The killings have taken place hundreds of miles apart."

"Ah, but we don't know what a lobox's natural hunting range

is, Miss Rhys-Whitney. If this creature has inherited the speed and intelligence we believe was possessed by its ancestors, then it could range over an extremely broad area, and it would be very wily. Even if it were sighted, it might be mistaken for a large dog." Button paused, took a deep breath through his open mouth, shuddered slightly. "If it's a lobox, or anything like a lobox, it is a most formidable creature. Perhaps the only natural enemy humankind has ever had. And if it's able to breed successfully with wolves or dogs . . ."

Nate Button turned back toward me, and for a moment the reflection of candlelight danced in his eyes' dark depths. Suddenly, I felt sorry for the man, as I realized how much emotion the cryptozoologist had invested in his quest to be the first to unmask this ultimate in hidden animals, a prehistoric creature rambling over the Great Plains, stopping on occasion to rip up and eat some unfortunate human.

"The prehistoric horses you mentioned are the result of years of work by humans, Dr. Button," I said quietly. "The herd represents generation after generation of offspring that are the result of very careful reverse breeding. What do you suppose the odds are against the spontaneous mutation that would create a lobox?"

"Astronomical, to be sure," Button said with a small sigh as he gathered the photos and sketches off the table and shoved them back into his worn leather briefcase. He made no effort now to hide his deep disappointment at my total lack of enthusiasm for his idea. "Perhaps you're right, Dr. Frederickson; perhaps the killing thing will turn out to be human after all. I've very much enjoyed meeting the two of you, and now I won't take up any more of your evening."

As Button rose from his chair, Harper rubbed her foot against my leg under the table. It felt like an electric shock, and I barely managed to stifle a groan.

"Good night, Dr. Button," Harper said evenly as she looked at me and raised an eyebrow provocatively. Her shoeless foot was working its way up my leg, past my knee, wriggling against my thighs. "Good luck with your search."

Button merely waved with his free hand as he made his way toward the exit.

"Well, Robby," she continued in her low, husky voice, "I think he was an interesting fellow, don't you?"

"Uh . . . yeah." Harper had now rested her foot in my groin, and I was starting to sweat. "Whatever you say, my dear."

"I say it's time we went to bed."

"Right. You're going to have to stand and walk right in front of me when I get up, or I'm going to be seriously embarrassed."

"It can be arranged."

Our lovemaking that night was well worth the wait.

CHAPTER FIVE

We flew to Topeka the next morning, rented a car, and drove south to Dolbin, where World Circus had set up for the week on the county fairgrounds. We arrived too late to catch the matinee performance under the Big Top, and we bided our time by wandering over the grounds. I would have liked to view the animals, perhaps say hello to my old friend Mabel, but a number of posted signs and the presence of security guards made it clear that visitors were not welcome in the penning areas.

As we approached a water spigot near one of these areas, Harper abruptly stopped, squatted down. She opened her leather purse, took out what appeared to be a wooden pillbox with an enameled cover that had perhaps a half dozen tiny holes punched in it. Next she produced a sealed plastic refrigerator bag, and I was rather startled to see that it contained a strange mix of dead flies and small, live beetles. The last item to come out of her purse was a small sponge encased in plastic wrap. She set the wooden box down on the ground, slid the top back a fraction of an inch, shook an ounce or so of the anteater's trail mix into the opening, closed it again. She straightened up, wetted the sponge under the spigot, squeezed a few drops of water through the holes in the cover of the box.

"Feeding time," she said brightly, smiling at me. "What's the matter, Robby? You look very strange."

"I may look very strange, love, but you *are* very strange."

"Why, thank you."

"Harper, what the hell have you got in that box?"

"Oh, I always bring a little friend with me when I travel," she said in the same bright tone as she wiped excess water off the top of the wooden box with a tissue, then replaced box, plastic bag, and sponge in her purse. "For some reason, having said little friend always makes me feel more secure. Does it make you nervous?"

"*You* make me nervous, Harper. You've always made me nervous."

"Come on, sweet thing," she said, slinging her purse over her shoulder, grabbing my hand and leading me toward the midway, which was set up on six or seven acres at the northern end of the fairgrounds. "First I want to ride on the Ferris wheel, and then you can buy me some cotton candy."

It didn't take much sight-seeing to establish that World Circus was well managed, a class act—at least as far as the midway and food concessions were concerned. The grounds were relatively litter-free, the mechanical rides all showed indications of proper maintenance, and the food stalls were clean. There were none of the seedy peep shows one finds in so many rural road shows, and I saw no evidence of cheating at any of the game stalls. A few inquiries later, we learned that the rides, games, and food concessions were all locally franchised, administered separately from the circus itself; a number of different booking agents were used all along the circus's great, circuitous route. Nobody we talked to knew any of the actual circus performers or roustabouts, since these people invariably kept to themselves. Still, all the concessionaires seemed happy with the arrangement and went to some lengths to police themselves; while insisting on honest, clean operations, World Circus paid a slightly higher percentage of profits than other road shows that came through the area, and the concessionaires were anxious to remain in good graces. Word of mouth was good, and attendance at the circus had tripled from the year before.

This was all very depressing. I'd been hoping to find a failing operation, a deteriorating mud show whose discouraged owners might be more than willing to dump it all off on anyone who made them a reasonable buy offer. What I'd found instead was a lean and efficiently run circus that might well be turning a small profit, if the costs for the performing talent weren't too high.

And I found myself growing depressed about other things. Wherever we walked, we immediately became the center of attention. People openly gawked at the dwarf and the beautiful woman, and not a few of the stares were hostile, as if the fact that we might be attracted to each other was a violation of some natural law. A few times I tried to remove my hand from Harper's, but she only tightened her grip as she kept up a constant stream of chatter, seemingly oblivious to the starers. In my frame of mind, her gesture took on heroic proportions. Falling in love with Harper Rhys-Whitney, I thought, was most definitely something I did not need. Through no fault of hers, she made me *feel* small and needy; her perfection only served to magnify, at least in my mind, my own imperfection. It was, of course, all quite neurotic, the kinds of unhealed scars we all carry with us from our childhood—but there it was, a terrible, and growing, insecurity. And I feared it was already too late to do anything about it. I was apparently still not sufficiently emotionally healthy to accept the love of a woman without risk of destroying myself with the gift.

I had the distinct feeling that I was being watched—which, I told myself, was absurd, since I *was* so obviously being watched. But I also sensed that we were being followed, and that was something different altogether. I abruptly turned around a few times, but in the crush of people it was impossible to pick out any one individual who might be tailing us.

Wandering around a circus midway set up in a vast field in the heart of rural Kansas, I was reminded yet again that a hole opened in my heart whenever I left New York City, with its crush of anonymity, and traveled into America's interior. The fields of Kansas reminded me too much of my childhood home in Nebraska. Out through that hole in my heart flowed my self-confidence; all that was left was a bilious, sour cloud of self-consciousness and paranoia. It was a lousy feeling, only exacerbated by the lovely creature holding my hand, and with whom I was sharing a bed. In my present frame of mind, I considered Harper—or, to be more precise, what I was feeling for Harper—all the more dangerous to my spiritual well-being. Being a dwarf was occasionally a pain, but I'd learned to deal with it; being a self-pitying dwarf was intolerable to me. It made me anxious to get on with my business in Kansas so that I could get back to where I felt safe, perhaps taking Harper with me. Yet I knew I couldn't afford to be—or seem—in a hurry. I owed it to Phil to try to keep myself together long enough to make the strongest effort of which I was capable in order to try to buy back his circus for him.

The evening show under the Big Top began at eight. At seven-thirty we wandered back in the direction of the enormous canvas tent, along with a crowd of what I estimated to be upwards of eight or nine hundred people. It wasn't at all a bad turnout, especially considering the fact that it was a weeknight and many of the families, most with small children, had undoubtedly driven a considerable distance over a countryside that was being terrorized by a vicious, insane killer.

As we got into the line that had formed in front of the ticket booth, I once again had the feeling that we were being observed, followed. I abruptly turned to my left, found myself staring into a pair of mud-brown eyes that framed a large, bulbous nose illuminated by networks of flaming, alcohol-ruptured veins. He was a big man, with a potbelly and legs that were slightly bowed, as if bending under the man's considerable weight. He looked like a roustabout, or perhaps the kind of thuggish security guard often hired by shows to remain in the background and provide muscle in case of trouble with town rowdies. Our gazes locked and held, and then the potbellied man flushed a deep red that almost matched the broken veins in his nose, turned, and walked quickly away.

Interesting, I thought. However, since I couldn't think of a single reason why anyone would want to keep tabs on us, I decided the man—roustabout, security guard, or whatever—had simply been more persistently curious than the others, or was more than a little interested in Harper. I turned my attention back to the line, which was moving more rapidly as showtime neared. Above the ticket window, a hand-lettered sign announced that National Rifle Association members showing their cards would receive fifteen percent off the price of admission.

World Circus carried no freak show, but the man selling tickets inside the booth at the entrance to the tent looked as if he was more than prepared to audition for the part of our sixteenth President in some "living museum" exhibit, and it occurred to me that he might actually be an actor, between roles, biding his time and picking up some ready cash by working for World Circus. It was impossible to gauge his height, since only his head and shoulders were visible, but from the way he was hunched over inside the booth I judged him to be over six feet, lanky. He looked like Lincoln, and he looked decidedly out of place wearing a dark suit of expensive material and a tie—the temperature was well over eighty. He had a gaunt, almost sad-looking face, piercing black eyes, black hair, a full beard. Although there was no gray in his hair, I put his age at over sixty.

"Two, please," I said as we reached the booth and I offered up a twenty-dollar bill.

The piercing black eyes, cool and glittering with intelligence, studied me; his gaze flicked to Harper, then came back to me. "Good evening, Dr. Frederickson," the man said in a pleasing baritone that echoed slightly inside the wooden cage. "It's an honor to have you join us."

I stepped back two paces and craned my neck in order to get a clearer look at his face. "You know me?"

"Indeed. You are the most esteemed alumnus of this very circus," the man who looked like Abraham Lincoln said. "Among other things. You are a very famous man, more than likely to be recognized even in the more sparsely populated regions of the nation. I'm afraid I don't recall the lady's name, but if I'm not mistaken, I've seen her likeness on posters dating back to the time of the circus's previous ownership. Ma'am, I believe you handled reptiles?"

"I'm Harper Rhys-Whitney," Harper said.

"Yes," the man replied, then turned his attention back to me. "You're a long ways from home, sir."

69

"Yeah. I just happened to be passing through the area, and I thought I'd check out the show."

"I see," the man in the ticket booth said, sounding as if he didn't see at all. Or that he didn't believe me.

I could hear some low grumbling from the people waiting in line behind me. A large hand holding my twenty-dollar bill and two green slips of paper emerged from the hole at the bottom of the screen in the window above my head. "These complimentary passes are for you and Miss Rhys-Whitney, Dr. Freckerickson," the man continued. "Your money is no good here. I think you'll be pleased with the seats. Enjoy the show."

"Who are you?"

"Oh, just an employee."

The grumbling behind me was growing louder, and I felt somebody press up against my back. "Thanks for the passes," I said quickly. "Listen, would you tell the owner that I'd like to have a few words with him afterward?"

"I'm afraid that would be impossible."

"Why?"

"The owner doesn't travel with the show."

"Who is the owner?"

"Oh, I'm afraid I'm not in a position to give out that kind of information."

"Then I'll talk to whoever is in charge. Would it be okay if we go back to the trailers after the show? I'd like to talk to the performers."

"I'm afraid not, Dr. Frederickson. We have a very strict policy against that. I'm sorry. Would you mind moving on, now? There are people waiting. Enjoy the show."

Pressed by the people in the line behind me, I took the green passes, walked with Harper through the open flaps behind the ticket booth into the great tent. An usher glanced at the slips of paper, then guided us along a narrow aisle at the base of a bank of bleacher seats to what appeared to be a VIP section with six folding chairs—all empty now—inside an oblong wooden box bedecked with red, white, and blue bunting, and set virtually flush with the sawdust track running around the perimeter of the Big Top and enclosing the one ring. The VIP box was a little too public for my taste, but we certainly weren't going to have to worry about having our view blocked by people sitting in front of us; we were close enough to the single ring to be part of the show. Almost as soon as we sat down, a six-piece band seated at the top of the bleacher section directly across from us began to play.

Harper leaned close to me in order to be heard over the music, said, "Is this the first time you've been back?"

"Yep."

"It must seem very strange to you."

It indeed felt strange, after so many years, to be sitting under the great canvas canopy where I had once been the center of attention, my acrobatic skills eventually being incorporated into almost half the acts, with a grand finale that saw me flying off a trapeze, soaring up and past the area covered by the safety net, into the steel, wood, and rope rigging actually holding up the Big Top. From there, I made my way around the perimeter of the tent, a single spotlight following me on my airborne journey, while all of the other acts gathered below in the three rings Phil had always used. Swinging through the rigging wasn't actually as dangerous as it looked, since there was a multitude of ropes, struts, and bars to grab hold of, but it was definitely a crowd pleaser. Especially at the end when I dropped twenty feet to land on Mabel's back.

So much was the same, yet at the same time completely different. I had tumbled through rings of fire in the center ring, soared through the air at the top of the tent, and yet now I couldn't even wrangle an invitation to visit backstage.

I said, "I'm sorry I didn't come back to visit when it was still Phil's circus."

"Hey, with a little luck, you may still get the chance."

"With a little luck."

The owner or owners of World Circus had invested some money in a new, modernized lighting system, which suddenly came on full force; a multitude of strobe lights began flashing over the audience while a single, powerful spotlight danced over the curtained-off entrance to our left. The band blared out a fanfare, the curtains drew apart, and the Grand Procession began.

Leading the procession were the elephants, minus Mabel.

These were the smaller Asians—Curly, Joe, and Mike—bedecked in thick leather harnesses with shiny brass buckles and streamers of brightly colored bunting and flowers. Atop Curly, who led the pack, waving to the cheering crowd in the center of the yellow spotlight that followed him, stood a man who was naked to the waist, wearing gold, spangled tights and black, calf-high leather boots. He held no reins to steady himself, yet he seemed perfectly balanced just behind the elephant's head, agilely bouncing and swaying in time to the elephant's rhythm as it led the parade around the sawdust track. I judged the man to be in his early to mid-forties, but he had the hard, sculpted body of a much younger man.

The public address announcer intoned: *"World Circus features Luther, world's greatest animal trainer!"*

I greeted the announcement with a skeptical clearing of my throat.

Harper, a slight catch in her voice, said, "God, he's magnificent."

I experienced a sudden, sharp pang of jealousy and was immediately angry with myself for feeling it. Harper Rhys-Whitney, I reminded myself, had always relished her men—and she'd gone through four husbands and countless lovers to prove it. Just because we had recently begun sleeping together was no reason for me to let my brains run out my ears. Our sharing of sexual delights meant absolutely nothing as far as any kind of long-range commitment was concerned. I was undoubtedly an exercise in nostalgia for Harper, and her seemingly boundless passion and willingness to give of herself was her gift, perhaps a homage to our close friendship in the past. I was just going to have to will myself to enjoy Harper as long as it was her pleasure to be enjoyed by me, and not tarnish that gift with anything as negative and presumptuous as jealousy.

But it wasn't going to be easy.

Besides, the fact of the matter was that Luther *was* magnificent. He appeared to be about six feet, a hundred and seventy or eighty pounds, all muscle. He had firm, sculpted features, a shaved bullet head, strong chin and mouth, glacial blue eyes that glinted in the yellow spotlight that was tightly focused on him as he passed in front of and above us on his mount's journey around the sawdust track. The man exuded charisma and control. I strongly doubted that the "world's greatest animal trainer" was a man I'd never heard of, performing in a third-tier road show, but I suspected he was certainly good, and maybe more than just good. Any successful animal act is a partnership, a collaboration, between beasts and trainer, and it takes a special kind of person, with a very special gift; watching Luther balanced atop Curly's head, I suspected he had it.

It didn't surprise me that Mabel wasn't in the Grand Procession. By default, I had become Mabel's "mahout" when she was a very sick baby, after Phil had bought her from a carnival owner who had mistreated her—and I had never, in the years I'd cared for, fed, and worked with her, felt sufficiently confident of her good behavior to take her out with the other animals at the beginning of the show. It appeared Luther had the same misgivings. Mabel was an African elephant, not Asian, and the difference can be described as relatively the same as between a pit bull and a spaniel. About the only things they have in common are color and those incredibly versatile appendages called trunks, living columns of flesh comprised of more than a hundred thousand muscles that can hold more than two gallons of water. From a scientific viewpoint, taxonomists do not even consider the two species closely related, although they obviously evolved from the same ancestor. African elephants, distinguished from Asians by their larger, floppier ears, are also bigger in overall size. In the African species, both sexes have tusks. The last time I saw Mabel, her tusks measured eight feet and had been permanently capped with stainless-steel hemispheres bolted to the ivory. African elephants are highly intelligent and—when they are in a cooperative mood—can be taught to do some amazing tricks. The problem is that you can never predict when an African elephant is going to feel in a cooperative mood; a misjudgment can get you killed. Africans are rarely trainable, always unpredictable, and potentially dangerous.

Both species are long-lived—the record, in captivity, being an eighty-six-year-old Asian elephant in Ceylon which was used to carry the sacred tooth of Buddha on ceremonial occasions. After twenty years, I thought, Mabel and I were growing old together, but—the stories about elephants having exceptionally long mem-.

ories notwithstanding—I doubted very much that she would remember me. The reason I knew she was still alive and with the circus was the fact that the program listed a special act featuring the "monster elephant." That would be Mabel; even more than most Africans, Mabel had always been a prima donna. I was most curious to see just what Luther was coaxing her to do to earn her considerable keep—besides using her as a living crane to raise and lower the Big Top, which she'd always enjoyed doing anyway.

The elephants looked well cared for, as did the six horses that followed them in the processional. The program listed a bear act and, of course, Bengal tigers; these animals would have to be well taken care of, or they simply wouldn't perform. It also meant World Circus had a good veterinarian traveling with them, not one that existed only on paper, as was the case with so many third-tier road shows and carnivals. The healthy look of the animals, and the generally robust feel of the operation, could mean that the owner really cared about his or her acquisition, which could make my mission that much more difficult.

The show started off with an equestrian act. Harper's friends in Palmetto Grove had mentioned the quality of the performers, and now I could see what they meant. The horses, all white bays, were expertly trained, the performers who jumped on and off their backs and raced with them around the ring, daring and skilled. This, I thought, was a circus in the European and Russian tradition—one ring instead of three, but with acts that deserved and got undivided attention to what was happening in that one ring.

Incredibly, every act that followed seemed even better than the one that preceded it—bears, jugglers, dogs, tumblers, aerialists. If anything, I thought, they were almost too good to be performing in a relatively small road show like World Circus, virtually unheralded, traveling in broken-down campers and semis over bumpy roads, going from one rural town to another. All of these performers could be with Ringling Brothers, Cole, or Beatty—the big boys—traveling in much greater comfort and presumably making more money, perhaps working fewer hours.

It was true that I'd stayed with Statler Brothers Circus even after receiving far better offers, but I'd stayed out of a sense of loyalty to Phil Statler. It was difficult for me to believe that all of the fine performers I was watching remained with World Circus out of loyalty to an owner who was, if the ticket taker could be believed, an absentee landlord. Then there was the question of where these people had come from, where they had learned and polished their skills. The world of the circus is a small one and should have included the performers in World Circus; word of exceptional talent spreads from show to show, people move from show to show, get to know each other, hang out in the same bars, vacation in the same places, or—especially in the case of freaks— retire to towns like Palmetto Grove in order to avoid the stares of the curious or simply to have neighbors with whom to relive old memories. None of Harper's friends had purported to know any of the World Circus performers or to have heard of them previously; it was almost as if World Circus had hired its people from another planet. I found it all quite curious and knew it was something I was going to have to try to look into; if our budding corporation was to make a successful bid to buy the circus, I would have to know the details of the operation, including the terms of the contracts held by all the performers.

Harper nudged me. I glanced at her, then looked in the direction where she was pointing, at a spot high up in the bleacher section to our right. I could see nothing but darkness.

"What is it?"

"It's a who. Your admirer, Dr. Button. Wait until the lights pass over that area again."

I waited. An animal act was in progress, with spotlights anchored at ground level sweeping back and forth across a woman and her dogs, and incidentally illuminating various groups in the audience. Suddenly a cone of white light swept across the top of the bleacher section where Harper had been pointing and I could indeed see Nate Button in the very top row, still breathing with his mouth open and still wearing his khaki safari jacket. However, he wasn't watching the action in the ring; he was staring off into space, absently tapping the right side of his head with a rolled-up piece of paper that was the same color as the handbills we had seen announcing the schedule of the circus for the next six weeks. I started to wave to him, but then the light passed, and he was once again lost to sight.

"He's come a long way for a little excitement," I said. "It must be better than four hundred miles from Lambeaux to here."

Harper shrugged. "Who can resist a circus?"

After the dogs came a trapeze act, and then a company of clowns took over, working the sawdust track and the aisles as a gang of roustabouts proceeded to throw up a huge, double-walled steel cage that would contain the Bengal tigers listed as the next act in the program. The double-walled cage was the same one Phil had used, but it now had a curious modification: an extra set of doors had been cut into the enclosure, and they extended all the way to the top of the cage, twenty-five feet in the air. I wondered what they were for.

The rigging completed, the small band struck up another fanfare; Luther, dressed now in black leather pants with matching vest and black boots, came bounding into the caged-in ring out of the mouth of the tunnel leading back to the penning area. As the music abruptly ended and the applause died down, Luther turned back toward the dark tunnel and casually clapped his hands together once. Instantly, a huge, sleek Bengal tiger emerged from the tunnel as if shot from the mouth of a cannon and raced toward the man standing in the center of the ring with his hands at his sides.

My initial reaction was that a critical mistake had been made—a missed cue or a mistake in timing by the handlers working the tiger cages backstage at the other end of the tunnel—and I sat bolt upright in my seat, sucking in my breath. Animal trainers rarely used blank-loaded guns any longer, but Luther had nothing in his hands, no whip, chair, or cane baton, and no sane man faced a grown tiger with nothing but his bare hands. Luther had absolutely nothing to interpose between himself and the savage missile of fangs, muscle, and claws hurtling toward him. The tiger bunched its hind legs beneath it and leaped at Luther's head as it extended its great paws.

At the very last moment, Luther put his hands on his hips and bowed slightly, no more than five or six inches. The tiger sailed through the air over him, its furred belly actually seeming to brush against Luther's shaved head, and landed on the padded platform directly behind the trainer. It immediately leaped down to a slightly lower platform to the left, sat on its haunches. Even a slight flick of the tiger's paws during its flight could have torn Luther's head from his shoulders, and then these few hundred people inside a circus tent in a desolate area of the Midwest would certainly have seen a lot more for their money than they'd bargained for.

Even as the first tiger was settling onto its perch, a second tiger burst from the dark mouth of the tunnel, and then a third. Each of the tigers executed the same maneuver, leaping through the air only millimeters over Luther's slightly bowed head to land on the platform behind him. As the tigers reared up on their haunches and pawed the air, Luther turned around to bow to them, then raised his arms to acknowledge the applause of the crowd.

Neither Harper—who, like me, knew more than a little about the difficulties and dangers of working with tigers—nor I was clapping. We'd both half risen from our seats in expectation of grisly tragedy, and only now, as the applause began to fade, did I realize that I had been holding my breath. "Jesus H. Christ," I said as I exhaled and slowly lowered myself back down onto my seat. "That is one fucking crazy animal trainer."

Harper said nothing as she too sank back into her seat. She didn't have to. When I glanced sideways at her, I could see that her face was flushed, her maroon, gold-flecked eyes gleaming. I wondered whether it was Luther himself that so excited her, or his masterful handling of the cats, and decided that it was probably both.

Spellbound, I watched Luther work his tigers, using only voice and hand signals. Damned if the man might not actually be the world's greatest animal trainer after all, I thought. Up to that point, the greatest I had ever seen was the justly celebrated Gunther Goebbel-Williams, now retired from Ringling Brothers, who'd worked with an elephant and up to a dozen tigers in a ring. Statler Brothers Circus hadn't had that kind of a livestock budget, nor did this one. Luther might only have three cats, but one tiger can kill you just as easily as a dozen, and I had never, ever, heard of a trainer going into a cage with tigers empty-handed. A whip or a baton might be a puny defense against a Bengal tiger, but the point was that the tiger didn't know that. The whip, chair, or baton was an important psychological barrier between man and beast, the man's scepter of authority. Luther managed to work without anything.

To the unpracticed eye, the tricks Luther did with his tigers would appear simple. In fact, they were anything but. He worked them very slowly, in elegant routines requiring perfect control and concentration on his part, and absolute cooperation and split-second timing on the tigers' part. It was the group equivalent of a top expert skier "walking," virtually in slow motion, down a precipitous mountainside while athletes of lesser abilities schussed past him to the plaudits of onlookers who did not understand that slow can be much more difficult than fast—in skiing, in working animals, and in life. It struck me that, alone among the World Circus performers, Luther would probably have the most difficult time being accepted by a larger circus—at least this particular animal act. The act was simply not sufficiently flamboyant to excite audiences used to faster routines. Luther had opted to turn animal training to an art form that could only be appreciated fully by the cognoscenti.

When he finished, he casually waved his cats, one by one, back into the tunnel leading to the penning area. There was only a smattering of applause by now, but I knew that Luther was the greatest animal trainer *I* had ever seen, and I found that I was deeply moved by this display of skill, courage, and absolute rapport between man and animal.

Now, standing alone in the center of the large ring, Luther produced a tiny whistle from a pocket in his black leather vest. He raised the whistle to his lips, blew into it. The resulting sound was inaudible to human ears, but the immediate response was the great, trumpeting bellow of an elephant somewhere backstage; the sound seemed to fill the tent with an almost physical presence, making the bleacher platforms vibrate. Luther spun around, then ran across the ring and disappeared into the tunnel.

"*And now* . . ." the announcer intoned over the public address system, ". . . *the monster elephant!*"

There was another trumpeting bellow from backstage.

"Neat," Harper whispered in my ear. "He's taught Mabel to speak."

I agreed that it was neat; getting Mabel to do anything on command, with consistency, was neat.

A few moments later, Mabel, outfitted in full, clanging "war elephant" regalia of steel-studded leather harnesses, marched regally through the parted curtains of the entranceway, with Luther riding atop her, while the band enthusiastically blatted out a souped-up version of the Triumphal March from *Aida*.

Whether or not Mabel was fully earning her keep, she was certainly looking real good; obviously putting away her vitamins and truckload of hay a day and getting her beauty rest. I felt a surge of emotion as I gazed up at the magnificent, multi-ton beast that I had nursed back to health and started to train when she weighed barely three hundred pounds. My little baby had made good. I felt like a proud parent, and I found I had tears in my eyes.

Luther stopped her when she was in front of the first bleacher section and she immediately began to turn in a circle, lifting her knees high as she did a kind of elephant prance I had never seen before. I could see that he was controlling her with a mahout stick, a mahogany pole with a steel hook at the end, prodding and goading her behind the ears to get her to go forward or to turn. As with Luther's performance with the tigers, I was more than a little impressed by his control of Mabel. The proper function of a mahout stick, despite its nasty hook, is not to hurt, for it's never a good idea to get an elephant angry at you, but to more or less focus the animal's attention on what it is you do or don't want it to do. I'd had an aversion to the mahout stick, so I'd used a baseball bat—a Louisville Slugger, Henry Aaron model. After Mabel had started to put on weight and pose a very real threat to my life and limb, I'd found it quite effective to get her attention by whacking her on the tusks with the bat if I was on the ground, or around the head if I was on top of her. Luther, however, seemed to be doing just fine with the hooked mahout stick—but I comforted myself with the thought that Luther was bigger than me.

Mabel finished her curiously dignified pachyderm pirouette. She obviously knew—and accepted—the routine, for with no further prompting from Luther she straightened out and came down the sawdust track, heading for the next bleacher section, opposite Harper and me. As the animal and her rider came abreast of the box, I raised my hands above my head and applauded. This was not a good idea. I'd no sooner raised my arms than Mabel's incredibly powerful yet delicate, sinuous trunk whipped around under my arms, encircling my chest, and plucked me straight up out of my seat.

"*Sheeit!*" I screamed as I was lifted high in the air and then deposited unceremoniously on my stomach, arms and legs splayed to the sides, in the valley between Mabel's two huge skull mounds, virtually in Luther's lap. The trainer looked even more startled than I was. "*Jeeesus Christ!*"

So much for my skepticism regarding the acuity of an elephant's long-term memory.

The fact that Mabel had decided to shanghai an old friend during the course of her performance obviously wasn't going to keep her from completing her star turn. Without missing a step, and with me bouncing around and with only a precarious grip on a strap of her head harness to keep me from falling to the ground, she reached the next bleacher section and immediately went into another pirouette.

The people, naturally assuming that this hilarious spectacle of the plucked-up dwarf dangling from Mabel's head harness was all part of the act, were out of their seats, screaming, stomping their feet, and clapping with wild enthusiasm. Mabel, of course, was loving it too, and she proceeded to raise her feet even higher as she "pranced." I could feel my fingers beginning to ache as I held on for dear life.

"Hey, look!" I said to Luther, shouting to be heard over the roaring cheers of the crowd. "I'm really sorry about this!"

Luther had gotten over his initial shock, and was studying me, his glacial blue eyes bright with amusement. "Frederickson!" he shouted back in a voice laced with a heavy German accent. "Mabel's first mahout! Obviously, you imprinted her! She loves you! You are her only true master! I must say I'm quite jealous!"

I looked into the hard features of his face to try to see if that was his idea of a joke, decided he was at least half serious. "Yeah, that's great!" I yelled, tightening my grip on the harness with my left hand and extending my right. "How about helping me get up in the saddle?"

He grinned, then reached out and gripped my right wrist with fingers that felt as strong as steel cables. He effortlessly dragged me on board, then helped me turn around so that I was sitting cross-legged, just in front of him, with a secure grip on Mabel's harness.

"Are you okay, Frederickson?"

"Yeah," I replied over my shoulder. "It's been some time since I've taken an elephant ride, but I think I can manage not to fall off. What happens now?"

The crowd noise was beginning to subside as people settled back in their seats to enjoy the spectacle of the "world's greatest animal trainer" and a foolish-looking dwarf sitting atop the "monster elephant," and Luther was able to speak in a normal voice.

"I'll let her finish the routine," he said evenly, "and then I'll take her back so that you can dismount with some dignity. It's a pleasure to meet you, Frederickson. I've heard and read a good deal about you. I regret that we never had a chance to work with each other. I understand you're now well known as a private investigator, but I must say I was most impressed with what you managed to achieve with Mabel here. People also told me you worked with Bengals when you were with the circus."

Mabel had reached another bleacher section and was going into her curiously dainty pirouette. I half turned so that I could look into Luther's face, his startlingly blue eyes. He still had a look and air of amusement about him; despite his compliments, I had the feeling that he still couldn't quite believe there was a dwarf riding along with him on Mabel.

I said, "I never got in a cage with any Bengals, Luther. I just played with them. I used to like to help raise them from the time they were cubs."

"Always the best way."

"With me, working with animals was always just a hobby. Strictly amateur hour." I paused, added: "There was a time in my life when I pretty much preferred animals to people—most people."

"Oh, I still feel that way," Luther said easily. "Did you ever think about working tigers in the ring?"

"No. I never felt like getting eaten."

Luther grunted. "I believe you would have made a very good professional animal trainer."

Mabel, still running on automatic pilot, finished her dance, moved on to the last bleacher section, started turning once again.

"I was having enough trouble getting people to take me seriously as a tumbler and aerialist, Luther. I just don't think too many people would have taken to a dwarf tiger tamer."

"The tigers must have taken you seriously. That's all that counts."

"What about you, Luther? Why is it that nobody ever heard of you until you came to work for World Circus? And why do you stay when you're so obviously ready for bigger things?"

He paused a few seconds before answering. "I'm quite happy with World Circus, Frederickson."

"Are you? Now that Goebbel-Williams has retired, you'd have top billing at Ringling, or with Clyde Beatty. Here you're just another act listed in fuzzy print in a cheap program. As a matter of fact, that's true of every performer with World Circus, and you've got top-drawer acts. It's almost as if the owner wants to keep the circus going—but just barely, without too much publicity. What's going on here, Luther?"

"It's a long story, Frederickson," he said carefully. "I wouldn't want to bore you."

"Oh, I'm sure I'd be interested. Where did you people come from, and why is it nobody seems interested in moving on to the bigger arena shows?"

Mabel finished her pirouette and started back around the sawdust track.

"*Ho!*" Luther barked, reaching over my right shoulder and rapping Mabel smartly on the top of the head with the blunt end of his mahout stick.

Mabel stopped dead in her tracks.

"*Back!*" Luther commanded, rapping her two more times. "*Ho! Back!*"

Mabel stayed where she was. Luther waited a few seconds, then rapped her twice again, this time harder.

"*Back, Mabel! Ho! Back!*"

Mabel still didn't move. The crowd began laughing again, hooting at the trainer and the dwarf atop the recalcitrant elephant. Luther reversed the stick in his hand, used the steel hook at the end to goad her as he repeated his command for her to reverse direction. There was still no response from Mabel. The crowd began to laugh even louder. They were loving this unexpected clown act.

I again glanced back at Luther, who now looked a good deal more surprised and frustrated than amused. I said, "I used to use a baseball bat on her; Louisville Slugger, Henry Aaron model. You wouldn't happen to have a baseball bat tucked away up here, would you?"

"No, Frederickson," Luther said somewhat tersely, "I don't have a baseball bat. If I'd known Mabel was going to arrange to have you join me up here, I'd certainly have brought one."

"Mabel was always such a prima donna, as I know you've discovered. She likes the crowd response, and she doesn't want to give up the limelight."

Luther shook his head. "That's not it. It isn't the crowd, it's you. She wants to finish out the act with you, to show you what she can do."

"The act isn't finished?"

"No. I told you: I was going to take her back and let you off before we continued."

"Well, Luther, what the hell? I'm already up here, so why don't we all just go ahead and do whatever else it is you do so that we can keep Mabel happy?" The fact of the matter was that I was thoroughly enjoying myself in this, my first return to my circus alma mater. *I* was enjoying the limelight. It was exhilarating to be riding this great beast, and I wanted to prolong the experience for as long as possible.

Luther, an enigmatic smile on his face, didn't answer right away. Finally, he said, "I thought you might prefer to get off."

"Nah. I'm fine, Luther. Go ahead and finish the act."

"You're sure?"

"Hey, it's not as if this is the first time I've ever ridden an elephant. Let her rip."

"As you wish," Luther said, and then prodded Mabel behind the left ear with the hooked end of the mahout stick. "*Go, Mabel! Ha!*"

Mabel went; she reacted immediately, heading up the track at a good pace to the accompanying cheers, laughter, and applause of the crowd. She started to make the turn around the caged-in ring, abruptly stopped in front of the huge, steel double doors. Luther reached over my shoulder and used the hooked end of his stick to release the safety latch on top of one of the gates. He pushed with the stick, and the portal swung inward. Mabel moved forward.

I was beginning to have serious second thoughts about my casual decision to stay aboard Mabel for this particular ride.

Mabel turned sideways in the relatively narrow corridor, and this enabled Luther to lean back, hook the top of the open gate, and pull it shut. Mabel moved again, and Luther opened the inner gate, which automatically closed behind us as Mabel, without any prompting, stepped smartly into the enormous cage. Two tigers bounded out of the tunnel and began to race around Mabel, through her legs. The third tiger joined them, and all three bounded to their leather-padded pedestals where they sat and—I was convinced—proceeded to eye me hungrily.

Mabel, unbidden, curled her trunk upward, as if inviting me now to get off. I wasn't going anywhere.

"Take this," Luther said, handing me his mahout stick as he stepped around me and settled into the muscled cradle formed by Mabel's trunk. "If any of the cats comes at you, poke it with this. Otherwise, my advice is to remain very still and try not to show that you're afraid."

Right.

Mabel lowered Luther smoothly to the ground, where he stepped out of the trunk's cradle and went immediately into his routine, again using only hand and voice signals. The tigers leaped off their perches and began a slow lope around the stolid Mabel, gradually speeding up their pace, occasionally darting under her belly, snaking in a figure-eight pattern through her legs. I thought the tigers seemed skittish, which would have been understandable under the circumstances, and I was certain I now knew exactly how Custer had felt at Little Big Horn. A new element—me—had been unexpectedly introduced into their routine, and they did not know what it meant, were not sure what was expected of them. Tigers not sure of what is expected of them are liable to do what comes naturally—defend their turf, tear and bite at that which is unfamiliar.

Animals aren't people, and nobody who's survived working

with big cats, bears, or elephants ever makes the mistake of anthropomorphizing his or her charges. The beast may curb its natural instincts for a time out of love for, or fear of, a human, but instinct always threatens to take over, and death can be just a sweep of a claw, a snap of armored jaws, away. You change routine at your own peril, and Luther certainly knew that; by allowing Mabel to carry me into the cage with him, he was not only putting my life at risk but greatly increasing the threat to his own. It was quite a shared experience, and I had mixed emotions about it.

I turned around so that I was looking out over Mabel's broad back. I braced the mahout stick across my knees, gripped it firmly with both hands, took a deep breath, and waited to see what would happen next.

Each tiger took a turn leaping up off a pedestal onto Mabel's back, which was protected by a thick leather pad. Each tiger spent a few seconds that felt like hours glaring balefully at me and growling; I held the hooked end of the mahout stick out in front of me and growled back.

The crowd loved it.

The most dangerous moment came during the finale, with all three tigers gathered on Mabel's back, the closest only a yard or so away from me—close enough for me to smell her, close enough for her to remove my smeller along with the rest of my head, if she were so inclined. We studied each other for a few moments, but then, at Luther's command, she reared up on her haunches and pawed the air along with the two others.

Once, in a rare moment when my rough, lofty perch was tiger-free, I took my eyes off the animals long enough to glance at Harper. She was watching me intently. I managed a grin and a weak salute, but she didn't smile back. Grim-faced and ashen, she obviously didn't find anything about the situation amusing, and she was right. She knew her animals, knew that by introducing an unusual element into the routine Luther was playing a dangerous game—dangerous not only for Luther and me but also for the extremely valuable piece of livestock that a nurtured-from-birth, carefully trained Bengal tiger represented; I had no place to retreat, and if one of the magnificent beasts lunged at me, I would have no choice but to poke at its eyes or throat, looking to kill or maim.

But then Luther signaled for the tigers to leap off, and they did—with only a parting, perhaps regretful glance in my direction. They raced in line to the tunnel, with Luther standing at the tunnel's mouth and whacking each animal affectionately on the flank as it passed inside. Then he slowly walked back to Mabel, stepped into the trunk's cradle she offered, and rode regally back up to the top of her head as he waved triumphantly to the appreciative crowd.

"It's true what I've heard about you, Frederickson," Luther said easily as he settled down behind me, and Mabel, satisfied now, strutted once around the ring, then exited through the double gates, which were being held open for us by two women in skimpy, spangled costumes that included plumed headdresses. "You have courage."

"You too, Luther. That stunt was even riskier for you than it was for me."

"True, but I'm getting paid to take risks. May I ask you to join me in my trailer for some schnapps?"

"I have a lady friend with me."

"I know. I'll have her brought to us."

"In that case, I'll be happy to join you. And you can make that a triple schnapps."

CHAPTER SIX

"I must ask you a question, Frederickson," Luther said as he sipped at his glass of chilled, pear-flavored brandy. His blue eyes revealed nothing as he stared at me over the rim of his expensive crystal snifter. "Are you here on the behalf of a . . . government agency?"

I glanced at Harper, who was sitting next to me on a banquette in the kitchen area of Luther's small but nicely appointed trailer. Luther, swathed now in a thick terry-cloth robe and with a Turkish towel around his neck, was seated across from us, his elbows on the Formica-topped table. Harper had arrived moments after Luther and me, escorted by the Abraham Lincoln look-alike; Luther and the ticket taker had exchanged glances, but not spoken to each other. Now Harper met my gaze, but merely raised one eyebrow as she sipped at her brandy.

"No," I replied, turning back to Luther. "Why do you ask?"

"The purpose of your visit isn't in your capacity as a private investigator?" he asked in a flat tone. "You haven't been hired to, as you Americans say, 'check us out'?"

"You people had us followed out on the grounds, didn't you?"

Luther sighed, picked up the cut-glass decanter beside him,

and refilled our glasses. "I will be frank with you," he said in a low voice. "In any case, there is no way I can keep you from discovering the truth, if that's why you're here. If your visit is innocent . . . Well, you're both circus people, and I think you can be trusted. There is a good reason for the way World Circus operates, with no headliners and a minimum of publicity despite the fact that—as you pointed out, Frederickson—our performers are exceptional. There is a good reason why we do not choose to go elsewhere."

"Which is?"

"There is no place else to go. You see, Frederickson, every performer you saw tonight, every usher, clown, and roustabout, is in this country illegally." He paused, as if waiting for me to say something. When I didn't, he pushed his glass away from him, leaned back on the banquette, and folded his arms across his chest. "So there you have it. If you're here investigating an individual, or the circus itself, I've just given you information that can be used against us. Yes, you were recognized on the midway, and yes, we had you followed. You see, you make all of us very nervous."

"Luther," I said, shaking my head, "the INS doesn't use private investigators. I'm not here to check up on anyone."

"I'm relieved to hear that."

"What the hell is this, some kind of sanctuary movement for circus performers?"

"Precisely—if I understand correctly what you mean by 'sanctuary movement.' There is a great circus tradition in Russia and the Eastern European countries, as I'm sure the two of you are well aware. Much has changed in that part of the world, but some traditions remain. The famed Moscow Circus, perhaps the foremost collection of circus talent in the world, is still, in fact, made up of the finest acts which have been culled from small, regional circuses in the Eastern bloc countries. Those small, regional circuses are where all of us come from, and that's why you've never heard of us before. You may also know that it is a great honor to be selected as a performer in one of those circuses—and, of course, the government in each country still provides the best circus performers with certain privileges and a life-style not accessible to the average citizen. Circus performers are considered artists in the countries we come from, and all of the hundreds of regional circuses are subsidized by their respective governments. I am from what used to be East Germany. Some years ago, before all the changes and when I was much younger, I was invited to perform with the Moscow Circus. I refused the invitation."

"Why?" Harper asked.

"Because I hate the Russian people in particular, and the communist system in general," he said simply. "I could not allow my talents to be exploited and used as propaganda for a people and form of government I loathe."

Harper took another sip of her brandy, studied Luther's sculpted, hard-featured face. "I would think that at the time refusing an invitation like that could be risky," she said evenly.

Luther smiled thinly, nodded. "I was fired from my own circus and sent out to the countryside to work on a collective farm. It was eight years before I was allowed to return to my work with animals—and only then after I had submitted to a formal political rehabilitation program. Then I was given the opportunity to escape to this country, and I took it. It was because of this circus that I had that opportunity."

I said, "World Circus has only been in existence a little more than two years. As you mentioned, much has changed in that part of the world."

"All of us left before the changes. In any case, walking across a border there is not the same as coming *here*, to America, which is where all of us want to be. You see, Frederickson, World Circus is, indeed, a sanctuary for circus performers and their families who have fled to the greatest free country of all. Now we want to stay here. Unfortunately, the vagaries of various immigration laws being what they are, none of us has had the luxury of being able to go through normal procedures to acquire proper documentation. If we had even applied for exit permits in our own countries at that time, none of us would now even have the luxury of freedom."

I asked, "Who actually owns World Circus, Luther?"

"I'm not at liberty to tell you that, Frederickson. It's not that I don't trust you—I obviously do, or I wouldn't have admitted that all the personnel of this circus are illegal aliens. I simply feel

I don't have the right to give you the names of the individuals and organizations that banded together to buy and fund this circus, and to provide the finances and logistics necessary to help us escape from our countries and then travel here."

"People defected from communist bloc countries all the time, Luther, and they were routinely granted asylum. And things are considerably simpler now."

"Not for us, Frederickson. In many ways, the changes in Eastern Europe have complicated our situation here. There is nothing routine about the granting of asylum. You see, as circus performers, we are outsiders; our plight, especially now, would not generate the interest or sympathy of that of a defecting ballerina from the Bolshoi, or a chess grand master, or a scientist. Circus performers are not taken seriously by politicians. If we were not immediately sent back to our countries, we would all probably be put in refugee camps, like the Haitians and Laotians. It could be years before we obtained proper credentials, if we ever obtained them, and by then our careers would be finished. So, you see, it's just a little thing we have here. We prefer anonymity to the risk of losing our freedom to live here and practice our art. We don't harm anyone, and we bring pleasure to a great many people. It's enough for us. The one thing every person associated with this circus shares is a desire to live in the United States, and . . ." His voice trailed off as he glanced back and forth between Harper and me, and he frowned slightly. "Is something the matter? You both look . . . disappointed."

"Luther," I said wearily, "the reason Harper and I are here is that we represent a group of people who were hoping to buy this circus; we were hoping that whoever picked it up at auction when Phil Statler went bankrupt would be ready to cash in if he or they could turn a profit. The situation is turning out to be a little more complicated than we thought it would be."

"Ah," Luther said, once again leaning forward on his broad forearms. "And now you understand not only that the circus wouldn't be for sale but also why. Or I hope you do. It was not purchased for the purpose of making a profit, but to provide a refuge for circus performers, workers, and their families fleeing what was then communist oppression. Now it exists to allow us to remain in this country. Were we to lose this, not only would we lose a means to earn a living, but we could be sent to refugee camps or even forced to return to the countries we and our families risked so much to escape from."

I said, "Right."

Harper said, "Do you mind if we look around?"

Luther seemed startled by our reaction—or by what he might have considered a lack of it—and by Harper's request. He swallowed hard, recovered. "I don't think that would be a good idea, Miss Rhys-Whitney. As I've just explained to you, all of the people here have reason to feel skittish about outsiders, and very few of them speak English. I wouldn't want to make them uneasy, and I wouldn't want to subject the two of you to any possible hostility."

"I understand," I said, rising and extending my hand across the table. "We certainly don't want to make anyone nervous, so we'll be leaving. Thanks for the ride and drink, Luther. And good luck to all of you."

"And to both of you."

Harper, who seemed surprised by my sudden action, looked at me quizzically for a few moments, then slowly rose and took Luther's outstretched hand.

Abraham Lincoln was waiting outside the trailer to take us back the way we had come.

•   •   •

It can get cold, even in summer, in the Great Plains states when the sun goes down. Knowing this, I had brought along a light poplin jacket, and Harper a sweater, which we'd draped over the backs of our seats. Mabel hadn't given me much of an opportunity to gather my belongings when she'd decided to include me in her act, and Harper had left her sweater with my jacket on the seats when she'd come back to join Luther and me. By the time we returned, the show was over, the lights in the Big Top dimmed, Harper's sweater and my jacket gone. Abraham Lincoln apologized profusely and offered to pay for the missing articles of clothing, but we declined.

It was cold, and the heater in the rented car wasn't working; that was bad. Harper was huddled next to me as I drove; that was good. "Why the quick exit, Robby?" she mumbled into my shoulder.

"I didn't want to wear out our welcome."

"I didn't notice that we had a real welcome to wear out. I kind of figured you were going to put a little heat on him."

"Why did you figure that?"

"You mean you believed that story about all of them being illegal aliens, refugees from communist tyranny traipsing through the Midwest in a kind of ghost circus?"

"No. First, I can't see how being with a circus would protect you from INS scrutiny. Second, and more important, there were no children; none in any of the acts that we saw, and none wandering around outside the trailers. It was Luther who mentioned families, and it's a little hard for me to believe that all those men and women just up and left their children behind— one or two couples, maybe, but not all of them. Have you ever seen a circus where the performers' kids weren't running around all over the place?"

"Hmm. Of course not. I hadn't even thought of that."

"That's the reason you're not a world-famous private investigator. Why didn't *you* believe him?"

"Because I know at least a half dozen performers living in Florida who are refugees from what used to be communist bloc countries, and they never had any trouble getting permanent resident status. I think our friend Luther was bullshitting us, Robby. He's a hell of a lot better animal trainer than he is a liar."

"Right."

"Then why didn't you press him on it?"

"What would be the point? It doesn't make any difference what's really going on there. The only thing that matters is that they own the circus, and they obviously don't intend to sell it."

"Then you're not going to check with the bank in Chicago?"

I shrugged. "Sure. Why not? It's on the way home."

"But you don't think any information they might give you could somehow help us get the circus back?"

"Highly unlikely. I just want the information, if I can get it."

"I don't understand, Robby. If the people who own World Circus are up to something fishy, I mean something besides providing a sanctuary for illegal aliens, then why wouldn't it be possible for us to expose them and perhaps put them out of business? We could pick up the circus the same way they did. They virtually stole it from Phil, so why shouldn't we steal it from them?"

"It might be possible; it just wouldn't be a good idea."

Harper lifted her head from my shoulder, peered at me in the dim light cast by the dashboard. "And just why not, Mr. world-famous private investigator? I thought getting Phil Statler's circus back for him was why we came here."

"Because, my dear, the people who own World Circus and who may be using it as a front for some kind of illegal operation might not appreciate having the circus 'stolen back,' as you put it, much less having their activities exposed. Let's suppose, for the sake of argument, that we're dealing with some heavy drug dealers here. That would be my guess as to what's going on; the circus is used as a front for picking up drug shipments and then distributing those drugs in lots to smaller dealers across the Midwest, all along a fifteen-hundred-mile route. They're able to keep everybody together, and everything buttoned up tight, because everyone has a piece of the action. They've probably bought protection from local police in the areas they travel through. Of course, we could always go to the DEA—assuming we had some kind of proof. So all of the people involved are busted and put in the joint, the circus is seized and eventually put up for sale, we buy it and turn it over to Phil to manage. You think the big boys behind the whole operation, assuming it is drugs, are going to let it go at that? The first thing they'd probably do is blow up the whole circus during the middle of a performance, and then they'd start knocking off every one of the listed shareholders in the Statler Brothers Circus, starting with you and me. Drug dealers don't take kindly to having their operations exposed."

"I see," Harper said in a small voice as she again rested her head on my shoulder. "I hadn't thought of that either. But what if we could expose them without their finding out who we are, or that it's really the circus we're after?"

"I've already told Luther we were interested in buying the circus. I want to do some checking with the bank in Chicago, and then I'll pass on anything I learn, along with our suspicions, to an

FBI friend of mine in New York. But for now, we stay away from the circus. We want to get Phil back on his feet, not put him under the ground."

"You're right, Robby," she sighed. "It's just such a shame . . ."

After a few more minutes, Harper began stroking my thigh—slowly and gently at first, then with increasing pressure and purpose. It was becoming just a tad difficult to concentrate on my driving.

"It's still a couple of hours to Topeka," I said hoarsely, stroking the back of her hand where it had come to rest in my groin. "You want to stop someplace for the night where we can be, uh, warm?"

"I think that's a wonderful idea, Robby," she said huskily. "I was beginning to wonder how long I was going to have to keep this up before it would occur to you. I was afraid I was losing my powers of persuasion."

Fifteen minutes later we came to a medium-size town and found a motel on the highway just beyond it. I pulled up to the main office, parked next to a newspaper vending machine and left the car running, went into the office to register. I'd just started to fill out a registration card when I heard the office door open and close. I turned, was surprised to find Harper standing just behind me, a wry grin on her face. She was holding up a copy of a local newspaper, and I was startled by the half-page photograph and the banner headline just above it.

Obviously, the story told by the photograph and the banner headline had, at least for one day, pushed news and rumors about the werewolf killings off the front page. Now the big news was UFOs, as well as the Big Question of what the message seen by a few million people across four states might mean, and who the message might have been intended for; none of the dozen pilots who had been hired to skywrite or tow banners professed to know.

The headline read: *Message to an Alien in Our Midst?*

The photograph was of a message in smoke written across the sky, and it read:

MONGO CALL HOME

"Robby, I think you'd better call your brother," Harper said drily. "He seems anxious to talk to you."

· · ·

"Cute, Garth. Really cute. Is something the matter with Phil?"

"Well, well, well." Garth's voice at the other end of the line carried more than a hint of exasperation. "No, nothing's the matter with Phil. What with Mary's cooking and a lot of walks along the river, I'd say he's looking quite healthy. I see you got my message."

"I got it, all right, along with a few million other people. Jesus Christ, Garth, just how many planes did you hire, and how much is all that skywriting and banner-towing going to cost Frederickson and Frederickson?"

"Don't ask. I wouldn't have had to spend any money if you'd simply checked in with me after a reasonable time, the way you're supposed to. How the hell was I supposed to reach you? I thought we had a standard reporting procedure we're both to follow."

"Our mother is alive and well and living not too far from here, Garth, and you're not her. This is more of a vacation than an assignment, for Christ's sake, and there's nothing dangerous involved."

"You should have checked in with me, Mongo," Garth said coldly. "You should have checked in within twenty-four hours. That's the procedure. We've agreed that we've made enough enemies over the years so that keeping tabs on each other, vacation or no, is a good idea."

"I've been distracted."

"Distracted, huh? You say you're in no danger? Well, I've got good news, and I've got bad news."

"Come on, Garth, get on with it. It's late."

"Oh-oh. Did I catch you in a bad mood?"

"Listen, brother, I'm the recipient of what's probably the most expensive three-word message in the history of communications, and I have to help pay for it. But am I in a bad mood? Not really. What I am is disappointed in recent events, and the previously mentioned distraction is waiting to give me comfort. So give me the good news first. Just thinking about what all that skywriting is going to cost us may be all the bad news I can take."

"I wouldn't have done it if I didn't think it was important, Mongo," Garth said evenly. "You don't think you're in any danger, and I think you could be. Have you been to that bank in Chicago yet?"

"No."

"Well, don't bother. I'd be very surprised if they tell you anything."

"That's your good news?"

"The good news is that I found out who bought that circus. The bad news is the owner. World Circus is a show you should steer clear of. There's no way you're going to be able to buy it, because they won't sell."

He'd gotten my attention. "Let's take it from the top, Garth. How did you find all this out?"

"The wonders of technology, brother. I thought I might be of some help, so while you've been traipsing all over America's heartland trying to find a circus to buy, I've been sitting in our air-conditioned offices punching up a few things on the computer and talking to some of our contacts. First, it seems that United States Savings and Loan got itself involved in the same financial difficulties and scandals that brought down a lot of other savings-and-loans operations a while back; there were lots of bad loans and a flirtation with bankruptcy. When it looked like they were going to have to accept federal receivership, all of their debts and assets went on the public record. I was able to access that information. It turns out that Statler Brothers Circus was picked up at auction by the Battle Eagle Corporation, an outfit operating out of Bern."

"Switzerland?"

"Yeah, that Bern."

"Who the hell are they?"

"Not 'they'; 'he.' And Frederickson and Frederickson had to cash in a few IOUs in order to get the rest of this information. Battle Eagle is wholly owned by one Arlen Zelezian, a German Swiss."

"And a drug dealer."

"No," Garth said after a pause, sounding slightly puzzled. "At least, not that anyone I talked to knows of. What the hell made you say that?"

"Just a wrong guess. Go ahead."

"Whatever reason Zelezian had for wanting a circus, it wasn't to flutter the hearts of ladies and gentlemen and children of all ages. He's not in the business of making people happy. Whatever's going on with that operation, I think it's a very good idea for you to steer clear of it. Your days of anonymity are long past, brother, and if Mongo Frederickson shows up on Arlen Zelezian's doorstep, out in the middle of nowhere, he's just likely to think you're checking up on him. That's why I was in such a hurry to get in touch with you; you're likely to put yourself in harm's way if you show up at World Circus. I'll fill you in on all the details when you get home."

"It's a little late for playing it safe now, Garth. Just go ahead and give me the gory details."

"Shit. You've been to the circus and talked to somebody?"

"I talked to one man. He told me World Circus is a kind of floating refugee camp for illegal aliens who've fled from the old communist bloc countries."

Garth snorted. "What bullshit. Arlen Zelezian is rumored to get some very large payoffs from the Russians, Mongo—and from the Western countries, including the United States, as well. In fact, letting him run whatever it is he's really running in this country may be a payoff—or a down payment—from one of our illustrious government agencies. Zelezian doesn't care who he does business with, and his customers obviously don't care either. Arlen Zelezian is definitely not in the humanitarian business."

"You've already belabored that point. Now tell me what business he is in."

"Bioweapons."

"Come again?"

"He's a combination super arms dealer and free-lance researcher whose specialty is biological weapons. I told you that there are rumors about his getting financing from both Western countries and the Soviets, primarily because they don't want to be shut out of the market if and when he comes up with more efficient methods of killing people. For the past decade, he's supposedly been holed up in Switzerland working on something really heavy, so it's a real surprise to find him—or one of his operations—here."

"Bioweapons. You mean like bugs? Diseases?"

"Yeah, but Zelezian works with bigger critters. I was told that the U.S. Navy stole—or bought—their idea of using dolphins to plant mines and attack enemy divers from Zelezian. Think of Hannibal using elephants to cross the Alps, attack dogs, that sort of thing. Bioweapons."

"Got it. Just what is this heavy thing that he's been working on for ten years?"

"Nobody that I talked to knows. Zelezian happens to be one of the world's foremost authorities on dog breeding, and he's a specialist in a particularly vicious breed of dog called a kuvasz. His son works with him. Besides being a top-notch animal trainer a lot of people say is good enough to work in any circus, the son is a noted conservationist. He spends a lot of time in Africa."

I grunted. "Some conservationist. World Circus gives fifteen percent off the price of admission to NRA members."

"Well, what can I tell you? I haven't got the slightest idea what he had in mind when he bought Phil Statler's circus, or what he's doing in the United States, but it doesn't sound like anything you want to get close to."

I thought about it, and suddenly felt I knew precisely why Arlen Zelezian was in the United States. "He's field testing," I said distantly, almost to myself. My mouth had gone very dry. "Jesus Christ. Forget the Navy's killer dolphins. He's got himself a bigger and better bioweapon, and he's here to field-test it on a lot of innocent people."

"Huh? What did you say?"

"You said he's a specialist in a breed of dog called a kuvasz?"

"Yeah, that's right. What's the matter, Mongo? What were you saying about—?"

"Nothing. Garth, listen: fax me everything you have, will you? There must be a terminal around here somewhere that I can rent for a couple of hours. I'll call you in the morning, tell you where to send it."

"I'll fax you *shit,* Mongo," Garth said tersely. "There's no need.

That circus isn't for sale, so there's no need for you to stick your nose into Arlen Zelezian's business. Some of the people I talked to think that his presence in this country may even have been approved by some Pentagon agency, or even the CIA, so we're talking heavy-duty business that you want no part of." He paused for a few moments, and when he spoke again, his tone had softened. "I know you're interested, brother, so as a reward for good behavior I'll have all the information I've gathered waiting for you on your desk. I even managed to come up with a photo of Arlen Zelezian, and you'll love it. That death merchant son-of-a-bitch looks just like Abraham Lincoln."

CHAPTER SEVEN

My conversation with Garth had given me more food for thought than I could digest, and the information he'd given me rested like a sharp, hard lump in my mind. Something evil had been loosed on America's Great Plains, and I suspected there was more than a fifty-fifty chance that Arlen Zelezian was responsible. But without proof, my suspicions were virtually worthless—especially if it was true that he was operating under the auspices of some government agency with a vested interest in whatever he was up to. Without proof, my suspicions would be dismissed as being even loonier than the notion that there was a "werewolf" wandering over the vast prairie stretches, slaughtering people. If I was right, it was not something I could turn my back on. I needed to check out the situation. If I was wrong, the only thing I risked was making a fool of myself, and I'd certainly done that before and survived. But if I was right, the lives of any number of innocent people could depend on how quickly I could gather the necessary evidence and then get the right people to take me seriously.

However, none of these distractions was sufficient to lessen my lust for Harper. When she slid into bed next to me, her naked flesh touching mine, my body mercifully paid no heed to what my mind was busy with—and soon my mind wasn't busy with anything but the enjoyment of the woman with me as we slid up and down each other, wallowing back and forth across the waterbed in our room.

Afterward, I closed my eyes and drifted off to sleep, but I had set my mental alarm clock to wake me up sometime in the middle of the night. When I did awake, the luminous dial on my wristwatch told me it was two in the morning. I very carefully withdrew my arm from under Harper's head, eased myself off the bed. I fumbled around in the dark until I found my suitcase, picked it up, and tiptoed into the bathroom, where I closed the door before turning on the light.

The darkest clothes I had with me consisted of a charcoal-gray business suit and black shoes, an ensemble I had brought in anticipation of a visit with the officers of the bank in Chicago. I slipped on a navy-blue T-shirt, then dressed in the dark suit and shoes. Finally, I turned off the bathroom light, opened the door, and edged out into the darkness, once again tiptoeing across the room. I stopped to pick up the keys to the rented car off the dressing table, went to the front door, opened it, and stepped outside. Then I slowly closed the door behind me, grimacing in disgust when the latch clicked softly. The last thing in the world I wanted or needed was to awaken Harper.

It was a cloudless night, with a full, golden moon that didn't suit my purposes at all. I walked over to a rose bed planted in the middle of a concrete island separating our motel unit from the next, scooped up a handful of black topsoil, and rubbed it over my face, the back of my neck, and my hands. I wished I had a gun, but you don't carry a gun when you go shopping for a circus; as usual, my Beretta and Seecamp were at home, locked in the safe in my office. I walked to the car, opened the door—and started when the interior light came on.

"Jesus! What the hell—?"

Harper, dressed in jeans, untied sneakers, and a blue silk blouse that was only half buttoned, was sitting in the front seat on the passenger's side. Her long gray hair was uncombed, hastily pulled back into a ponytail held in place with a blue ribbon. Her face was still puffy with sleep, but her maroon eyes nonetheless glowed with curiosity—and what might have been a glint of triumph.

"It looks to me like you forgot to wash your face, Robby," she said wryly, stifling a yawn. "Or maybe you're on your way to a very kinky late night party. I like that dirt all over your face. Nice touch. You look like a very well dressed commando. But I'm afraid you're going to have to have that nice suit cleaned after the party."

I didn't get into the car. "Harper," I said with a deep sigh of exasperation, "what the hell are you doing here? I thought you were asleep."

"Oh, I know you did. I was—but I'm a light sleeper. I woke up when you took your arm away. When you got up and took your suitcase into the bathroom, I figured you planned to do more than just pee. In fact, I got the notion that you might actually be planning to sneak off somewhere without me. As you see, I can get dressed pretty fast when I have to, especially when I'm afraid I might miss something. I've got a dark scarf I can use to cover my hair. Do you want me to rub some dirt on my face and hands?"

"No, I do not want you to rub dirt on your face and hands. What I want is for you to go back to bed."

"And have you slip off without me into the night with dirt on *your* face and hands? No way. This definitely looks to me like it's developing into one of those bizarre Mongo Frederickson cases you told me you don't get involved in any longer. If so, you think I'm going to miss out on all the fun and excitement? Uh-uh."

"Harper, this isn't a game."

"I'm aware of that," she replied evenly. "Robby, I think you fibbed to me earlier. That message from your brother involved more than the fact that he was pissed off because you hadn't touched base with him, right? He told you something about World Circus that got you into that commando outfit. Right?"

"This isn't the time, Harper. Please go back in the room and wait for me."

"No, Robby," she said with a firm shake of her head. "If I can fly you all over the countryside in my plane, then I can go off with you on your post-midnight sojourns."

"It could be dangerous."

She narrowed her eyelids, thrust out her dimpled chin. "Robby, you're very close to sounding sexist. Not only do I handle poisonous snakes, but I've been married four times. You don't think I can take care of myself?"

"Your husbands didn't shoot at you, I trust."

It was absolutely the wrong thing to say to Harper Rhys-Whitney. Her maroon eyes went wide, glowed even brighter. "Wow. It's *that* dangerous, is it?"

Seeing that there was no sense in arguing with her, I got in the car and started up the engine. "No, it's not that dangerous," I said, hoping it was the truth. I put the car into gear, pulled out of the motel parking lot onto the highway, and headed south, back toward the county fairgrounds and the circus. "There's not going to be any shooting. All I want to do is look around."

"What's this all about, Robby? What did your brother tell you?"

"Something that makes me suspect people in that circus may be hurting people. That's what I want to check out; I can't go home until I do. If they have been hurting people, then I want to try to get proof so that it can be stopped as quickly as possible. If I'm wrong, then all I've lost is a little sleep and the cost of having my suit dry-cleaned."

"Robby, you haven't told me a damned thing."

"Not now, Harper. Please. It has to do with concentration. To tell you the truth, I already feel more than a little foolish, and I'm going to feel even more foolish if I have to explain why I have to go back to the circus. After I've had my look-around, I'll explain my reasons. Okay?"

I thought she was going to argue. Instead, she simply said, "All right, Robby. I don't want to disturb your concentration, because I don't want you to be hurt."

We didn't talk any more during the remainder of the fifty-mile drive back to the fairgrounds. Something I'd said had seemed to make an impression on my traveling companion, or perhaps a full realization had come to her that I wasn't outfitted in my very-well-dressed-commando costume for fun and games. I could feel the tension in her. Once, I put my hand in hers, and she squeezed my fingers hard.

I pulled off the shoulder of the highway a quarter mile from where the darkened circus tents and midway rides stood out against the moon-washed sky like some ancient ruins.

"If the highway patrol comes by, tell them you stopped to rest for a few minutes. Drive off, and come back here to pick me up in an hour or so."

"Robby," Harper said in a tight voice, "what if something happens to you and you can't get back?"

"Don't worry."

"But how will I know?"

"I'll be back. But, just in case, if I'm not back in two hours—"

"One hour, Robby. The circus isn't that big."

"Ninety minutes. If I'm not here, call the highway patrol or the county sheriff."

"But what are you looking *for*, Robby? What am I supposed to tell them?"

"Tell them the person or persons responsible for the so-called werewolf killings travels with the circus, as well as the werewolf itself, and that they should come in to get me in a big hurry."

Harper's mouth dropped open, but before she could say anything I got out of the car, quickly closing the door so as to shut off the interior light, and walked across the highway. I hopped over a steel guardrail, navigated a water-filled ditch, and began running, keeping low, toward the circus.

I reached the midway, stayed in the moon shadows next to the huge Ferris wheel for two minutes, watching and listening for guards. There didn't appear to be any, at least not in my immediate vicinity. I made my way past the still rides and shuttered concession stands, angling around toward the penning area at the far side of the Big Top. I was more than a little curious to see what animals, if any, Arlen Zelezian was keeping in his pens or his semis, besides the usual circus menagerie. I was fairly certain Mabel was going to smell me, but I could only hope she wouldn't cause a fuss; it was definitely not the time for a reprise of our earlier reunion scene.

As I moved around the perimeter of the Big Top, I noticed a pale sliver of light spilling out into the night from beneath a loose flap. I could think of no reason why a light should be on in the tent in the middle of the night, and it seemed worthwhile investigating. I got down on my belly, crawled under the canvas flap, and found myself beneath a bank of bleachers. There was a single spotlight turned on in the rigging above, and it was shining directly down into the ring. I moved to the aisle between bleacher sections, eased myself up to where I could peer over the seats and get a clear view of what was happening in the ring. When I did, my heart began to pound in my chest.

Luther, dressed in jeans, brown leather boots, and a gray sweatshirt, was crouched in almost the exact center of the ring. He was facing and talking in low tones that were at once soothing and commanding to a creature that looked like a huge dog or wolf, but which I knew was neither.

For one thing, this animal had extended canines that Nate Button had never mentioned, saber teeth that reminded me somewhat of the kind of wax vampire fangs children wear at Halloween—except there was no doubt in my mind that these teeth were very real and very sharp. There was a cage on wheels, its door open, at the far end of the ring, and from the tension exuded by both man and beast, I suspected the creature had just been set free. The animal was about the size of a large mastiff, with a very broad rib cage, but it had the long, spindly legs and enormous paws of a wolf. Its coat was a rusty, buff color, and it had black stripes running lengthwise down its back. There was a thick ruff around its neck, like a lion's mane. It had a squarish face, a large muzzle marked by gaping, black leather nostrils, and a predator's close-set eyes.

Luther had faced bears and tigers without so much as a stick in his hand, but he now wore a .357 Magnum in a holster strapped around his waist.

I now regretted even more the fact that I didn't have a gun as the animal looked away from Luther—toward me.

The damn thing knew I was there.

Luther, never taking his eyes off the creature in front of him, slowly straightened up. He removed the Magnum from its holster, cocked the weapon. The animal seemed to be familiar with the gun, and perhaps even had some idea of what it could do; it reacted to the loud click of metal on metal by stepping back a pace and baring its fangs. The enormous saber canines glistened with saliva.

"All right," Luther said loudly over his shoulder, still never looking away from the creature in front of him, "bring her in."

The backside of the heavyset man with the potbelly and bulbous nose who had been following Harper and me on the midway suddenly emerged from the tunnel leading to the penning area. The rest of him—clad from head to toe in a heavily padded uniform and wearing a baseball catcher's mask—emerged, and then I could see that he was dragging a heavy, wheeled cage identical to the one already in the ring that had held the first creature. This cage contained a smaller version of the animal standing in the ring—grayer in color, more like a wolf, lacking the heavy ruff, sharply delineated black stripes, and with less pronounced canines. It was a bitch of the species, and she was in heat. Draped over the end of the cage was the soiled khaki safari jacket Nate Button had been wearing.

The huge buff-colored male stiffened at the sight of the bitch, and a tremor ran through its body, but it did not move from its position. The man with the potbelly glanced nervously in the direction of the male, then quickly stepped around behind the cage holding the female.

I felt a hand touch my shoulder, and I thought I was going to have a heart attack. I jumped, but somehow managed to stifle a shout. I wheeled around to find that the hand belonged to Harper, who was standing just behind me.

She leaned very close to me, whispered, "That's a lobox, isn't it? And that's the jacket that professor was wearing."

It was not the time or place for a conversation, whispered or not. I put my finger to my lips and shook my head, then pushed her back and under the bleachers before turning my attention back to the tableau in the dirt ring.

The creature certainly was a lobox, or something very close to it—as close as Arlen Zelezian was likely to get after a decade or more of teasing and leaching past horrors from present genes, breeding wolves and dogs, matching for tiny retrograde genetic factors, bringing this creature back from extinction by mining the shadowy genetic repositories of its closest modern ancestors. Despite my revulsion at what I was certain Zelezian had opted to do with the creature, I could not help but be impressed. The lobox, this beast with a taste for human flesh that had terrorized early man and perhaps contributed to the Neanderthal's extinction, was absolutely magnificent.

The presence of the lobox bitch in estrus continued to have a galvanizing effect on the male; it stood very stiffly, ruff slightly raised, its hide quivering—but it remained where it was. A powerful tribute, I thought, to Luther Zelezian. The trainer, still keeping his eyes fastened on the creature, sidled backward toward the closed cage, ignoring the sudden growling and thrashing of the animal inside it. He took the safari jacket off the top of the cage, dipped a corner of it in the bloody estral fluids at the bottom of the cage, then nodded to the potbellied man, who quickly wheeled the lobox bitch back into the recesses of the tunnel.

"Kill," Luther said in an even tone as he casually tossed the soiled jacket off to his left.

The lobox sprang forward like something shot from a rocket launcher, then leaped high in the air in a stiff-legged manner that reminded me of a fox pouncing. In the brief moments that it arched through the air, I could see long, curved claws—including one at the rear of the footpad—unsheathed, claws that were more like a tiger's than a wolf's or dog's.

The rear, opposable, claw was exactly where Nate Button had said it would be.

And then the creature was at the jacket, using its claws to pin the material to the ground while it tore at it with its long, gleaming fangs. Within moments the jacket had been ripped to shreds—just as its owner, the man whose body odor permeated the fabric, would be if and when this animal was released to track him down. Luther had found a most effective technique for priming the killer beast to track and kill a selected victim by using elemental forces—the pleasure, the promise, of sex, combined with a fear of whatever punishment the animal understood to be represented by the gun, probably the ear-shattering report that would result if the Magnum was fired.

I hoped Nate Button was a long way from the area, but I strongly suspected he was not. The fact that Luther had his jacket, and was using it to prime the lobox, had to mean that the scientist was a captive, or was somewhere within the lobox's scent range—which Button had indicated might be as much as ten miles, or even more. It meant Button, despite my discouraging remarks, hadn't given up on his lobox theory. What he had undoubtedly done was to get a map and compare the killing sites with the location of the circus on each date, and then speculated correctly just where a large predator could hide out between killing onslaughts. It was why he had been in the audience earlier in the evening. After the performance he had decided to look around for a "werewolf" and been caught at it. An article of his clothing had been taken from him.

Just as articles of clothing had been taken from Harper and me. The Zelezians, father and son, were taking no chances.

"Back," Luther commanded, and again cocked the hammer of his weapon.

The lobox hesitated, caught between the frenzy whipped up by his natural instincts, the smell of the estral fluids, and Luther's training.

Luther reached around with his left hand to put his index finger in his right ear, aimed the revolver into the dirt, and pulled the trigger. The explosion of the gun reverberated throughout the tent. The animal jumped back, stood for a few moments with its hide quivering, then slowly walked back to the position where it had previously been standing.

"Sit," Luther said evenly.

The animal sat down on its haunches—and once again turned its head to look in our direction. Then it bared its fangs and growled.

Luther, who had started across the ring to retrieve the shreds of Nate Button's safari jacket, suddenly stopped, tensed, looked up in the direction of where we were shrouded in darkness.

The lobox growled again, louder.

It seemed like an excellent time to beat a hasty retreat; but it was, of course, too late.

"Here," Luther commanded. When the lobox's head turned in his direction, he first pointed out in the darkness, then squatted down and slowly drew a line in the dirt with his finger. "Track! Now!"

The lobox rose from its haunches, ambled across the ring, jumped over the six-inch-high wooden apron defining the dirt ring, then loped lazily down the sawdust track, heading directly toward us. It definitely did not bode well, I thought.

"Oh, God," Harper said in a strangled, thoroughly frightened voice as she grabbed my right arm with both her hands and tried to pull me back down the aisle.

"No," I said in as normal a voice as I could manage under the circumstances. I grabbed her wrist, pulled her up beside me. "We can't outrun it. Don't move at all, Harper—unless it comes at me. If it does, then get back out under the tent, run like hell, and climb the first tall thing you come to. Otherwise, stay very still."

"Robby, I'm—"

"Don't move," I repeated, and then stepped out from the darkness between the bleacher sections into the twilight aura at the edge of the pool of light cast by the arc lamp above the ring. I stood in the center of the sawdust track, hands at my sides, and faced the beast coming at me. "All right, Luther," I continued evenly, "you've got me. Call Fido off."

"Actually, Frederickson," Luther said casually, "I'm almost as curious as you are to see what's going to happen." He walked across the ring, put one foot up on the apron, rested his left hand on his hip. The hand with the gun was hanging at his side. "We haven't spent much time at all practicing this particular procedure. It will be interesting to see what the animal does."

The lobox kept coming at me at a steady pace, its mouth open. With its gaping nostrils and saber teeth, its facial expression reminded me of something like a loony grin; I would almost have found it amusing if I hadn't known that this was death's smile.

When the animal was about ten paces away, Luther cocked the gun. "Stay!" he commanded.

The lobox kept coming until it was only five paces away, then abruptly stopped, sat on its haunches, and stared at me with golden eyes with black irises that were bright with intelligence and seemed almost human. Its mouth opened even wider in a kind of yawn, and its pink tongue lolled from its black leather lips. Its huge nostrils quivered slightly, as if it wanted to get a new, improved, sniff of me. Its head was at about a level with mine, and again it struck me how the damn thing almost looked as if it was smiling.

I tensed as I felt, rather than heard, Harper come up behind me, and a moment later I felt her hands on both my shoulders.

I appreciated her courage, her willingness to stand with me in the face of a totally unpredictable creature that could tear us both apart in seconds, but her action wasn't the thing to do; now, if one of us died, the other was certain to die also. Once, just once, I wished she would do something I asked her to. There was no longer any possibility of escape for her—if there ever had been.

Luther stepped over the wooden apron, strolled down the sawdust track toward us. I followed his progress with my peripheral vision, never taking my eyes off the animal squatting on its haunches in front of me; one lunge, and it would have my face in its jaws.

"I'm sorry I can't offer you and Miss Rhys-Whitney a drink this time, Frederickson," Luther continued, a hint of what almost sounded like genuine regret in his voice. "You've created an impossible situation."

"What's the problem, Luther? I don't care what hours you keep, and I've seen trainers work with, uh . . . dogs before."

Luther slowly shook his head. He knew, of course, that I knew the creature with the golden eyes, gaping nostrils, and saber teeth was no dog. I'd wanted to at least try to give him an out, but he obviously felt he couldn't afford to take it. "You should have minded your own business, Frederickson. And you should have been more patient. I wasn't entirely truthful with you earlier this evening."

"You don't say?"

"We're almost finished with the circus. It will be up for sale. You could have had it. But then, you haven't been entirely truthful with us either, have you? I can't help but wonder if you were ever truly interested in buying this circus."

"If you're all getting ready to move out, does that mean you think you've killed enough people?" I nodded in the direction of the magnificent, bright-eyed animal in front of me. "How many of these little cuties do you have?"

"A sufficient breeding stock."

"All as well trained as this one?"

Luther shrugged, pursed his lips, ran his free hand over his shaved skull. "I'm not sure 'trained' is an appropriate word to use with this animal. It's controlled."

"By the promise of sex, the cocking sound and report of your gun."

"Yes," Luther said easily.

His response seemed to indicate that he didn't at all mind talking about what he had done and how he had done it, and I thought that was probably a bad omen. Still, I was curious, and I couldn't see how we could get into any deeper trouble than we already had. "Interesting," I said.

"More interesting than you understand, Frederickson. It's not just the sounds of the gun that control the animal. It understands that the gun kills."

"What have you killed with it?"

"Chickens. Killing a chicken with a Magnum makes for a most effective demonstration."

"I'll bet. You're saying that you think it understands death, that it can make a connection between the thing that was blown apart and itself?"

"Yes. It's very intelligent; it's probably the most intelligent creature on the face of the earth today, with the exception of humans—although I'm often led to question just how intelligent, as opposed to instinctual, humans really are."

"Intelligent is one thing, true self-awareness is another. To understand death is to have self-awareness. You think this animal has that?"

Again, Luther shrugged his broad shoulders. "I suspect so. Indeed, I'm quite certain whales and dolphins have a strong sense of self. I suspect all of the large mammals have more self-awareness than we give them credit for. Also language."

"Well, we've seen the results of your successful training methods, Luther; they've been splattered all over the countryside. Innocent people."

The trainer smiled thinly. "Not so innocent, Frederickson. NRA members, super-macho types to a man, hunters who have slaughtered innocent animals, driving many of them to the edge of extinction, using high-powered weapons. Didn't you notice our discount sign outside the ticket window? I don't care, or have any sympathy, for people who kill other sentient creatures and call it sport. Human beings are the most arrogant and destructive species that has ever lived, and the idiots in the NRA are the worst of the lot. I consider it simple poetic justice that these men who've derived satisfaction from blowing out the lives of deer, elk, bears, or whatever, many using automatic weapons, should have a taste of what it feels like to be stalked and killed by a creature that is, in many ways, their equal as a predator."

"You're crazy, Luther. You're right out of your fucking gourd."

"Perhaps I am," Luther said in a flat voice. "It's certainly true that I don't have a high regard for human life; at least I don't have the regard for the lives of *those* men that you do. All of those victims, in all likelihood, have butchered dozens of magnificent creatures that had as much right to live on this earth as the hunters, and all so that they could hang a trophy in their den or feel sexual excitement. They're no loss, Frederickson."

"But *why*?" Harper asked in a voice that quavered with horror. "What's the *point* of training an animal to do that?"

"Assassination," I said, watching Luther's face—and knowing I was right. "This animal is a pitiless killing machine, virtually impossible to defend against under the right conditions. It's more accurate than a missile, or even a whole flotilla of bombers, and it's presumably cheaper. It can be fired—released—by a handler who's ten miles or more away from the site where a president, king, dictator, senator, or whoever else you want to kill may be living, speaking, or even simply passing by in a motorcade. And all you need to load up this assassination weapon is an object, preferably an article of clothing, that's been permeated by the victim's scent. Then you find out where the intended victim is going to be, just the general area, and you're in business. This thing tracks better than a bloodhound, and its natural instinct is to kill people. It's been trained to kill specific human beings through the manipulation of its sexual urges, fear of loud noises, and the possible knowledge that it can cease to exist. But this thing won't worry about the presence of Secret Service agents or bodyguards; it will just relentlessly go at its target. If it survives and returns, that's fine; if not, only the investment it represents is lost. Even if it should be shot or captured, and even recognized for what it is, there would be no way to determine what individual—or government agency—ordered its use. It's just a great assassin's weapon with brains. Right, Luther?"

He wasn't going to bother denying it. He was staring very intently at the lobox, which was staring very intently at me. I wondered if Luther was considering giving the lobox an order to kill—an order I had no doubt the creature would respond to immediately. Instead, Luther said in a soft voice, "What you can't appreciate, Frederickson, because you've never seen it, is its tenacity in tracking a given subject. That tenacity seems to be a genetic trait that couldn't have been predicted. It seems that once this creature has taken it into its head to kill a particular subject, it won't be stopped by anything but its own death; it will eat and drink only sparingly while tracking spoor, refuse to return, and continue to stalk indefinitely until it has found its target. They are elusive, and far more intelligent than any other animal I've ever worked with. I'm not sure how much you knew before you came here, or what you've guessed, but I will tell you that the lobox is a creature from the past, in a manner of speaking. Before my father went to work on the problem, using a variety of reverse breeding techniques, this animal did not exist any longer anywhere on earth."

"Do tell. The families of the men you targeted to train and test these animals might not agree that the deaths of their fathers and husbands was no great loss. Why did you have to kill so *many*, Luther? Why string the whole thing out for almost two years? You knew just what you had after the first killing."

He dismissed my suggestion and questions with an impatient wave of his hand. "I think you already knew what I just told you, Frederickson. I think you know a lot of things."

"Some things aren't all that difficult to figure out. You chose the Great Plains of the United States as an area in which to field-test that thing because of the wide-open spaces, and you bought a midsize circus because it seemed a perfect cover—it gave you an excuse to move around, and you could keep the lobox breeding stock with all the other animals. You were probably telling the truth about the performers' countries of origin. Eastern bloc countries provided you with serious circus artists who wouldn't ask any questions because their families were being held hostage; in return, those governments would get the chance to purchase your new weapon. They want a piece of the action. I also have to wonder if people in our own government might not be involved somehow, maybe by making sure nobody inspects this circus too closely, in exchange for the right to bid on the finished product."

"You're a fool, Frederickson," Luther said softly. "You're a fool for even allowing yourself to think such thoughts, much less to utter them aloud."

"Why? What difference does it make? Some of the nastier power players in this country and I have been dancing with each other for a long time. What bothers me the most is that right now it looks like you're getting ready to sic this lobox on the man who was wearing that safari jacket, wherever he might be. You're the monster, Luther, not the lobox. The lobox is just doing what comes naturally—and what you've taught it to do in order to survive."

"You consider me a monster because you have a romantic, overblown notion of the value of human life, Frederickson," Luther said in the same soft tone. "Politicians and professional soldiers certainly don't; people in charge of developing and manufacturing weapons don't. Governments, including the United States, have been testing the effects of weapons systems on their own civilian populations for some time; the politicians and the Army sent soldiers into radioactive areas of the Nevada Proving Grounds to test the effect of radiation on human tissue; the CIA once tested a bacteria-laden aerosol spray in the New York City subway. Of course, you wouldn't consider the whole-sale slaughter of whales, porpoises, rhinos, and elephants as outrageous, would you?"

"Hey, Luther, I'll match my contributions to the Audubon Society and Save the Whales against yours anytime. We're talking something different here."

"It's only different in your mind. I have been forced to use human test subjects—but I, at least, have chosen them discriminately. I have loosed loboxes to hunt men who are themselves hunters and pride themselves on it. I chose my subjects carefully and haven't inflicted harm on a whole population. You know, there's a school of thought that says the real reason atomic bombs were dropped on Hiroshima and Nagasaki was not to win the war, which was already won, but simply to see what would happen. The scientists who'd built the weapon, and the politicians who'd approved the vast sums to finance it, couldn't bear the thought of not seeing, in the real situation for which it was intended, just what they had wrought. Not only did the CIA test sprays in New York City, but they secretly financed so-called researchers who doped up unsuspecting psychological patients with LSD and other mind-altering drugs. The list goes on and on. Hundreds of weapons research programs are going on at any given moment, all over the world, and any number of civilians will die as a result of that testing. So spare me your naiveté and outrage."

"You seem to be implying that you're working under the auspices of the United States government, or think you are, maybe under the wing of the CIA. Is that the story, Luther?"

"I'm saying that you're a fool if you think this is some rogue operation run by mad scientists. There are very powerful interests, in this country and around the world, which have always been keenly interested in research projects like this one."

"Luther, just how much are you and your daddy going to charge your killer customers for one of these damn things?"

Luther stiffened. "What do you know about my father? *How* do you know?"

"It's not enough to own one, though, is it? Somebody's going to have to handle the damn thing and then carefully prime it for a specific assassination victim. Are your services part of the sales package with each lobox?"

There was the loud click of a gun being cocked somewhere in the darkness behind me. The lobox reacted, getting up off its haunches, backing away a step. Growling.

"Don't say any more, Luther." It was the elder Zelezian's deep, rich baritone. "You've already said quite enough. I do believe you're looking for Dr. Frederickson's respect. You're wasting your time. It was you who mentioned my reverse breeding program. Stop giving him information."

Luther flushed slightly, stepped back a pace. Arlen Zelezian moved forward into the dim light, a few feet off to my left. He was still wearing his suit, and still looked like an actor ready to step on some stage as Abraham Lincoln, always on call. He too held a cocked Magnum aimed in the general direction of the lobox, but he seemed less attentive to the animal than Luther—probably because he knew his son was on guard for him.

"You've somehow gained a great deal of information about me and my operations, Frederickson," he said, staring at me intently with his coal-black eyes. His deep voice echoed slightly in the empty tent. I stared back into the eyes, which I now noticed were curiously blank, with less life in them than in the golden eyes of the creature he had conjured up from the past. "Considering your reputation, I suppose that shouldn't surprise me. In your tenaciousness, there is much of the lobox in you. How did you discover that Luther and I are father and son? Who are you working for?"

I said nothing, desperately trying to think, to calculate whether it was to my advantage or disadvantage for Arlen Zelezian to think I had been tracking him, or for him to know how much I actually knew or was merely guessing at. I couldn't come up with an answer, and I found it depressing to think that it probably didn't make a difference anyway. Harper and I had some serious trouble, and I couldn't see how any amount of fast talking was going to get us out of it. Still, I knew I was going to have to try; I figured I had about as much chance of surviving hand-to-claw combat with a lobox as I did of catching a bullet between my teeth.

Arlen Zelezian continued, "Why did you tip your hand by showing up here earlier, Frederickson? Who else knows, or suspects, what we're doing?"

Plan A.

"Look, Zelezian, your boy here said you'd just about finished your field tests and are ready to close up shop and go home with your pets. This 'werewolf killings' thing has to be wearing a bit thin. No matter whose auspices you're working under, sooner or later somebody else besides Nate Button and me is going to tumble to the fact that the reason the werewolf can't be found is that it's sleeping and traveling with your circus. Kill us, and you're likely to find there's more heat coming down on you than you can handle. Maybe you should close up shop right now—tonight—and get back home to Switzerland while you can. Let Harper go, and keep me as a hostage to ensure her silence while you're packing and en route. Then I'll tell you what you want to know."

"Don't be silly, Frederickson. We can't do that."

"Try this one, Mr. Zelezian," Harper said tersely. "Keep *me* as a hostage to ensure Robby's silence until you're away."

Zelezian ignored her. "Who are you working for, Frederickson? Who is it that seeks to interfere with my business?"

Plan B.

"Let's negotiate."

"But you have nothing with which to negotiate."

"Wrong. You want to know what I'm doing here, where I got my information, who I may have been reporting to, and why my hypothetical employer should want to know your business. You may think nothing of using human beings as test victims in your experiments, but somehow I don't think you're into killing for the sake of killing—especially if it could be bad for business. I guarantee you that killing us will be bad for business. Miss Rhys-Whitney is a member of a very wealthy and influential family, and I'm not exactly your average midwestern farmer. You and I both find ourselves in what might be described as an uncomfortable situation, but I say we can make an arrangement."

"What kind of an . . . arrangement?"

"First, you've already determined that a lobox can be trained, with deadly consistency, to do what you want it to do. There's no need for any more testing—and I still can't understand why you've kept at it so long. So pass on Nate Button—the man who was wearing that safari jacket."

"That may not be possible," Arlen Zelezian said carefully.

"Because he made the link between the lobox and the circus and came snooping around? So what? He's been touting the case for a lobox from day one, and nobody's taken him seriously. How much more evidence could he have had than the hair and saliva samples? Did he actually see something here? The man is considered a crackpot, even in academic circles. Nobody will pay the slightest attention to anything he has to say. I don't know whether you've already got him on ice somewhere, or simply know where to find him, but there's no need to kill him. There's no reason now to kill Harper and me. We have no proof of anything, and we'll keep silent about what we know—as long as you take yourself and this whole insane operation out of the country."

The elder Zelezian's thin lips curled back in a sneer of contempt. "You'll say nothing?"

"You have my word on it."

"I agree," Harper said evenly, squeezing my arm in what I took to be a gesture of encouragement.

"You expect me to believe that?"

"Why not? If you know so much about me, then you know that I keep my word. It may piss me off to see you murderers get away, but I have to live with a lot of things that piss me off, and it's a bargain I'm forced into in order to save our lives. Bear in mind also that the value of this particular bioweapon decreases radically in proportion to the amount of information that leaks out about it. Kill us, and I guarantee that lots of people are going to be on your ass, trying to find out things. You really have no choice but to take my word that no leaks will come from us. You'll be other people's problem."

Zelezian thought about it, finally shook his head. "No. Afterward, you might decide that breaking your word is something you can live with also."

"You've got loboxes and the capacity to breed more. We're both aware of what a lobox can do. You've got articles of clothing from both Harper and me. That's your insurance policy. Now, you give Harper's sweater back to her, but you keep my jacket. If I break my word, if you ever have any trouble you think I caused, you can cart one of your loboxes into my neighborhood, prime it with my jacket, and let it loose. If I break my word, I'll know I run the risk of one day walking down the street and having one of those things jump out from some alley to tear my throat out. I know I can't defend myself against a lobox; even if I wanted to put a stop to you, I'd know that the price would be a horrible death. I certainly don't want to be constantly looking over my shoulder for a prehistoric creature that has nothing more on its mind than making a meal out of me. *That's* your guarantee that I'll keep my mouth shut."

Zelezian glanced first at the lobox, then at his son. Luther Zelezian, who I somehow suspected might be on our side, nodded to his father. He said, "If I loosed one anywhere in New

York City, it would keep stalking, no matter how long it took, until it found and killed him. We know that from the trials. Frederickson seems to have a strong argument."

"All right," Arlen Zelezian said, looking back at me. "Agreed. Now answer my questions."

"Ah. Now, how do I know I can trust you to keep your part of the bargain?"

"Even if you are no longer, as you Americans say, on my case, who else might be?"

"How do I know I can trust you, Zelezian?"

"You don't have any choice but to trust me. Now, tell me how you came to know so much about me."

"Computer," I said, watching the lobox. "The bank that sold you the circus ended up with all its transactions on the public record because they were in financial trouble and under investigation by federal regulatory agencies. That's how I got the name of Battle Eagle Corporation. Then it was just a matter of checking out Battle Eagle with contacts I have in Interpol, the CIA, and the FBI."

Arlen Zelezian grunted. "What about your brother? Why isn't he out here with you?"

"My brother's back in New York State working on other matters. He has no part in this. He doesn't even know I'm here."

The tall, gaunt, bearded man raised a large hand, cocked his index finger, and pointed it in my face. "A lie. The Frederickson brothers always work together. Indeed, if he were to fail to hear from you for any length of time, it's a certainty that he would come looking for you."

He paused, as if waiting for me to respond to what he'd said, or try to refute it. I remained silent. It seemed he knew as much, or more, about the Fredericksons as I knew about the Zelezians. But then, a lot of people knew about the Fredericksons. It was the price of success—and why we constantly tracked each other.

Zelezian continued, "Suppose we were to work out some arrangement whereby you and the woman would be free to go in exchange for your promises of silence? How would we manage to keep the other half of Frederickson and Frederickson out of our business?"

"I'll call him and give him some kind of story about how I've lost interest in the matter. You can listen in on the conversation."

"Oh, I most assuredly would. Now, you've already told me one lie. Another lie will cost the prying man who wore this jacket his life, so be very careful what you say. I don't bluff. Who else knows about my business here? What individual, private firm, or government agency hired you to check up on me?"

"I'm not working for anybody but myself, Zelezian. Phil Statler had a breakdown after he lost the circus. I found him a few days ago, sick and dying, an alcoholic who'd been living on the streets of New York City. I feel I owe the man. I figured that if I could find a way to buy back the circus for him, it would give him a reason to live and clean up his act. My first stop was a circus community in Florida to see if I could line up some financial backers, which is how I happen to have Harper with me. Check with your son. He'll tell you I tried to sound him out about buying the circus."

"I'm aware of that, Frederickson. Luther told you the circus was not for sale. Did you think you could somehow get him to alter that decision by sneaking around here in the middle of the night? I think you had a pretty good idea of what you might find here."

There was something in his voice and manner I didn't like at all. "Just hold on and listen, Zelezian," I said quickly. "I did have an idea what I might find here, but not because of any official or extensive investigation. Nate Button, the man you're threatening to kill, approached me in Lambeaux, the last town you were in. He was investigating the killings, which you already know, and *he* assumed I was in this part of the country to do the same thing. He was the one who said he was convinced it was a lobox doing the killing, and he told me what a lobox was. I didn't pay any attention at the time—the same as nobody is going to pay any attention to him now. It was only after *I* started thinking of your background, bioweapons, and where a large mammal that would kill over such a large range could remain hidden that I thought of the circus, and then decided that it was my civic duty to check out the situation. Nobody else, with the possible exception of Nate Button, has any notion that World Circus has any business other than making its paying customers happy, and nobody will care what Nate Button thinks. That's it."

Arlen Zelezian stared at me with his black, dead eyes for a few moments, then slowly shook his head. He turned toward Luther, nodded in the direction of the shredded jacket back in the ring. Luther, who looked uncomfortable, hesitated a moment, but then turned around and walked to the ring. He picked up the torn fabric, slowly walked back.

The lobox quickly rose off its haunches, and its ears stiffened as it turned and looked at Luther. This was a routine, obviously, with which it was well familiar, and its hide had again begun to quiver.

"What are you doing, you sons-of-bitches?" I said tightly, having to force the words out of a constricted throat as I looked back and forth between father and son. "I've told you what you wanted to know, and now you keep your end of the bargain. Don't kill that man."

Arlen Zelezian nodded once again to his son.

"Kill!" Luther commanded as he threw the tattered remnants of Nate Button's jacket toward the main entrance to the Big Top.

Harper screamed as the lobox, its driving paws kicking up clots of sawdust, bolted away, racing toward the far end of the tent. I watched in horror as it disappeared into the night, wondered just where Nate Button was at the moment as death raced toward him like an express train from hell, ready to disembowel him and tear out his throat.

"I warned you that your next lie would cost that man his life," Arlen Zelezian said to me in a low, calm voice that had a slightly reproachful tone. "And I warned you that I didn't bluff. Did you really expect me to believe an absurd story about you wanting to buy back this circus to give to your poor, old, sick ex-boss? Do you take me for a fool? Come, now. Tell me the truth, or the woman will be next. Who sent you to spy on me? Who else knows I'm in this country, and why?"

For a few moments I was too paralyzed with shock and horror to speak, but then the words erupted out of me in a half shout, half scream. "That's the truth, you dumb fuck! Do you think I'd have brought a woman along with me if I'd known I was going to find a crazy killer like you! Jesus Christ, you just killed that man for nothing!"

I stood trembling with rage, fists clenched at my sides, as the bearded man hovered over me, looking down into my blood-engorged face. Finally, he shrugged. "Yes," he said evenly, "I see your point. Perhaps I was a bit too hasty. Now I think you may have been telling the truth after all."

I lunged for him, going for his kneecaps and groin. The barrel of his Magnum came up fast and hard, catching me on the side of the head. I was probably unconscious long before I hit the ground, but there was the sensation of a considerable amount of time passing as I floated down a long, black well shaft echoing with screams, growls, and the gnashing of teeth until I finally landed in an ocean of blood that drowned out everything.

CHAPTER EIGHT

Arlen Zelezian apparently hadn't thought much of my story—or, more likely, he had never intended to keep his part of the bargain. Whether or not he'd believed me was impossible to tell, but it was obvious that he was willing to kill us and take his chances.

I regained consciousness only to find myself in a drugged stupor—the result, I suspected, of having animal tranquilizers injected into my right arm, which was sore. I was imprisoned in what looked to be an old-fashioned circus cage, mounted on a flatbed truck. The bars of the cage were covered on all sides by wooden shutters, but faint illumination was provided by a naked light bulb dangling on the end of a frayed cord suspended from the ceiling and presumably running on current off the truck battery. I slept most of the time, managed to occasionally awaken with just enough energy to relieve myself in a galvanized steel pail set up in a corner near a locked trapdoor. I knew that we were traveling, for through my drug-induced dreams I could feel the cage swaying and bumping over potholes, could hear the muffled roar of the truck engine. It seemed we were on our way to the next stop, wherever that might be.

I wondered what they had done to Harper.

I wondered where we were going and what was going to happen when we got there.

I wondered where Garth was.

Finally, I awoke with my head relatively clear, but with a splitting headache and a taste in my mouth like rotten blubber. My cage and my body had been hosed down, and I was lying naked on the rough, splintered wood floor in a corner of the cage, covered with a towel. On the floor over by the trapdoor, neatly folded, were my charcoal suit, blue T-shirt, shorts, socks, and shoes. I found the discovery ominous.

Clean clothes could mean that execution day had arrived.

As if in response to my foreboding, the wooden shutters at the front of the cage suddenly flew open, banging against the sides of the enclosure. Wherever we were, it wasn't with the rest of the circus; with the truck engine turned off, it was completely still. It was night, the darkness pierced by what I presumed were car or truck headlights shining into my prison.

"Get dressed, dwarf," a voice with a heavy East European accent said.

I stepped back a pace, shielded my eyes from the headlights with my hands, and squinted. Now I could see that the voice belonged to the potbellied roustabout with the bulbous, Technicolor nose. With him was another man, gaunt and unshaven, who was dressed in ill-fitting coveralls and a stained Greek seaman's cap. Both men were holding guns.

"Where's the woman?"

The potbellied man raised his pistol and aimed it at my chest. "I told you to get dressed."

I got dressed. The gaunt man in the coveralls and seaman's cap said something to the potbellied gunman in a language I thought might be Polish or Hungarian, then produced a key which he used to open the padlock on the wooden trapdoor at the side of the cage. The potbellied man motioned with his gun, indicating that I should get out. I ducked through the opening, descended to the ground by means of a short wooden ladder, then turned toward the two men. Now, without the headlights shining in my eyes, I could see that the potbellied man had a huge shiner; his right eye was swollen shut, and the whole right side of his face was a dark rainbow of black, purple, violet, and muddy yellow. He motioned with his gun toward the car off to his left, and I started walking.

"I like the looks of your eye," I mumbled to the potbellied man as I passed him. "Too bad whoever did that to you didn't take your head off."

"Shut up, dwarf," the man said, his thick accent making his words just barely intelligible. "That fucking big brother of yours is going to get his guts spilled just a little while after you lose yours. Next stop."

I stopped and stiffened, started to turn, then froze when I felt the bore of a pistol suddenly press hard against the base of my skull. It was the gaunt man in the coveralls; he was good with the gun—and watchful. It wasn't going to do anybody any good for me to get my brains blown out; I knew I was going to have to be patient and pick exactly the right time to make a move on these two men. "You have Garth?"

It was the potbellied man who answered. "Whatever the big fucker's name is, we've got him."

"How do you know he's my brother?"

"Because Mr. Zelezian told me."

"What happened to the woman who was with me?"

"Shut up and get in the fucking car, dwarf, or Janek will put a bullet in your brain."

I continued walking toward the car, at the same time looking around me. Not only had we left the circus, but we appeared to be in the middle of nowhere. As far as I could see in all directions, there was nothing but flatland, with no lights to indicate any houses or a town. Arlen Zelezian's men had chosen a completely isolated spot to let me out of the cage, and I was pretty certain I knew why. I wondered how many miles it was to the nearest tree.

I opened the back door of the car. The interior light came on, and I could see Harper sitting in the back seat, hands folded in her lap. She was wearing the same outfit—jeans, silk blouse, and sneakers—as when I had last seen her. Her face was ashen, the hollows under her eyes dark from sleeplessness, but she looked otherwise unharmed. She saw me, and her maroon eyes went wide.

"Robby! I was so afraid you were . . ."

I got into the car, slid across the seat, and wrapped my arms around her. I held her tight, buried my face in her hair. "God, I'm glad to see you," I murmured. "Did they hurt you?"

She shook her head. "They just kept me tied and gagged in the back of somebody's trailer. What are they going to do with us?"

"I don't know," I lied. In fact, I was virtually certain I knew exactly what they planned to do with us.

"They have your brother."

"So I hear. Our friend with the black eye just told me."

"They trapped him. I heard it from the trailer. He confronted them. He seemed to know they had you."

"Yeah. Garth has quite a nose for evil."

"No talking!" the potbellied man snapped as he got into the back seat next to me, pressing me hard against Harper. I felt the bore of his gun dig into my ribs, on a direct line with my heart. The position didn't leave me a lot of room for maneuvering.

The gaunt man called Janek got into the front seat, behind the wheel. He started up the car, an ancient Plymouth, put it into gear, and started forward; apparently, even the area we were in wasn't considered sufficiently isolated. The car's engine sputtered and coughed, and there was a strong smell of exhaust seeping up through the floorboards.

"Are you going to kill us?" Harper asked the potbellied man sitting next to me.

"Shut up, lady. We're just going for a little moonlight drive."

"It would be a terrible waste to kill somebody like me, wouldn't it?" Harper's voice had suddenly grown even huskier than usual, pitched at its most alluring. As she spoke she leaned forward slightly in order to look across me at the potbellied man—in the process giving him a good glimpse of bra and breasts. I could see now that her blouse was unbuttoned, and I felt a shudder of disgust as she reached across me with her right hand and placed her palm on the inside of the man's thigh, just above his knee. "Can't you think of something better to do with me?"

"Don't bother, Harper," I said, trying to keep my disgust and disappointment out of my voice, and failing. "That's not going to do either of us any good. He'll just use you, and you could get hurt."

"Mind your own business, Robby," Harper said curtly. She didn't look at me, although her face was only inches from mine as she leaned across me. "I know what I'm doing; I'm doing what I want to."

Now Harper took the man's hand, brought it across me to her chest, pressed it down inside her bra. The potbellied man began to breathe heavily as he kneaded her breast.

I loathed the sight of what was taking place almost literally under my nose, and if it was a ploy to allow me to make a move on the man, it wasn't working; the potbellied man had transferred the gun to his left hand and was pressing the bore up hard under my chin, right over the carotid artery, forcing my head back. I certainly hoped the weapon didn't have a hair trigger, for I could feel his whole body beginning to tremble with passion. Having my head accidentally blown off by a cretin whose mind was elsewhere seemed a particularly bad joke considering some of the scrapes I'd survived, and I closed my eyes so that I couldn't see the man savoring the same flesh I had been savoring not long before.

Harper moaned softly.

"You're a hot little bitch, aren't you?" the man said in a hoarse, quavering voice. His breath smelled of onions, his body like an old sock.

"I want it," Harper said in her low, husky voice. "I want it now. Let's get out."

The man in the front inclined his head back slightly and said something in Polish or Hungarian, sharply; the man with the gun to my neck replied in Polish or Hungarian, sharply. I didn't need a translator to tell me that the potbellied man wanted Janek to stop the car. An argument ensued, during the course of which my unwelcome seatmate often chose to emphasize a point by jabbing the bore of the gun even harder against my carotid artery. My companion apparently won the debate, because Janek abruptly braked and pulled off to the side of the potholed road. Then he turned around in his seat and aimed his pistol at my head. The potbellied man took his gun away from my throat, shoved it into the waistband of his trousers. He got out, started around the car, stopped in the back to unzip his pants and relieve himself.

Harper cast a quick glance at the man in the front seat, then leaned toward me. For the first time since she'd started playing whatever game she was playing, she looked directly into my eyes.

"Remember what I said about wild things, Robby?" she asked softly.

"You've talked a lot about wild things," I replied tersely, averting my gaze. I was feeling surly. Incredibly, I was also feeling hurt. Of all the things I should be feeling at the moment, I thought, hurt was the most inappropriate. But there it was.

"You tame wild things, Robby. It's your nature. But wild things can take care of themselves. From everything I've read and heard about you, you're likely now to try something impossibly heroic because you think you have to try to save me from being degraded. I've also read that you're deceptively quick and powerful. You might even be able to take this skinny guy with the gun on you."

I glanced back through the rear window. The potbellied man had finished relieving himself and was zipping up his pants. In response to our whispered conversation, the man in the front seat had stiffened and was concentrating even harder on keeping his pistol aimed at the exact center of my forehead; if there had ever been a chance of surprising and disarming him while his companion had his way with Harper, it was gone now.

"Thanks a lot, Harper," I said with a deep sigh, looking up at the car roof. "I can always use that kind of encouragement."

"You're angry with me because you're thinking that I've put this other jerk-off on guard and made it harder for you to put some kind of move on him," Harper whispered urgently as the other gunman came around to her door. "Well, you might have succeeded in taking away his gun, and then again, you might have been killed. Do me a favor, Robby. Let this wild thing take care of herself. For a woman who's known as many men as I have, I'd be most surprised if the fat jerk-off has anything new to show me, unless his whang has polka dots. You may be surprised to see how this works out. So just sit still."

There was no way I was going to try to put a move on anybody; any plans I might have had to take advantage of the potbellied gunman's temporary distraction were canceled now. Not only had Harper put Janek doubly on his guard, but she'd taken the heart out of me. So I sat still, staring off into space, as the fat man jerked the rear door open, grabbed Harper's arm, and started to drag her from the car.

"Easy, big guy, easy," Harper said, abruptly pulling out of the man's grasp and stepping out of the car herself. "I want you as much as you want me, remember? So there's no need for any rough stuff. Now, let's go find us some nice private place. I've got a few tricks I want to show you."

Harper slammed the door shut, then took the man's hand and pulled him away into the night, toward a clump of bushes about seventy-five yards away that stood out in silhouette like an atoll in a sea of darkness against the flat, empty horizon. I sank back in the seat, crossed my arms over my chest, and stared back at the man in the front seat who was aiming his gun at my head.

"Fuck you," I said with a big grin, just to see if he understood any English at all.

He either didn't understand or didn't care. He just kept staring and aiming his gun.

In my disgust and hurt and general all-around disappointment with Harper, another thought was clearing its throat in the back of my mind, trying to get my attention. It finally did. Harper was indeed a wild thing, I thought, but unless I had completely read her wrong, her behavior in the last few minutes was totally out of character. She was sexy, yes, and certainly passionate, but I simply could not understand why she would seduce a man she had to know fully intended to see her dead, no matter what she did.

And how could I possibly be surprised by how it was going to work out?

Suddenly, there came from the darkness in the direction of the bushes a sharp, high-pitched shout that could have been a cry of passion. The gaunt man in the front seat started, momentarily took his eyes off me to look out the window toward the bushes. We waited together and didn't have to wait long. Half a minute later, Harper, flushed and out of breath from running, appeared at the side of the car. She began pounding her fists against Janek's window, apparently heedless of the gun in the man's hand.

"Come with me!" she shouted at Janek, pointing to her chest and making gasping sounds. "Quickly! There's something wrong! I think your friend has had a heart attack! Come on!"

The gunman, obviously torn between the need to attend to whatever emergency had come up and the imperative to guard his charge, kept looking back and forth between Harper's twisted face at the window and me, nervously licking his lips as his pronounced Adam's apple bounced up and down in his throat. Harper hurried things along by finally yanking his door open and grabbing his arm—an action that made me wince and duck down. But the gun didn't go off.

"Come on! Your friend's dying!"

Janek made his decision. He got out of the car, grabbed Harper. He put the gun to her head, then spoke to me rapidly in Polish or Hungarian, pointing first to me, then at the car.

"I think I've got it, Janek," I said drily, emphasizing my words with slow and elaborate sign language. "If I get out of the car, you'll shoot the woman. Bang-bang."

The man nodded enthusiastically as I again leaned back in my seat and crossed my arms over my chest. Then I watched through the window as Harper pulled him off in the direction of the bushes.

Things did not bode any better for Janek than they had for his potbellied colleague, I thought with a grim smile. I knew that I had been a fool.

Two or three minutes; there was another sharp cry, this one louder than the first, and then some enthusiastic but abbreviated cursing in Polish or Hungarian. I waited another minute, then got out of the car and walked slowly toward the black outline of the bushes.

I found Harper behind and slightly to the right of the clump of bushes, squatting down in the grass between the corpses of the two gunmen. In the faint moonlight I could just make out the men's faces, and it was obvious that they had died not only quickly but unpleasantly; the flesh on their necks and the lower parts of their faces was swollen and black. Harper's head was bowed, and she seemed to be fighting for breath. In her right hand she held the small, carved wooden box I had previously seen her take from her purse. She was holding her right wrist with her left hand. I stayed a distance away.

"Harper?" I said quietly.

She looked up at me, and in the moonlight I saw her wry smile. "What's the matter with you, Robby? Don't you understand Polish? Didn't you hear that man tell you you were supposed to wait in the car?"

"Is your little pet and traveling companion back where it belongs?"

Still holding her right wrist, she shifted around and slipped the wooden box into the left front pocket of her jeans. "Yeah," she said thickly. "It was kind of hard to find the little guy the second time; the first time, he just jumped right out of the box onto the guy's neck. Pretty effective—better defense than Mace, huh?"

"No question about it."

She sucked in a deep breath, slowly exhaled. "God, I was so afraid it was dead—I hadn't fed or given it water in a long time. I was able to put it in my pocket when they let me go to the bathroom. I told them I had my period and needed my purse."

I went to her, put my hands under her arms, and gently lifted her to her feet. She had begun to tremble violently, and I held her tight, stroking her long hair, kissing her lips, neck, cheeks, and forehead. "God, Harper, you're a pisser," I whispered hoarsely in her ear. "All that talk about wild things; you wanted to make certain I didn't get hurt trying to rescue you, because you were about to rescue me. You knew they were dead men."

Now she pulled away from me, stared hard into my face. There were tears welling in her maroon eyes, sliding down her cheeks. "You should have heard your voice back there, Robby. You sounded like you hated me."

"I'm so sorry, Harper," I said, pulling her back close to me, kissing away her tears. "I was going for the world-class professional stupid cup. Please forgive me."

After a few moments she sighed heavily, nodded, leaned hard against me. The tears had stopped, but now I noticed that her flesh felt cold and clammy, and I wondered if she was going into shock. I pushed her away, looked into her face. Her eyes seemed slightly out of focus.

"Harper, are you all right? Did either of them hurt you?"

"No," she said, shaking her head. "I'm all right."

I looked around me in the darkness and shuddered as I suddenly felt a stab of fear. I walked quickly over to the dead men, neither of whom had even come close to making it a hundred feet after the krait had bitten them. I searched their bodies until I found their guns, put the weapons in the pockets of my suit jacket, then took Harper's hand and started to lead her back toward the car. She stumbled, and would have fallen if I hadn't caught her.

"Harper?"

"I'm all right."

"Come on. We have to get back to the car. Quickly."

"Robby? Why—?"

"Unless I'm seriously mistaken, we were brought out here to empty city to serve as lobox bait. They probably would have let us out of the car, maybe with a warning to go and sin no more and to count our blessings. We'd have been wandering around out here looking for a house, and then the thing would have been on us. I still have my wallet in my pocket, and your purse is probably somewhere in the car; werewolves don't have much use for credit cards or money, so they didn't want those items to be missing from our corpses. You and I were scheduled to be the werewolf's next victims. Zelezian has used your sweater and my jacket to prime the lobox, and I'm certain it's on its way now, tracking us—or the scent of the car."

"Oh, God, you're right," Harper said, and then she too began looking around.

We walked quickly to the car. I helped Harper into the passenger's seat, then hurried around the rusting Plymouth and got in behind the wheel. I made sure all the doors were locked, turned on the interior light, and checked the weapons I had taken from the gunmen. One was a .45 automatic with a full clip, and the other a snub-nosed Colt Cobra with a full cylinder. I put the safety on the Colt, which I judged would have the least kick, and offered the weapon to Harper, who was turned slightly away from me. "Can you use this, babe?"

Harper turned her head to look at the gun, hesitated, then finally shook her head. "Not right now, Robby," she said in a small voice. "I'm a little shook up, and I'd rather you had both of them. Can we get going?"

"We can, but I don't think we should. If I'm right, and we were brought out here to give that lobox another trial run, it's not going to do us any good to drive away. It will follow the smell of this damn car, and it will keep searching for us, coming at us, no matter where we are. Luther said it was incredibly tenacious, and I believe him. Maybe it's tracking us now, maybe not, but I do know that we'll never have a better chance than this to turn the tables and nail the son-of-a-bitch if it is coming at us. If we go, then there's no telling when and where one or both of us may find the fucking thing leaping out of some shadow to tear our guts out. If it's been primed, then it will keep searching until it finds us, and then we're dead. Now, at least, we know where it is. We're ready for it. I say we solve our lobox problem while we have the opportunity and the advantage. Then I have to give some thought to the problem of getting my brother away from them."

"I say we go back and kill the Zelezians. That will solve the problem."

I blinked, surprised, somewhat taken aback by the purpose and ferocity in her voice. I was at once pleased, because her outrage and obvious willingness to take extreme risks meant that I had an increased number of options. At the same time, her rage made me a bit nervous. I did not want Harper Rhys-Whitney, this woman I certainly lusted after, and feared I loved, to be harmed. I couldn't do anything about the extreme danger she already faced, but I didn't want her anger to put her in any more danger or to provoke her to harsh or hasty action.

"That's certainly a possibility to consider," I said carefully. "But that might not be so easy, and if we failed, we'd be in an even worse situation. Even if we succeeded, we'd still have a lobox on our trail. We don't have a lot of time, and things could get very complicated. If we decide to go to the police, it would help a great deal to have a dead lobox in the trunk of the car as proof of our story. But even then, I'm not sure I'd trust the police or the state troopers to get my brother out of there safely. Along with your safety, Garth has to be my number one priority."

"Damn right," Harper said with the same quiet intensity. "But

I still say we just go right back there—wherever 'there' is—and kill the bastards now. Just give me a little time to get myself together, and I'll be able to handle one of those guns. You show me how it works, and I'll kill the bastards myself. I'm a lot madder at them than I am at any lobox."

I reached across the seat and gently stroked her back. "One step at a time, Harper," I said softly. "We—and Garth—can't afford for us to make a mistake. Let's wait to see what's hunting us before we decide how we're going to hunt the Zelezians."

"Okay," Harper said quietly, after a pause. She was silent, breathing rather heavily, for some time, then added, "Where do you suppose we are?"

"I haven't got the slightest idea. I was drugged most of the time. But we can assume that the circus has at least moved on one more stop. I was bouncing all over the cage they had me in for what seemed like hours."

"It *was* hours—almost eight. There was a clock inside the trailer where they kept me."

"Then they've made just one move?"

"Yes."

"Then, according to that schedule we saw, the circus is out of Kansas and into Nebraska—home sweet home for me. It should be set up near a town called Stonebridge, and we can't have been driven too far from it. That's where we'll find Garth and the Zelezians—when we're ready to call."

I waited for a response, but there was none. Harper's breathing, although still ragged, was more regular than it had been; exhaustion, rage, fear, and tension had finally taken their toll, and she had fallen asleep. I put the .45 and the Colt on the seat beside me, took off my suit jacket, and covered her with it. Then I turned around, got up on my knees, and, resting my chin on the back of the seat, stared back the way the car had come, looking for a dark shape moving on the horizon, a deadly shadow in the moonlight, listening for the sound of scratching or sniffing at the doors.

•   •   •

The clock in the car wasn't working, and I'd lost my wristwatch, but I estimated that more than two hours had passed when the horizon off to the east began to glow, and the surrounding landscape became dimly visible in the first light of the false dawn. Although I was certain that a lobox, by now, would have easily covered the ten miles or so that comprised its scent range, I had still not seen or heard anything.

Perhaps, I thought, the gunmen had planned to simply shoot us and dump us in a ditch by the side of the road after all.

It was certainly good news that we were alive, but I was disappointed not to find a lobox on our trail. The Zelezians had articles of our clothing; just because a lobox had not been primed and sent to kill us on this night didn't mean that it wouldn't happen in the future, when we would not know the beast was coming, or where it was coming from. Also, I would have dearly loved to have a dead lobox for show-and-tell with the local police or the state troopers; eventually, we were going to have to explain the two corpses with swollen black necks and faces lying in the grass seventy-five yards away.

Already, with the failure of the two gunmen to return to the circus, Arlen and Luther Zelezian had been warned that something was wrong. Perhaps they were, even at that moment, hastily shutting down the whole operation, moving their breeding stock of loboxes. Perhaps preparing to kill Garth.

Shit, I thought as I stared out over the still, silent landscape. In fact, double shit.

"Robby," Harper said wearily, stirring, "I've got to pee." She sounded terrible.

I studied the landscape some more, turning all the way around in my seat. There was still no sound, except for an occasional birdcall, no sign of movement, and yet the muscles in my stomach ached from tension. I said, "Climb over the seat and pee in the back."

"I think I may have to do more than pee."

"Do it in the back."

She laughed weakly. "Robby, I really don't think I know you well enough to exercise my excretory functions in front of you. I hope I never know you that well. How would I maintain my mystique?"

"Harper, this is really no time to worry about your modesty or

137

your mystique. I promise I won't peek or listen. I don't want you to get out of the car."

"You haven't seen or heard anything, have you?"

"No, but that doesn't mean there's nothing out there."

"I have to go, Robby. I'll only be a minute."

"All right," I said, reaching for the key in the ignition, "just hold on a little longer. Let me drive ahead a few hundred yards to the top of the hill up there where I can get a better view."

I turned the key in the ignition. The engine of the old Plymouth ground and whined, but didn't start. I shut off the ignition, gave it a rest for thirty seconds, and tried it again, with the same result. Cursing under my breath, I pumped the accelerator—and knew I'd flooded the engine when I smelled gasoline.

Harper sighed, shifted in her seat. "I'll be all right, Robby. Don't worry. There's nothing out there."

When Harper raised her right arm from her side where she had been cradling it and reached for the door handle, I could see that the flesh of her wrist was a mottled gray, swollen from wrist to elbow to more than the diameter of her hand. I grabbed her left arm, pulled her across the seat to me as I felt my heart begin to pound.

"Harper, you've been bitten! *Jesus Christ!*"

She apparently didn't have the strength to struggle, for she simply slumped against my shoulder, weakly nodded her head. "It got me when I was trying to get it off the second man's neck. Careless of me."

"I have to get you to a hospital!"

"Too . . . late, Robby. I mean, it would have been too late hours ago. There's nothing you, or anybody else, can do for me. There's no specific anti-krait venom in the United States. If the people at the hospital knew what they were doing, the first thing they'd do is put in an emergency call for an airlift of a pint or so of Harper Rhys-Whitney's blood to use as an antitoxin serum. Well, I already have more of Harper Rhys-Whitney's blood than anybody else, so there's no sense in my going to a hospital. I told you I've been bitten dozens of times before, Robby. I have resistance. If I was going to die, you'd have found my corpse over there in the bushes beside the two men. I'm having an allergic reaction to the venom, but it will pass. I'm not going to die, I promise you—but I am going to severely embarrass myself if you don't let me out of this car so I can go to the bathroom."

"*Damn* it!" I shouted, again trying—and failing—to get the Plymouth's engine to turn over. "I'm taking you to the hospital anyway! Just as soon as I can get this fucking car started!"

Harper shook her head. "Not a good idea, Robby. By the time we find a hospital, the police are likely to have found those two men over by the bushes—and they're liable to find out quickly that they both died of snakebite. Do you want to try to explain to the police how *I* happened to have been bitten by the same kind of poisonous snake?" She pulled away from me, pressed down the handle on the passenger's door. "Now, I've *got* to go to the bathroom. Don't leave without me."

"Harper!" I said, once again grabbing her left arm and yanking her back toward me just as she shoved the door open. "I just don't want to take the ch—!"

The juggernaut of fur, fangs, claws, and bunched muscles hurtled through the area in space where Harper's torso had been just before I'd pulled her back, and I heard the distinct click of fangs snapping on empty space just before the lobox crashed into the side of the door, driving it back and springing it off its hinges. The metal's screech mingled with a sound from the lobox I had never heard before, a sound other men may have heard only a brief moment before they died, a kind of high-pitched, almost human-sounding cry that was somewhere between a growl and a roar.

The lobox bounced off the door, its killing scream turning to a yelp of pain, surprise, and frustration. It hit the ground just outside the door and lay there on its side, momentarily stunned, as I desperately grabbed for the nearest gun on the seat, the Colt. I sprawled across the seat, atop Harper, in order to get a better shot at the lobox, aimed the weapon dead center at the animal's head, and pulled the trigger. Nothing happened; I had forgotten to deactivate the safety mechanism after Harper had declined the gun.

As I swiped at the safety catch with my left hand, a second, tawny head suddenly appeared in the doorway, its saber fangs only inches from my face. Now, with the animal in a killing rage, the thick ruff around its neck stood on end all around the head with the golden, curiously human eyes, reminding me of a hooded cobra.

Not one but two loboxes had been primed and sent, one for Harper and one for me. With its extended ruff, the head of the lobox in front of me filled the entire doorway, blocking the sun.

The lobox snapped at me just as I managed to draw my head back out of the way. I released the safety catch on the Colt, brought the gun up, and fired. The report of the weapon in the closed space slammed against my eardrums, and I felt a stabbing pain in both ears. The head was gone—but I knew I hadn't hit anything; the beast, apparently recognizing the danger posed by the gun, had, with incredible quickness and agility, ducked and bounded away a split second before I had fired the bullet that would otherwise have gone right into its gaping maw and exited through the back of its skull.

Something thudded hard against the side window on the driver's side, right behind me, shaking the car and cracking the glass. Instantly, I twisted around, raised the Colt, closed my eyes, and fired. Powdered glass sprayed over my face and chest, but there was no spurting blood, no animal howl of pain; once again, the lobox had bounded away just before I had fired. I desperately wiped the debris away from my eyes, sat up, switched the gun to my left hand, and used my right to push Harper off the seat, down into the well beneath the dashboard. Then, in a near panic, I blindly pumped three bullets into the open space on the passenger's side when I thought I caught a flash of movement. But there was nothing there. I swiped more powdered glass away from my face, picked up the automatic, then lay down on my back on the seat, my cheek pressed against a section of the steering wheel, as I aimed the Colt at the empty space just above my head, and the automatic out the open door.

It sounded like a hive of bees was buzzing around inside the car, but I knew that it was just ringing in my ears from the firing of the gun. I could feel blood trickling out of my left ear, but it was impossible to tell whether it came from a shattered eardrum or a nick from a stray piece of glass.

"Cover your ears!" I shouted over the ringing in my own head as I put my hand on Harper's shoulder and shoved her even further down into the cramped space under the dashboard.

I heard a thump, and then the scratching of claws on metal at the rear. I glanced between the seats, saw the head and shoulders of one of the loboxes standing on the trunk of the car. I poked the Colt between the seats, squeezed off a shot. I missed the lobox, which had darted off the car as I'd aimed, but the rear windshield exploded under the impact of the bullets.

The Colt was empty. I shoved it aside, gripped the .45 automatic with both hands, swept it around me in a series of arcs—back and forth, up and down, the empty spaces to my rear, the side, and at the back of the car.

Harper was sobbing hysterically, but there was nothing I could do at the moment to comfort her. Mongo the Magnificent was, I thought, currently being outsmarted by two overachieving animals, ancestors of the wolf. So far, in what was probably less than a minute, the two beasts, using their incredible agility, had managed to get me to shoot out most of the glass in the car, removing that barrier between their fangs and our flesh. And at the same time I was using up bullets.

They couldn't *intentionally* be suckering me, I thought. Two animals couldn't possibly have the intelligence, or the communications skills, to coordinate an attack like that; they couldn't *plan* to make me keep wasting ammunition until we were defenseless and they could easily get at us. The damn things couldn't possibly be thinking things out, working together to inexorably close a killing trap.

Or could they?

I remembered Nate Button's photographs of the recently discovered cave paintings at Lascaux, the utter terror radiating from those primitive people's rendering of the hunter-killer beast they had probably worshiped as a god . . .

Humans appeared to have a primal fear of wolves, I thought, and now I had a pretty good idea where it had come from.

Wolves hunted in packs, and I recalled that they had been observed to cooperate in complex ways that were astounding to their human observers. If wolves cooperated, why not loboxes? And why should I be surprised if loboxes did it a hell of a lot better? These two had, after all, sneaked up on us, totally undetected, during the night, recognized that Harper and I were in the car, and then waited patiently just outside the car for one of us to make a mistake, open a door . . . and let them in.

Not too trashy for an animal, I thought. It seemed that the lobox was, indeed, a pretty smart cookie, a savage merciless killer, a most formidable opponent. I had a sudden image of two or more loboxes escaping from the Zelezians, slipping their psychological leashes, to run off into the wild. Then humanity would have its own very special natural enemy for the first time in tens of thousands of years of unfettered trampling over the flora and fauna of the planet.

The woods would certainly be empty of hunters during deer season, I thought with a grim smile—and every other season. A lot of human behavior would change, for better or worse, at least in North America. And all because of a beast genetically retrieved from the past to serve as an advanced weapon of assassination. If these things ever got loose in the wild, there would be many changes in the way human beings did business.

In the meantime, Harper and I were trapped in the confines of a car with most of its glass shot out and one door hanging open, and I had seven bullets left.

A giant, tawny head with gaping maw, quivering nostrils, and expanded ruff suddenly appeared at the open door. I squeezed off a shot, missed again as the lobox ducked back.

Six bullets.

All together now, children: *If you go out in the woods today you're sure of a big surprise* . . .

Suddenly there was the thump of something heavy landing on the hood of the car, the grating of claws on metal. I twisted around on the seat and aimed the gun at the front windshield, but there was nothing there.

A thump at the rear. I twisted again, glimpsed a tawny shape on the trunk, squeezed off a shot between the seats, hit nothing.

Five bullets left.

Things were not working out at all.

"Harper, I'm going out."

She looked up at me, her maroon eyes swimming with terror. "Robby—?"

"I'm just telling you what I'm going to do so you won't be

surprised and maybe try to come after me. I've already wasted too much ammunition. Going out is the only way I can get a clear shot at those damned animals. If we stay in here, we'll die; if one of those things comes sailing in through a window while I'm looking the wrong way, it's all over. I have to go after them."

"No, Robby! Please don't leave me!"

I shoved her back under the dashboard, sucked in a deep breath, then quickly flopped over onto my belly on the seat. I braced my feet against the door on the driver's side, pushed, and slid across the seat on a slippery carpet of powdered glass, out the door. As I fell out of the car, I did a half twist, landed on my left shoulder, rolled forward, and came up on my feet with the automatic in both hands, sweeping the space in front of me. I had five bullets left; since I didn't know how many bullets it would take to bring down a lobox, I couldn't afford to waste any of them. With both of them, I would go for nothing less than a head shot.

A huge head with great black leather nostrils and gleaming saber fangs poked out from behind the rear of the car. I swung my gun in that direction, and the head ducked back.

The head of the second beast poked out from behind the front. I swung my gun that way, and it too ducked back.

The damn things were smarter than a lot of people I knew, and that probably included me.

My little offensive maneuver was indeed proving to be a good defense, but it wasn't good enough. It was too static. Right now it looked like a standoff; they wouldn't come out into the open where I could get a clear shot at them, and I couldn't risk going around to the other side because it would leave Harper, crouched only inches from the jammed-open door, exposed to a quick, deadly sweep of razor-sharp claws.

But I wanted the damn things dead, and I didn't feel like standing around for a couple of hours waiting to see what *they* would do next.

I couldn't walk around the car, but I could go in another direction—up—and still have a line of fire on the right side of the car. I had stepped back a few paces in order to improve my angle in the event they both came at me at once. Now I ran forward, leaped up on the hood of the car, jumped to the roof.

What I saw was the two loboxes, ruffs now flat to their necks, running flat out, side by side, toward a field of tall grass two hundred yards away. They seemed as fast as greyhounds, for in only the two or three seconds it had taken me to get up on top of the car, they had raced almost half the distance to the grass—and then, only after they had instinctively reacted to the sense that my position above them meant death, and after they had made the decision to run.

Not bad for animals, I thought; but, considering the fact that the two of them had been intent on slashing Harper and me to bloody pieces, I was beginning to take the bad attitudes of these otherworldly creatures just a bit personally.

"You fucks!" I screamed as I went down on one knee, aimed, and squeezed off a shot, sighting between the two of them. Dirt kicked up just to the right of them, and I squeezed off two more shots.

I was rewarded with a piercing howl. The animal to the right stumbled, fell, and rolled over, but was almost immediately on its feet again and running. I debated firing the last two bullets but decided not to.

I was almost convinced the two creatures would somehow know my gun was empty.

I put the automatic in the waistband of my slacks, jumped back down to the hood of the car and to the ground. I walked around to the open door, leaned in, and placed my hand on Harper's neck—even as I stared back at the spot in the landscape where the loboxes had disappeared into the grass.

"It's all right, Harper," I said softly, gently stroking her neck, her hair. "They're gone now. We're safe."

For a few minutes, at least.

She couldn't stop crying. I hated to take my attention off the ground behind the car, but it seemed I had no choice; I needed Harper alert and watchful while I attended to the balky Plymouth. I slid onto the seat, wrapped my arms around her, held her tight. Her black, swollen arm was resting on the seat, only inches from my face, and I groaned inwardly at the sight of it. It looked ready to burst. I kept hugging and kissing her, and finally the sobs subsided. I helped her get up on the seat, and she leaned her head on my chest.

"Robby, are we . . . are we . . . ?"

"They're gone, Harper. I think I may even have hit one of them."

The problem, I thought, was that they probably wouldn't be gone for long, and with only two bullets left in my gun and a car that wouldn't start, I wasn't feeling too secure. There was, of course, always the possibility that they'd hightailed it back to the circus, but somehow I doubted it. They had been trained well and were smart enough to *know* they had failed at what they were expected to do. As Luther had pointed out, they *were* tenacious. I was sure they'd be coming back at us, tracking again, waiting for the right moment to pounce. Even now they were undoubtedly resting in the high grass, waiting . . .

Harper raised her head, smiled wryly. "I peed in my pants, Robby."

"I won't tell anybody. Most people in that situation would have done a lot more than just pee in their pants."

She giggled nervously, held her hand to her throat in a choking gesture. "I was so frightened, everything else went in the opposite direction. I don't think I'll be able to go to the bathroom for a month." She paused, shuddered. "My God, Robby, if you hadn't grabbed me and pulled me back when you did . . ."

"Well, they didn't get you, and you're safe."

"For now," Harper said in a small voice.

"Don't dwell on it, sweetheart. It's the stuff nightmares are made of. Just hang in there, and we'll get through this."

Harper studied me for a few moments, then kissed me, hard. "That's right," she said in a stronger voice. "I was the one who said I wanted to get involved in one of Mongo the Magnificent's bizarre cases, as I recall. You've been through horrible things before, haven't you?"

I smiled, shrugged. "This business ranks pretty high on my horribility scale. I must have bad karma."

She shook her head emphatically. "You have good karma. And I want to see those men *dead*, Robby. I can't believe they planned to leave us out here to die like . . . that. So horribly. I'll kill them myself. I want them to meet *my* pet."

"Stay cool, my dear. Our first priority has to be concentrating on getting out of range of those things, at least for a few hours, and then I have to figure out a way of getting my brother out of that circus."

"What do we do now?"

"We can't do anything until I get the car started," I said, and got out.

The first thing I did was to step back from the car and again sweep my gaze across the landscape, especially the area where the loboxes had disappeared. There was no sign of them. Next, I put my shoulder to the sprung door and, after a good deal of huffing and puffing, managed to get it shut. Then I walked to the front, opened the hood, climbed up on the fender, and looked down at the engine.

A mechanic I'm definitely not, but even I could tell that the hose hanging down next to the carburetor wasn't in its proper place. I reconnected the hose to the carburetor, then got back behind the wheel and turned the key in the ignition again. After some coughing and sputtering, the Plymouth started up. Around us, for as far as I could see in all directions, there was nothing but what appeared to be wheat and corn fields, and, far to the west, what might have been a grain elevator jutting up into the sky. I put the car into gear, made a U-turn across the shoulders of the narrow dirt road, and started driving back the way we had come, leaving behind an old, rotting circus wagon and two corpses. I was more than a little anxious to put as much distance as possible between us and this killing ground.

CHAPTER NINE

We found Harper's purse in the trunk, and my cash and credit cards were still in my wallet. It was some relief.

We reached a main highway in twenty minutes. Except for the assumption that we had crossed into Nebraska, I had no idea where we were. I arbitrarily turned right. A few miles down the road there was a sign announcing that we were seventy miles from the town of Quigley. I came to a gas station just as the needle on the gas gauge settled on the E. The attendant who filled the tank kept glancing curiously at the broken windows of the Plymouth, but he didn't comment. I hoped he wouldn't call the police, but knew there was no sense wasting time and energy worrying about it. I paid for the gas, then went into the adjoining convenience store to buy a map, a couple of hero sandwiches and a six-pack of beer, and a bag of ice for Harper's arm. I kept harboring a notion of taking her to a hospital, but she kept insisting that the danger had long since passed, and that with a bag of ice to reduce the swelling she would be fine. In fact, she did look considerably better, and I decided that she was probably right; we would pass on the hospital. First, there was the danger of her being connected to the snakebitten corpses we had left behind; second, as long as there was a lobox hunting for her, I did not want to leave her alone in any situation I could not control.

There was a gun shop in Quigley. I stopped, bought ammunition for the handguns, and a shotgun and a box of shells. I also checked the map, found I had turned the wrong way. Stonebridge was about eighty miles behind us, to the west. At the moment, that was just fine with me. We both needed some rest.

"These are for you," I said, handing Harper the shotgun and box of shells as I got back into the car. "We'll stop at the first motel we come to, eat our sandwiches, and rest up. I'll also show you how to use that thing at close range. If we play this right, there's a chance you may never see a lobox again, but in an emergency, that shotgun will be a lot more effective than a handgun."

She nodded, took the shotgun, and clasped it tightly across her laps. "When are you going there, Robby?"

"Tonight. I'd like to go there now, but I'm tired, and it's just too risky trying to do anything during the day. I figure I'll go in looking for Garth when they're putting on tonight's show—if there is going to be a show. By now, there are going to be a lot of nervous people in that operation, and they may be closing up shop fast. But I don't think they'll just go away without the two loboxes, and I have a strong hunch those animals are still on the prowl, hunting for us."

"Maybe you should go to the state police, Robby."

"I've given it a lot of thought. That option could lead to a lot of sticky complications. For one thing, what—and how much—can we tell them? And would they believe it? I don't want to risk having you arrested and charged with the murder of those two charmers back there."

"But those men were taking us out to be killed, Robby."

"Sure, but we can't prove it. There's no guarantee they'll believe us. I could be charged along with you, or held as a material witness."

"Robby, I'm more than willing to risk facing charges if it means your brother will be safe."

"There's no guarantee of that at all. If I get entangled with the law around here, Garth could be dead by the time I get untangled. Also, Zelezian almost certainly is being sponsored—protected—by some heavy-duty agency in Washington or very powerful individuals. It's possible local law enforcement people wouldn't be allowed to move on the circus until it was too late. I don't know if that's true, but I don't want to take the chance. There are just too many questions, too many uncertainties. It's why I have to go myself and hope that I get lucky. If it doesn't work out, and they nab me again, then you'll still be free to exercise the option of calling the troopers."

"Robby, they may be looking to nab you now, to trap you the same way they trapped Garth. And if they do, they may just kill you out of hand. Even if they do go ahead and put on a show tonight just to keep up appearances, they're certainly going to be on guard, watching for you."

She was probably right. "Maybe," I said. "Maybe not."

"Not only will they be looking for you, Robby, but you'll be going right back into the loboxes' sensory range."

"We don't know where they are, Harper. In any case, I don't feel I have any other choices."

"Okay," she said evenly. She paused, staring at the shotgun, then continued, "How did I do last night, Robby?"

"You did real good."

"Then there'll be no argument about my going to the circus with you tonight."

"Harper," I said with a sigh, "if I were to tell you that having you with me would be a distraction because I'd be worried about you, you'd call me a sexist, and then remind me that it was you who saved our asses last night. Right?"

"That's very good reasoning," she said, and smiled. "So thank you for not being a sexist, and thank you for not forcing me to remind you that it *was* me who saved our asses last night."

"I need you some place safe, Harper, so that you'll be able to call the police if I don't come back."

"In some motel nearly a hundred miles away? I want to be *there*, Robby. This time I promise I *will* wait in the car, but at least I'll be close by, close enough to actually hear or see—maybe—if anything goes wrong. You know I'm right. We're in this together. I'll be useless a hundred miles away, and you know it. I just might mean the difference between you and Garth living or dying."

"Harper, the loboxes . . . As you pointed out, we *will* be going back into their sensory range."

She wrapped her hands around the shotgun, hefted it. "I won't pee in my pants next time, Robby. If a lobox comes after me again, I'm going to have me a lobox rug. Let me watch your back. I really will feel safer if I'm with you."

I reached across the seat, took her hand, and squeezed it hard. "Thank you, Harper," I said simply. I didn't know what else to say. The fact of the matter was that she was right, and I was grateful to her for her resolve and courage.

* * *

I'd definitely had just about enough of dread and circuses, but this was a command performance. It was show time—both for World Circus and for me.

If the Zelezians were worried about anything—dead gunmen, missing multimillion-dollar assassin-beasts, or their cranky intended victims on the loose—it wasn't evident in the setup or atmosphere on the county fairgrounds outside the town of Stonebridge; lights blazed on the midway, where all the rides and games were in progress, and music blared from inside the Big Top, where the show had just begun. It could mean that they weren't at all concerned about what Harper and I might tell the authorities—or anything else we might do—and that tended to make me even more nervous.

As it was, I was soaked with sweat, although it was a relatively dry, cool night; walking around knowing that at any second horrible, clawed death may leap out from the shadows to rip out your throat and bowels can have that effect on a man.

We'd left the ruined Plymouth in an alley beside a supermarket and rented a station wagon, which was now parked, with Harper and her loaded shotgun inside it, at the edge of one of the three parking fields where there was enough radiated light for her to be able to see anything and anybody that might approach. With the Colt in my suit jacket pocket and the .45 automatic in my right hand, I was working my way through lines of parked cars and pickup trucks toward a roped-off area behind the Big Top. There

I knew I would find the penning enclosures as well as the parking field containing the trailers and the enormous Mack semis that hauled the circus around the country.

There was a man in a gray suit standing in the moonlight near the roped-off area. He was holding a walkie-talkie near his mouth, and there was a pronounced bulge in his suit jacket, near his left armpit. He was definitely not a circus roustabout, and I strongly doubted that he was a plainclothes state trooper. Rather, the man's presence suggested to me that the Zelezians had appealed to their government or corporate sponsor for a little additional help in case of any emergency I might try to cause. As I watched, the man spoke into the walkie-talkie, in English, and there was a crackling response.

In the section of the field just beyond the gunman in the gray suit, a dozen semitrailers were parked in rows of four, virtually nose-to-nose, with one row flush to the rear of the Big Top. That was where I wanted to go. I had been kept inside an old circus wagon, but there were no more of those in evidence. Garth was too big and obstreperous to try to keep in any mobile home, so I figured they might have him locked up in an animal cage inside one of the semis. In any case, the rows of parked trucks seemed the logical place to start looking. He would, at least, be in a position to return a signal.

If he was conscious.

Trying not to think of what might be slinking toward me in the darkness of the parking lot, I angled to my right, away from the gunman in the suit. I stopped fifty yards away and waited for him to look in the opposite direction, then darted out from behind a car, ran across a narrow dirt track, and ducked under a rope into a dark area near where the semis were parked. I crouched down in the night, forcing myself to take deep breaths and try to relax as I looked around me in the darkness and wiped sweat away from my eyes.

I had to hope Garth hadn't been drugged into unconsciousness; I had to hope he could respond to a signal. I could only start worrying about how to get him out after I found out where he was.

It was time to get off the ground, where I was vulnerable to a lobox attack from all sides. I hustled on over to the trucks, climbed up on the running board of the first one in the first line, clambered up onto the roof of the cab. Then I put the .45 in my other suit jacket pocket, jumped up, and caught the edge of the roof of the box with my fingers. I hauled myself up and over the edge onto the corrugated steel roof, then lay down in the darkness and again forced myself to take a series of deep breaths, seeking release from the terror that had gripped me from the moment I had left the relative safety of the station wagon. I kept reminding myself that I was safe from the loboxes, at least for the time being. The suited gunman was still pacing back and forth on the dirt track, speaking into his walkie-talkie, which meant that I hadn't been seen. I was still in business.

I began to feel better.

I was even beginning to feel just a tad of optimism.

I worked my way across the length of the box on the first semi, softly tapping out a Morse SOS code on the metal with the barrel of the automatic as I went along. When I reached the rear of the box, I eased myself over the edge and dropped to the hood of the tractor parked behind it. I hauled myself up to the roof of the box of that truck, again started tapping out the SOS code as I worked my way down its length.

On the roof of the box of the third semi, I hit pay dirt. I was halfway down, tapping out my signal, when I heard Garth's voice.

"Mongo?! That damn well better be you, brother! I need rescuing!"

I rested my head against the cold metal and breathed a sigh of relief. My brother didn't sound drugged, only angry. I tapped again.

"Mongo?! Is that you, you little fucker? I want you to know that I'm seriously pissed at you! And Mary's pissed at you, too!"

His words filled me with a new fear. It had never occurred to me that Mary might have come along with Garth and been captured too. If she had, it would present a host of new problems.

My knowledge of Morse was limited at best, and I didn't know if Garth knew any of it at all. I screwed my eyes shut, trying to recall the pages of dots and dashes from my Cub Scout manual.

Tappety-tap. M-A-R-Y H-E-R-E.

"No! Just me!"

W-A-I-T.

"Mongo, when I find out what you've gotten yourself into this time, I'm likely to tear your fucking head off?"

S-H-U-T U-P W-A-I-T.

I crawled on my belly back toward the front edge of the box, where there was an air vent, gently tapping all the way so that Garth could follow my progress. I could only hope that Garth had all of the interior of the box to move around in. When I was near the edge I paused to look around, but I didn't see any guards or roustabouts. I leaned over the edge, put my mouth close to the air vent.

"Garth? Can you hear me?"

"Yeah." His voice sounded as if it was directly below me, which meant that he had not been locked in a cage inside a cage. Good. "Sorry about all that yelling I did. It was just my way of letting you know I was happy to hear from you. It's getting a little stuffy in here."

"Yeah, I know. You're forgiven."

"When I didn't hear from you again for two days after our last phone conversation, I knew you'd gone and stuck that big nose of yours into Arlen Zelezian's business—just like I'd warned you not to. Christ, I was afraid you were dead."

"Not yet."

"But you're working on it, right?"

"That isn't exactly the way I'd put it."

"What the hell's going on, Mongo?"

"You know about the loboxes?"

"What are loboxes? I don't know anything, except that you and your girlfriend are in deep shit. The police are looking for the two of you."

"Yeah, that figures."

"I take it they're missing something, but I could never make out just what it is. I only heard bits and pieces of conversation."

"They're missing something, all right: two things. Look, have you got any lights in there?"

"No. This truck's filled with spare equipment, from what I can make out. I almost broke my neck following you over here."

"Okay, you've got double doors that swing out at the rear of the box and in the middle, on your left as you're facing toward the cab—the way you're facing now. They're padlocked. I'm going to try to shoot the lock off the doors at the rear, because I have more cover there. The trucks are parked nose-to-ass, but there should be enough room there for you to squeeze out. The shot is going to attract some attention, so be prepared to move fast. I've got a friend waiting for us in a car, but we may have to shoot our way out through the parking lots. You ready?"

"And then some."

"Here I come."

I crawled back to the rear of the box, taking care not to let myself be silhouetted against the sky, lowered myself to the hood of the tractor parked just behind. The padlock on the double doors of the trailer box ahead was just about at waist level. I straddled the hood ornament, took the automatic out of my pocket.

"Hey, Mongo? You out there?"

I gently tapped the door in response, then aimed the gun with both hands at the padlock and waited. The gray-suited gunman and his colleagues were going to come running at the sound of the shot, and I needed something to at least partially mask the report. Inside the Big Top, the band was striking up the Triumphal March from *Aida,* signaling Luther's entrance on Mabel. The music was building up in a crescendo that would end in a blare of trumpets, a drumroll, and a cymbal crash. It might just be enough. I aimed the gun, waited for the right moment.

There was no sound of warning, no characteristic roar; as I began to squeeze the trigger, I caught a flash of tawny color and blurred movement out of the corner of my right eye. I yelled in sheer terror and went flat on my back, throwing my arms across my face and throat, in the process losing my grip on the gun, which clattered across the hood, fell to the ground on the other side. I felt the breeze generated by the lobox's flight through the air just over my body, felt a sharp tug as its claws caught the lapels of my suit jacket, shredding them.

"Mongo! What's the matter?! What's happening out there?!"

What was happening was that the lobox that had been primed to kill me was back on my case, and I really didn't have time to explain to Garth what that all meant. In fact, I might not have much time left for anything. When I reached for the Colt, I found my suit jacket pocket empty; when I had thrown myself back on the hood, the heavy gun had slipped out, fallen to the ground along with the automatic.

The lobox—which had hurtled across the tractor hood and landed on the ground to my left—leaped to its feet at the same time I did. The beast wheeled on the grass in the narrow alley between parked trucks, bunched its legs under it, and sprang up at me the same time as I sprang for the edge of the roof of the trailer box. My fingers caught the steel edge and I pulled, hauling my legs up just as I heard the snap of jaws below my feet. It was a motivating sound. Terror and adrenaline propelled me up the side of the box, and I rolled over onto the roof as I heard claws scratching at the steel in the spot where my body had been only a moment before.

There was a sharp crack of a gun, and a bullet bit into the steel at the side of the box. I glanced in the direction from which the shot had come, saw a gray-suited gunman running across the field in my direction.

It was just what I needed. Mongo the Fumble-fingered was being given the choice of having his throat torn away or his brains blown out.

Gunman or no, I wasn't about to hang around to see how many leaps it was going to take the lobox before it managed to get up on the roof; its body was repeatedly banging against the steel, claws desperately scraping at the metal, and each leap seemed to bring it closer to the roof's edge. Whatever killed me, human or animal, was going to leave me just as dead, and at the moment I was more worried about the animal than the human. I scrambled to my feet as another bullet whizzed over my head. Keeping as low as possible, I bounded three steps, leaped across the bridge of space separating the truck I was on from the one parked next to it. If I could make it across the roofs of two more rows of trucks, I thought, I just might be able to leap onto the Big Top's canvas and crawl up to where there was a hole at the top, around the great center pole that was the tent's main support. I didn't have the slightest idea what I was going to do when I got there, or what good it was going to do me in the long run, but it seemed an infinitely better spot than the one I was in.

My only other alternative was to jump down to the ground, where I estimated I would last about five seconds.

I might last only slightly longer than that where I was, I thought as I leaped through the air again and landed on the next truck. I could hear the lobox's claws clicking and scraping on the steel behind me. It had gotten up to the roofs, and it was gaining on me. Fast.

One more leap, and I was on the roof of a semi parked right next to the Big Top. I sprang out into the air, arms extended full length, and my fingers caught the hard edge where a support cable ran horizontally along the length of the tent, beneath the canvas. I pulled, feet scraping on the canvas, and managed to haul myself up and over the cable, onto the incline leading up to the top. Immediately, instinctively, I rolled to my left.

The lobox landed right next to me—and would have landed on me if I hadn't rolled away. The claws of both its front paws punctured the canvas, and I knew I was finished. I was like a novice rock climber in sneakers on an ice sheet trying to escape from an experienced, fully rigged mountaineer; there was no way I could scramble up the steeply inclined canvas fast enough to escape the lobox, which had built-in pitons on all its feet. I flinched, every muscle in my body knotting as I waited for it to pull itself up the rest of the way, get its hind feet under it, and then proceed to use me for a quickly disposable scratching pole. I was close enough to it to see that it had a new dark stripe on its coat, this one running vertically down off its left shoulder, perpendicular to the black stripes running down its back on either side of its spine. But the stripe on its shoulder wasn't natural; it was dried blood from the gunshot wound I had inflicted on it. Not that wounding it had done me any good; as far as I could tell, getting nicked by the bullet hadn't slowed the beast down one iota and had probably only served to make it more determined to get me. I stared back into the all-too-human golden eyes; they were only inches from mine, and they seemed alive with an all-too-human glow of triumph.

I'd been beginning to feel like the Road Runner, the big difference being that it looked like Wile E. Coyote now had me, and I would really bleed, hurt, and die.

Then there was the sound of ripping canvas. Incredibly, the

head of the lobox began moving in the opposite direction, away from me. Its ruff, which had been fully expanded, slowly fell, and I let loose a burst of hysterical giggles as I realized what was happening; the creature's saber claws were so sharp that they couldn't hold their owner's weight in the fabric, as thick as it was, and they were slicing like razors through the canvas.

The triumphal glow in the golden eyes had changed to what I swore was a look of astonishment, chagrin, and frustration as the broad-ribbed torso inexorably slid backward toward the edge of the tent defined by the support cable.

"Take that, you fucking overachieving furball," I said, still giggling hysterically as I shifted my weight and kicked the animal in the side of the head.

The creature uttered a very unloboxlike yelp and, to the sound of ripping canvas and the click of claws on steel cable, disappeared over the edge of the canopy.

Of course, it wasn't that I didn't have other things to worry about: there was the crack of a gun, and a bullet tore into the canvas three feet to the right of my head. I glanced to my left, saw two gray-suited gunmen standing in an open area of the roped-off field, well out beyond the four rows of semis. One man, presumably the one who had already taken the potshot at me, was aiming again, using both hands.

The second man grabbed the first man's wrist, forcing the first man to lower the gun. Words were exchanged, and then they both broke into a run toward the main entrance to the tent and disappeared from sight. I presumed that it had occurred to at least one of the men that it might prove tacky, if not downright difficult to explain, if a patron of World Circus were killed by a stray bullet in the air, and so they were going to come at me in another way. They certainly had plenty of options; I wasn't about to jump to the ground and try to run away while there was a stray lobox down there licking its oversize chops at the thought of my doing precisely that.

The only direction I had to go was up. I rolled over on my hands and knees; gripping the hard edge of a guy cable running upward just beneath a fold in the canvas, I scrambled up to the very top of the tent, where the center mast, a wooden pole nearly a foot in diameter, thrust up through a steel-reinforced circle in the canvas, almost four feet in diameter, where dozens of guy wires and ropes were anchored to concentric steel rings attached to the center mast. I lay down on my belly and, gripping the uppermost steel ring, peered over the edge of the circle onto the layout and doings below me.

Directly beneath me was a maze of ropes crisscrossing one another, pulleys, trapeze rigging, and a number of platforms holding lighting and sound equipment. The position of the lights made it impossible for anyone on the ground inside the tent to see me, but I could see down well enough.

The ground was about a hundred and twenty feet below me, and I was almost directly above the great curtain separating the performing area from "backstage." The section where the lobox's claws and the bullet had torn through the canvas was well away from the audience seating area, and it seemed nobody inside the tent had noticed all the commotion outside. Far below, everything looked to be business as usual. The enormous, double-walled steel cage had been thrown up around the ring, awaiting the entrance of the tigers. Mabel, with Luther astride her head, was halfway through her star turn, going into one of her pachyderm pirouettes at the far end of the tent.

While I was pondering just what it was I planned to do next, I had the good fortune to glance behind me just in time to see one of the ubiquitous men in gray suits reach the top of a ladder that had been set up against the vertical drop of the tent. Our eyes met, and as he started to reach inside his suit jacket for his gun, I waved and blew him a kiss just before reversing my hand grip on the steel ring and rolling forward, down through the opening. If the man wanted to follow me, assuming he didn't mind shooting me in front of a few hundred spectators, I would see how he enjoyed doing his act a hundred feet above the ground. I ended up on the rear edge of a wide wooden platform, just behind a bank of spotlights.

I moved along the platform a bit further, away from the opening above me, then squatted down and again looked down at the audience below, the rigging that surrounded me. *Déjà vu.* I was back in the Big Top, high up in the rigging, where I had so often performed as a young man so many years before. I was amazed at how comfortable I felt, still, so high above the ground.

There was a pleasant tension in my muscles, almost as if they anticipated hurling me through space once again.

Easy does it, I thought; those tingling muscles of mine no longer had the tone they once had when, nearly two decades before, I'd swung around the perimeter of the tent on trapezes and guy ropes. Still, to get out of this one, I was going to need a goodly amount of Mongo the Magnificent's old circus skills. I could only hope that a few of those skills were left, still alive and kicking in my muscle memory.

There was trapeze rigging about twenty feet to my right, but to get to it I was going to have to negotiate a tangle of guy wires, ropes, and electrical cables.

I leaped for a taut rope above my head, caught it, then began swinging hand over hand toward the relatively secure platforms, bars, and ropes of the trapeze rigging.

Mabel was the first to notice my presence. I was about halfway through my hand-over-hand journey at the very top of the tent when she suddenly stopped in the middle of a pirouette, abruptly turned in my direction, lifted her trunk, and trumpeted. Even from as high up and far away as I was, I could see the look of consternation on Luther's face. Then he looked up, saw me, and his jaw fell open.

Next, the audience noticed me; hundreds of heads turned to look at me. There were a few startled gasps, then applause for the dwarf in a ruined suit dangling from a rope at the top of the tent with no net below. They liked it. Along with the applause came laughter. They thought I looked funny.

There was nothing funny about the appearance of the lobox, and the laughter and applause slowly died as the creature emerged from the shadows between two bleacher sections, padded to the center of the section of sawdust track directly below me, stopped. Its ruff suddenly expanded as it squatted on its haunches, raised its gaze to look at me, opened its jaws, and uttered its keening killing scream.

The audience didn't much care for that. Whatever it was they thought the lobox might be, they didn't like the fact that it wasn't in a cage, or at least on a leash. They sensed that it was dangerous, and it wasn't difficult to figure out that it was after me. No longer certain that this action was part of the show, the people in the tent fell silent. The music from the band tapered off. When the utter quiet was broken by another lobox scream, people began to mutter nervously. I continued along the rope until I reached the trapeze rigging. I sat down on the top platform to catch my breath and try to think.

Never in the history of the world, I thought, had an attempted escape been watched by so many people, the vast majority of whom didn't have the slightest notion of what was going on. I felt like a very small fugitive in a very large cage. For the time being, the fact that my progress was being monitored by a few hundred people as I moved around the top of the tent would—I hoped—guarantee my safety from snipers, but that situation couldn't last forever. Very soon now would come an announcement that the remainder of the show had been canceled due to an emergency, and the audience would be asked to leave. And then the firing would begin, with the corporate types in their gray suits lining up below me and vying to see who would be the first to pick me off.

In addition to those distractions, my concentration was being affected by an overriding fear for Harper. If this lobox was about, the one primed for Harper couldn't be far away—for Harper wasn't far away. I was certain that at that very moment Harper's lobox was crouched somewhere in the shadows of the parking area, its gaze locked on the station wagon, waiting . . .

And, of course, there was also the problem, remaining, of having Garth locked inside the box of the semi parked outside the tent. It was a problem that was going to have to be solved, since I couldn't leave him behind; after this night's performance, the Zelezians would definitely be concentrating very hard on their own plans for escape, and they would want to erase all evidence, eliminate all witnesses. To leave Garth behind would be to condemn him to death.

The fact that World Circus used only its own people, or its sponsor's people, for security could, it seemed to me, be turned to my advantage under the right circumstances. There would certainly be no radio calls to the local police for assistance, and thus no roadblocks. It was simple, I thought: all I had to do was find a way to exit the Big Top without being shot, or torn up by a lobox, free Garth, and then go to where Harper was waiting, avoiding her lobox, so that we could all make our getaway.

All I really needed to bring this unfortunate episode to a satisfying conclusion, I thought, was a tank.

A tank, or something like a tank.

Ah.

I got to my feet, crawled up even higher in the trapeze rigging where I couldn't be seen, then looked around me for something that would serve as a suitable replacement for a Louisville Slugger, Henry Aaron model. I finally settled on a bar from one of the three trapezes. I undid the safety releases on the bar, shoved the four-foot length of hickory through two belt loops. Then I glanced around to see where Mabel and Luther were; they seemed a long ways away, still down at the far end of the tent. To get to them, I would have to have a mode of transportation that would carry me to the other end of the tent and to the ground—or close to it. That would be the climbing ropes used by the aerialists, and all three of the ropes were tied up on the trapeze rigging on the opposite side of the tent. I figured I would probably be able to climb over to that section of rigging on guy wires and ropes, but it would take too long.

We do what we have to do.

Without giving myself a whole lot of time to think about the folly of what I planned to try, I grabbed a trapeze bar from its catch-rigging, gripped it, took a deep breath. Then I swung out into space, heading for the triple platform across the way. If there was any sound from the crowd below, I didn't hear it; I was conscious only of the wind whistling past my ears, the creak of the rigging, and then my own half-uttered, half-screamed "*Shit!*" when I realized that I was, in much more than just a manner of speaking, going to be short. The rigging, height, and distance between the platforms had simply not been designed for a flying dwarf.

I didn't much like the idea, or the image, of me swinging helplessly back and forth until I came to an ignominious stop, dangling in the air where it would be easy enough for anybody to climb up on top of the steel tiger cage and pluck me off the bar like a piece of ripe fruit.

There was only one other option, and I took it. Somehow, at

the apogee of my swing, I kipped my hips up into the air and willed my fingers to release their grip on the trapeze bar. I soared up and out into space. There was nothing elegant about my flight; with a scream in my throat, I was all flailing arms and legs until I finally collided with a support rope. I grabbed the rope, swung around it, then finally managed to get my feet on a platform. I released the rope, stood up.

There was scattered, uncertain applause—which immediately tapered off as the lobox, which had trotted around the steel cage and positioned itself once more directly beneath me, raised its head and uttered another killing scream.

And now for my next trick.

I was dimly aware of pain in my lower back where the hickory bar I carried in my belt loops pressed against my spine, but I didn't have time to worry about that; the important thing was that I still had the bar. Once again I couldn't afford to give myself any time to think about what I was going to do, or I wouldn't do it. Mabel and Luther were still in the same position, with Mabel having turned to face me. I reached out, released one of the climbing ropes. I could only guess at what point I should grip it; if I guessed wrong, I could end up swinging rather ingloriously right into the ground, where I would smash every bone in my body, or—equally ingloriously, if considerably less painful in the short run—sailing right over my target. I arbitrarily pulled up four armlengths of the rope, checked to make sure that the hickory trapeze bar was still in my belt loops, then gripped the rope tightly and leaped into space.

I fell vertically, then was jerked hard when the slack of the rope was taken up. Even as I flew forward, I gauged that I was too far down on the rope. Desperately fighting gravity and the G-forces I was building up, I pulled myself hand over hand up the rope—one foot, two feet, three feet. It was enough. I lifted my legs as high as I could, and the ground swooped by barely an inch or two under me. Then I soared upward in an arc that turned out to be a near-perfect path of flight for my purposes; my apogee came when I was about five feet above Mabel's head. I released my grip on the rope, dropped lightly to my feet just behind the thoroughly startled Luther. He half turned, his glacial blue eyes filled with shock as he stared at me.

"Say good night, Luther," I snapped as I snatched the hickory bar from my belt loops and struck him on the side of his shaved head with what I fervently hoped was sufficient force to kill him.

The animal trainer had ducked away at the last moment, but the bar still hit him in the head with a most satisfying *thunk*. With a little help from my foot in his ribs, he slid off the side of Mabel's head and fell to the sawdust track below. I quickly moved forward and gave Mabel a sharp rap with the hickory bar just above her brow.

I had my tank, and now I had to see if I could make it go where I wanted.

My need for escape was made even more urgent by the muffled but distinct sound of a shotgun blast in the night outside the tent.

Mabel, obviously excited by all these strange doings and raring to go, lifted her trunk high and trumpeted. She was facing in the right direction, toward the main entrance, and so I once again used both hands to raise the hickory pole above my head, then brought it down as hard as I could on the front of her skull, hoping it would stir fond memories of the love taps administered by her former master with his Louisville Slugger, Henry Aaron model.

I needn't have worried. Mabel surged forward in what was the equivalent of an elephant sprint. I'd forgotten how difficult it can be to ride an elephant going at full tilt; I fell backward, and would have fallen off if I hadn't managed at the last moment to dig my heels into folds in the gray, wrinkled hide. I finally managed to get myself back up into a sitting position just in time to duck as we headed out through the entrance, taking pieces of canvas, ropes, and two support poles with us. Now she was heading straight for the ticket booth, and she showed no signs of wanting to veer away.

Arlen Zelezian suddenly emerged from a door in the rear of the booth. The Abraham Lincoln look-alike barely had time to throw his arms up over his face before the gray juggernaut I was riding ran over him and through the booth, leaving behind a bloody pulp and a pile of splintered rubble. African elephants on the run are most definitely things to steer clear of.

Another shotgun blast, this one much louder and closer.

I whacked Mabel on the left side of the head, just behind her great, flapping ear, and she immediately turned in that direction, rumbling along a dirt track on the perimeter of one of the areas used for parking. I raised myself up as much as I could in an effort to spot the station wagon at the far end of the furthest parking lot, but I couldn't. And I had to resist the temptation to immediately go to Harper's aid. I had to stick to my plan, hoping that Harper was able to defend herself with the shotgun, for this would be the only chance I had to rescue Garth.

There was no way to warn Garth of what was about to happen, so I could only hope that my brother wasn't standing around next to the side doors in the semi scratching himself. As we approached the trucks I swung Mabel out into a great arc in the field, and then homed her in on the side of the second truck from the right in the first row. She had never been more responsive to my strike-commands, and now I gave her two good thumps on the front of her forehead to indicate full speed ahead.

Mabel had surely missed me, or else she had mellowed a lot since she was a young lass, for I seriously doubted that in the past I could have gotten her to even consider ramming herself headlong into a truck. But now she rumbled right ahead, if anything increasing her speed. I thumped her again as a sign of encouragement, then dug my knees and heels into the wrinkles in her hide, leaned forward, and braced myself as the rambunctious Mabel collided at full speed with the side of the trailer box dead in the center, one steel-capped tusk hitting each of the doors, bursting the padlock that held them closed, collapsing them inward.

The impact was tremendous, and it was all I could do to keep from being thrown off my mount. The box of the trailer had been wrenched off its fittings to its tractor and was tilted on its side, apparently resting on the trailer box next to it. When I recovered my senses and my vision came into focus, I could see my startled, ashen-faced brother slumped where he had been thrown on the opposite side of the box, staring wide-eyed at the great elephant's head that now occupied the space where the double doors had been.

"Hey, brother!" I shouted, leaning over Mabel's brow and

waving the hickory pole to get his attention. "Up here! Let's go! Time's a-wasting!"

I strongly doubted that Garth had ever been this close to an elephant, but he seemed to know exactly what he had to do, and—once his somewhat glassy gaze came into focus—never hesitated. He struggled to his feet, scrambled up the tilted floor of the trailer box, and leaped out onto Mabel's trunk, spreading his arms wide to catch her great, curved tusks. He landed and started to climb, but it wasn't necessary. Mabel, who seemed to be thoroughly enjoying herself as she got the hang of this rescue business, curled her trunk and lifted him effortlessly, if just a bit too rapidly, into the air, and I had to duck as he sailed past my head and landed unceremoniously on his stomach a few feet behind me. He got up on his hands and knees, turned around, and sat down with his legs spread to the sides, bracing himself. He was laughing uproariously.

"What the hell are you laughing at?!" I shouted over my shoulder as, flailing away with my hickory bar, I backed Mabel up and turned her around.

"I love it, Mongo! I absolutely *love* it!"

"Is that supposed to be some smart-ass remark?!"

"No!"

"Well, I hope you're suitably impressed! Because if you're not, I'll have Mabel pluck you off and throw you back in the truck!"

"I'm impressed, I'm impressed! This is the most outrageous rescue you've ever engineered!"

"Save your congratulations until we're out of here! We've got one more stop!"

We'd reached the far edge of the first parking lot, and I turned Mabel right. A gray-suited gunman was standing directly in our path, starting to raise his gun; he thought better of trying to bring down Mabel with a hand gun and barely managed to dive out of the way as Mabel thundered past. Now I could see the station wagon up ahead; the front windshield had been blown away. The driver's door was open, the interior light on.

There was nobody inside the car.

I started to curse in rage and frustration, but then I saw the bloody, tawny shape lying still in the grass a few feet to the right of the station wagon's left front fender. Harper had killed her lobox.

A moment later Harper herself appeared, darting out from between two parked cars. She threw the shotgun to one side, sprinted toward us. For a moment I was afraid that Mabel would run her over, but Mabel certainly seemed to sense the proper drill. She slowed, and then laid out the length of her trunk like a welcoming mat. Harper jumped onto the trunk and Mabel lifted her up, depositing her on a spot behind me and just in front of Garth.

I found I didn't even have to thump Mabel any longer; a touch of the stick on her forehead, left or right ear, was enough to get her to go in the desired direction. She was obviously enjoying her newfound freedom, and having a grand old time. I touched her on the left ear. She turned. I tapped her on the forehead and she lumbered ahead through a wooden picket fence, across the highway, and on into a vast, darkness-shrouded corn field that seemed to stretch away to the horizon.

Somewhere in the night behind us, so close that it made me start and the hair rise on the back of my neck, a lobox screamed. It was not only human pursuers we were going to have to worry about.

CHAPTER TEN

Our most immediate need was to put as much distance between us and our pursuers—human, at least—as possible, and so we rode through the night, traversing vast fields planted with corn, wheat, and sorghum, avoiding farmhouses. Mabel was finding this vast cornucopia very much to her liking: she would frequently stop to graze and then drink whenever we came to a river or stream, which was fairly frequently. Clouds covered the moon, which was to our advantage—at least in the few remaining hours of darkness left to us. Occasionally, I thought I heard the distant *whump-whump-whump* of a helicopter, but it might have been my imagination; whatever was making the sound never came close to us, and there were no searchlights piercing the velvetlike darkness. We remained shrouded in night.

Dawn found us on the gently sloping bank of a shallow river, with Mabel sucking up gallons of water to wash down her recent, predawn repast of a quarter ton or so of hay. Harper's head was resting on my back, her arms locked tightly around my waist, even in sleep. Mabel continued to be completely cooperative and responsive to my commands, and even seemed to be aware of the tawny death following us; throughout the night, she had occasionally stopped of her own accord, turned to raise her trunk and flare out her enormous ears—the clear warning signals of an African elephant.

Across the river, to the northeast, a forest of the giant silos of a grain elevator complex rose into the gold-streaked blue sky of what looked to be the beginning of a clear, dry day. The lobox that had been trailing right behind us through the night now brazenly emerged from the dawn shadows and tall grass a hundred yards or so to our right, ambled unconcernedly up to the river's edge, and began to drink. When it finished, it lay down on its belly and fixed me with its eerie, humanlike gaze. Perhaps instinct, a kind of racial memory percolating in its retrieved genes, told it that it wasn't a good idea to get too close to a beast that was even bigger than a mammoth or mastodon, which meant that we had a kind of standoff. The lobox seemed to be smart enough to know that sooner or later I was going to have to get off the elephant or fall off in sleep, and then it would have at me.

Whether or not Garth and Harper might be able to get off with impunity was an open question that seemed better left unanswered, especially in light of the fact that by now the animal probably associated the two of them with me, and it simply liked human flesh. In any case, there was no place to go even if they could get off.

What it could not know, this creature waiting patiently to kill me, but what I was certain of, was that it would not have its home, and customary sexual reward, to return to.

"Where is everybody?" Garth asked.

"A good question," I replied, gazing around me at the empty fields, sky, and horizon.

There was a pause, then: "How do you suppose a formidable critter like that lobox ever managed to get itself extinct?"

"How the hell do I know? What am I, the answer man? You're just full of good questions this morning."

"Oooh. Do I detect a note of crankiness?"

"Sorry, Garth. If that little old guy down there was waiting around to eat *you* for breakfast, you might be a little cranky too. I know you're having a great time, and I don't mean to spoil it."

"I think somebody here woke up on the wrong side of the elephant."

"I said I was sorry."

When Mabel had drunk her fill, she sucked up one last twenty-gallon load of water, curled back her trunk, and proceeded to spray all twenty gallons over the riders on her back. It was a trick she'd picked up during the night, and judging from the deep, vibrating rumble that shook her belly each time she did it, I guessed that it gave her enormous pleasure. Only Harper, curled up behind me, had managed to stay relatively dry.

"Hey, Mongo."

I glanced back at my brother, who was wiping his wet face with a sodden shirt sleeve. His long, wheat-colored hair was pasted to his forehead, his shoulders. It was my turn to smile. "Yes, dear older sibling?"

"I'm getting a bit tired of this spraying shit. Is there any way you can get your gray lady friend here to shut off the tap?"

"She's just playing," I said, turning back and looking over at the lobox; if I didn't know better, I'd have sworn the creature with the saber teeth was amused.

"Well, how about getting her to play some other game? I'm soaked. I'd hate to think that I'd escaped from whatever peril Zelezian had planned for me only to die of pneumonia on the back of an elephant wandering through Nebraska. It's positively undignified."

I shrugged, replied, "I don't know how to get her to stop—and I'm not sure it would be a good idea to try. Mabel only does what she wants to do, and I wouldn't want to get her irritated. If it wasn't for her, we'd all be back there somewhere in cages, waiting for the Zelezians to dispose of us at their convenience. You shouldn't look a gift elephant in the mouth."

"Jesus, brother, half the time you're whacking the shit out of her to get her to do what *you* want her to do. So why don't you just whack the end of her trunk the next time she shoves it up here to squirt us?"

"You weren't listening, Garth. She might not like it if I did that. Mabel only *thinks* I'm whacking the shit out of her. Actually, she hardly feels it. The whacks are commands which she only obeys if she's in the mood. I've never known Mabel to be this mellow, but don't ever forget that she's an African elephant. The showers may be her way of reminding us—me—who's really in charge. If she gets cranky, we're all liable to end up on the ground as lobox food."

Garth grunted. "Your point is well taken, Mongo." He paused, and I could sense that he was looking around. "Besides, it probably won't be too long before we have more serious things to worry about—like being shot off Mabel's back."

"You got that right."

Harper stirred, then hugged me tight, sat up, and glanced around her. "Shit," she said when she saw the lobox. "He's still there."

"Oh, yeah."

"Where are we, Robby?"

"Somewhere in Nebraska."

"What are we going to do?"

"Now, there's a subject Garth and I were just warming up to."

Garth said, "The lobox is only part of the problem, Harper. The police don't seem to be after us; maybe they were called off. If they were after us, there'd have been helicopters with searchlights after the first hour, and we'd be in custody right now. If that was a copter we heard during the night, it was privately owned. It might have belonged to the people Mongo keeps referring to as Zelezian's sponsors. It wasn't really equipped for night flying."

Harper shuddered. "I wish we were in custody."

"That makes three of us," I said, shielding my eyes against the rising sun as I glanced again toward the northeast. My attention kept wandering back to the grain elevators. "With that lobox trotting along behind us, we'd have the proof we need—and an explanation for two snakebitten gunmen, one squashed Zelezian, and disturbing the peace with a purloined elephant. That's why the cops aren't after us. But, for sure, Luther and the people backing that whole weapons development operation are going to be seriously on our case now that the sun is up. We certainly won't be hard to track, considering the stomped crops and the tons of elephant droppings we've left behind. If they use a plane or helicopter, they'll pick up our trail two minutes after they're in the air."

"Maybe we should start looking for a phone," Harper said, and laughed nervously. "Since we can't get down, we'll ask Mabel to make the call."

"Luther closed down that circus five minutes after we disappeared into the corn field," Garth said, half to himself. He was musing, thinking like the cop he had been for so many years. "Since troopers aren't swarming all over the countryside, Mongo's right about their being protected by some powerful people. There'll probably be an established escape route for getting Zelezian, his people, and the lobox breeding stock out of the country—probably into Canada by tractor-trailer and then a plane back to Switzerland. Everything else in the circus would be abandoned, the animals left in pens or trucks. The breeding stock may already be on its way to Canada, but Luther and a posse of gunmen will most definitely be searching for us."

"Why would Luther take a chance on being caught?" Harper asked. "Why wouldn't he just leave too, while the leaving is good?"

"Maybe because I killed his father," I said, "but certainly because of that lobox over there." The beast raised its head, as if it knew it was being discussed, and yawned lazily; at that moment, except for its six-inch-long canines, it could have been mistaken for somebody's family dog. "Luther's the only one who can control it. He trained it too well—or he never fully realized just how really tenacious a lobox can be when primed to track and kill. He might be willing to leave us alive as long as we had no proof to back up anything we might say, but a live—or even a dead—lobox changes the whole equation. That's too much of a loose end to leave behind. He needs to either get it back or see it destroyed completely—say, by fire, or any other method that will ensure there won't be an autopsy.

"A lobox is a multimillion-dollar weapons system, valuable in its own right—in some ways, probably a lot more valuable than your average missile. But even more important than the dollar value of a single lobox is the fact that they can't allow that weapons system to fall into the wrong hands—meaning anyone's but their own. Also, if we have a live lobox for show-and-tell, the entire Zelezian weapons empire could fall apart; Switzerland will turn a blind eye to a lot of things involving money, but not for a resident or citizen who embarrasses them by running a Swiss company that would turn a savage, wild beast loose on innocent people just to see what will happen. Interpol would probably get involved, and in this country, congressional committees will probably be falling all over themselves trying to find out who's responsible for the fact that a band of foreign assassins slipped into this country so easily and then had virtual free rein of the place. If it turns out that the CIA is involved, which it probably is, all hell will break loose. For those people, an awful lot depends on getting that lobox back and seeing us dead. Which leaves us with the problem of finding someplace safe to hide with an elephant, and doing it quickly."

Garth asked, "What about those grain elevators over there?"

"I've been looking at those," I replied, giving a noncommittal shrug. "An empty grain elevator, or maybe some other building in a grain storage complex, could certainly solve our problems, at least for a while. But what about the people there?"

"Don't you think somebody would call the police if they saw three people riding around on the back of an elephant?" Harper asked. "That's what we want, isn't it?"

"Sure," I said, reaching behind me to squeeze her thigh. "But more innocent people could die if we go over there. So far, the lobox only seems interested in me, but that could change. Nobody really knows what a lobox will do. This one's been out of the barn a long time now, and Nate Button said that its natural instinct is to kill people. If it gets bored hanging around waiting for me to get down, and there are other people around, it might just start ripping them up. As far as we know it hasn't eaten for a couple of days, so it's got to be hungry. I don't see how we can take a chance with other people's lives."

"Agreed," Garth said. "But I'd say there's a better than even chance there's nobody there. You don't come home to these parts as often as I do, Mongo. Farms are in bad shape. I'll bet that half those farmhouses we passed during the night are abandoned. There are a lot of empty grain elevators in the Midwest, so that complex we're looking at may not even be in use. By the time we're within a mile or so, we should be able to see if there's anybody around. If there is, then we turn Mabel around and ride away. The way that lobox has been dogging you, there's no reason to believe it will run off now. If the silos are empty, we take up residence in one; if there are people around, at least somebody may call the police. It seems like a reasonable course of action. We're going to have to do something quick, Mongo, because we're running out of time."

"Right," I said, and tapped Mabel low on the forehead with the end of the hickory trapeze bar.

Mabel still seemed to be enjoying her strange outing and feeling cooperative, because she unhesitatingly lumbered forward into the river. The water in the middle reached her chest, but then began to grow shallower. It was the deepest body of water we had forded, and it certainly would have been a pleasure to discover that loboxes couldn't swim, or positively hated water, but there was no such luck; when I leaned out and looked back, I could see that the creature was still tracking us at a distance of fifteen yards, swimming through the water with powerful strokes.

"It looks like loboxes are good swimmers," Garth said wryly. "You might want to write that down in your notebook."

"If I did have a notebook, I'd probably throw it at you. If and when we do find a safe place to hole up before the bad guys come and shoot us all, we have to start giving some serious thought to what we're going to do about that damned thing behind us."

Harper yawned, then once again wrapped her arms around my waist and rested her head on my back. "Make him yours, Robby," she mumbled sleepily.

"Say what?"

"Make him yours; take control away form Luther. Tame him."

"You've got to be kidding me."

I could feel her shaking her head. "You know I'm not."

"That sounds like a hell of a good idea to me, Mongo," Garth said.

"Hey, brother, are you still enjoying your elephant ride? Anyone who ever met the Fredericksons always said you were the biggest kid in the family, always making jokes like that. I was always too busy being a dwarf to have any fun."

Harper laughed. "Do you two always go at it like this?"

Garth said, "Mongo always acts like this when he thinks there's some beastie that wants to eat him. He can't take pressure." He paused, then added seriously: "I do think it sounds like a good idea, Mongo."

"That's because she didn't suggest that *you* tame him."

Naturally, Garth paid no attention to me. "Now, that would really be something, you managing to put that thing on a leash. It would also solve a lot of our problems. Can it be done?"

"No," I said curtly. "It already has a master. I'm just a meal to it, and it has to be getting very hungry by now."

"Yes," Harper said in her dreamy voice. "Robby could do it if he really put his mind to the problem, Garth. You've never seen him work with animals; I have. I've seen him work tigers, bears, elephants—you've seen what he managed to do with this big thing that's our current mode of transportation."

"I didn't work them," I said tersely, glancing up at the sky for signs of a plane or helicopter, "I played with them. It was just a hobby, Harper. They were dangerous, sure, but their primary instinct wasn't to look on me as an entree. Those animals hadn't been trained to kill, and they certainly hadn't been specifically primed to kill me."

"My money's on you, Mongo," Garth said, and I didn't have to look around to see the grin on his face; it was in his voice. "The more I think about it, the more I like the idea. I'd love to see the look on Luther's face if you brought his pet back to him. The son-of-a-bitch would probably have a stroke."

"I'd love to see the look on his face just before the lobox he trained bites his face *off*," Harper said. She no longer sounded sleepy.

"I don't have the time or inclination to explain to you people the dozen or so good reasons why it can't be done," I said impatiently. "You're both out of your minds."

*   *   *

Garth had been right about the grain elevators. When we were still at least two miles away, it was possible to see not only that the complex was abandoned but that it hadn't been used in years. Half of the enormous silos were crumbling or had holes in them. All the windows in the various buildings had been boarded up.

We came out of a field onto what had once been the main

access road to the complex; it was now mostly washed out and filled with potholes. Mabel rambled up the road, and we entered the complex at almost the same time as a black speck that was a small airplane appeared on the horizon, to the south. The plane could have been a crop duster, but somehow I doubted it.

We moved around a network of dirt roads through the complex, past broken ramps and conveyor belts leading into broken silos, rotting buildings, rusting equipment, enormous chutes hanging uselessly in space. It was beginning to look as if the grain elevator complex, which looked so promising from a distance, was a false Eden. It would, of course, be rather foolish to try to hole up in a building pocked with holes that the lobox could come through anytime it chose.

Mabel seemed to be having some racial memory of her own working for her; she apparently sensed that the lobox was an enemy. The lobox, for his part, seemed to be suffering from hubris; it had been following us at an ever-decreasing distance throughout the night; since there had been no consequences, it had decided to close that distance even further. It was now trotting alongside Mabel's left flank, occasionally looking up at me as it raised its ruff and bared its teeth. It's a mistake to threaten an elephant's mahout; without warning, Mabel abruptly stopped, pivoted to her left, swinging her trunk and murderous tusks around. The lobox, despite its lightning reflexes, was caught off guard. First, Mabel's trunk whacked the creature hard on the right shoulder, and then one of her capped tusks caught the lobox in the ribs, the force of impact lifting it off its feet and hurling it through the air. It landed hard on its side, twenty feet away. It immediately got to its feet, but it swayed unsteadily for a few moments. I hoped to see it start coughing blood from a punctured lung and go down, but it didn't happen; the lobox was shaken, but not severely hurt. It shook itself, moved off even further, then raised its head and screamed in fury and pain. When it looked at me, I thought I detected something new in its expressive, golden eyes—fear. The lobox wasn't going to come too close to Mabel again, and that was to our advantage.

But that was all the good news there was.

We could survive without food for a few days, but lack of water was entirely another matter. Mabel could always wander off on her own to forage for food and water in the elephant heaven that surrounded us, but we would essentially be stuck in the place we set ourselves down in. Neither Garth nor Harper had said anything, but I knew they had to be as thirsty as I was—and I was very thirsty. Aside from an occasional spray from Mabel, we hadn't had any water in hours; we'd all been dehydrated by the physical and emotional stress of escaping from the circus, and we would be in deep trouble very soon. We not only needed a hiding place big enough to contain an elephant, but one that had water, and I wasn't at all sure we were going to find it in the grain elevator complex. I just didn't savor having to choose between dying of thirst, in a hail of bullets, or under the fangs and claws of a lobox.

It appeared that all of the water for the complex had been supplied by wells, and there were plenty of these around—but the electric pumps that had driven them had been shut off long ago; even if they could be manually operated, we didn't have any water with which to prime them. To make matters worse, almost all of the pipes leading from the wells into the silos and buildings looked to be broken. It was not a happy situation.

Twenty minutes later we came to three silos connected to one another by covered passageways. The structures appeared to be intact; a tour around the buildings didn't turn up any holes in the silos or connecting passageways, and the pipes leading into the buildings also seemed intact. It didn't mean that we would be able to find a way to draw water from the wells, or that the lobox wouldn't manage to find a way to get in, but we were rapidly running out of real estate, time, and options.

There were huge double doors cut into each of the connected silos, but the doors on two of the silos were padlocked; the third set of doors was held closed only by a length of rusted chain wound around two bolts. It took some doing, but by balancing on the upper part of Mabel's curled trunk I was able to stay out of lobox range while at the same time using the end of my hickory trapeze bar to unwind the chain, which I slung over my shoulder. I got Mabel to partially open the doors with her tusks, then turned her around and backed her through the opening.

The lobox, under Mabel's baleful gaze, kept a respectful distance away. We found ourselves inside a huge, circular bin, its floor covered with an inch or two of grain. Above us, the various levels of the silo were spiderwebbed with scaffolding holding rusting equipment. Tools were strewn about, and it appeared that this particular silo, at least, had ended up being used as a kind of gigantic toolshed and garage.

The next step was tricky and dangerous, considering the amply demonstrated quickness of the lobox, but it had to be done, and I was in the best position to do it. Without indicating to Garth or Harper—or Mabel—what I intended, I slid down Mabel's trunk, grabbed the edge of the open door on the right, and pulled. The door had rusted on its hinges, and it closed with agonizing slowness. The lobox had begun to quiver as it stared at me, now on the ground and helpless before it—helpless except for Mabel, towering in the air right behind me. She lifted her trunk and trumpeted a warning just as the creature sprang forward, running at full tilt at me. The doors gave, and I slammed them in the lobox's face just as it leaped. As I secured the doors with the chain I had brought in with me, there was the sound of furious scratching and growling just outside. Although it seemed to me an eternity, only a few seconds had passed. When I looked back and up, I found both Garth and Harper balanced far forward on Mabel's head, staring down at me. They were both ashen-faced.

"You're out of your fucking mind, Mongo," Garth said tightly. "That wasn't necessary. That thing is after you, not me. You should have let me close the doors."

"We can't be sure that it's not after you too by now," I said as I reached out to help Harper as she slid down Mabel's trunk, "and you don't climb an elephant the way I do. Besides, you have a more important job. You're the mechanic in the family. While Harper and I check this whole place out, you see if you can't find a way to get the water flowing. I don't know about you people, but I'm a little parched."

•   •   •

It took Harper and me three quarters of an hour to investigate the three silos and their connecting tunnels. The walls all seemed whole—a very good thing, since I could hear the lobox outside scratching, sniffing, and growling its way right along with me as

I inspected our sanctuary. That animal, I thought, was really getting to be a pain in the ass, and I was having to give ever more serious thought to what it was I planned to do about it. The lobox could go off for food and water anytime it wanted, if it wanted, and we would remain trapped inside the silos.

There was the sound of a plane passing overhead, low to the ground. We tensed, waiting to hear it start circling, but it continued into the distance.

The problem of the lobox had to be solved as quickly as possible. I didn't much care for the only solution I could think of, but there it was.

When we returned we were most pleased to find that Garth had found a way to use a bucket of rainwater to prime a pump and then get it to work manually. Water was gushing from a tap, and he was filling the first of three empty barrels he had found and rolled over to the tap. When the barrel was full, Mabel, without any prompting, ambled over, pushed me aside, thrust her trunk down into the cool, clear water inside the barrel, and promptly emptied it.

Garth, Harper, and I slaked our thirst as Mabel waited patiently for the barrel to fill again. I kept on drinking after Garth and Harper finished, sucking up water until my belly was distended and sore. I stopped just as I began to feel the urge to vomit.

"Jesus, brother," Garth said, "you must have been *really* thirsty. You're going to burst if you drink any more."

"I need all the water I can store," I replied, and decided that it would serve no purpose to tell Garth and Harper just why it was I wanted to tank up, and save myself repeated trips to the well.

I also decided it would serve no purpose to tell them that my primary sensation at the moment was not thirst, but fear.

CHAPTER ELEVEN

Standing on a narrow catwalk at the edge of a man-high adjustable vent cut in the side of the silo I was in, I watched the stream of my urine arc out and fall to the ground thirty feet below. The lobox was squatting on its haunches off to the side, just out of range, watching me with a good deal more than casual interest. Using the catwalks and vents, I was working my way around the perimeter of the three-silo complex as fast as my bladder would allow. This was my third evacuation, and now I knew I would have to go back to the working tap and tank up again. Mine was an execrable job, I thought with a grim smile, but somebody had to do it. By nature of expertise and—I hoped—talent, I had elected myself.

I heard my brother clambering up the steel ladder leading to the catwalk. "There you are," he said as he reached the walk and came up to stand beside me. "You've been gone more than an hour, and I've been looking all over for you. Harper's worried. What the hell are you up to?"

"I'm pissing."

"Don't be a smart-ass. I can see that you're pissing. If you hadn't drunk so much water, you wouldn't be pissing so much."

"You got that right. Thank you, Doctor."

"Come on, Mongo, what are you doing back here? I thought you and Harper checked it all out before. If there was any place that thing could get in, it would have been on us by now."

"I told you; I'm pissing—or I was. I'm finished now."

Garth shrugged, stepped to the edge of the vent, and reached for his fly. "Sounds like a good idea. It must be the power of suggestion."

"Not here," I said quickly, grabbing his sleeve and pulling him back from the edge.

"Huh?"

"Use the privy in the second silo. I don't want anyone pissing on the ground around here except me."

Garth stared at me, obviously baffled, and slowly blinked. "You're saying you can piss on Nebraska, but I can't?"

"Not this particular part of Nebraska, if you please."

"Why the hell not?"

"Because there can only be one leader of the pack, and both you and Harper decided it should be me. I don't want our friend down there to get confused. I'm scenting—spotting my territory. It's the essential first step."

"Mongo, what the hell are you talking about?"

"Go take care of your *toilette*, and I'll tell you when you finish. I'll meet you at the water tap."

Garth shook his head. "I don't have any *toilette* to take care of now; you've shocked the piss out of me. I want you to explain to me now why you can piss anywhere you want to in Nebraska, but Harper and I can't."

"Nobody, with the possible exception of Luther Zelezian, knows a whole damn lot about lobox behavior, except for what we've already observed. I'm assuming that loboxes passed on some of their natural traits to their modern heirs—dogs and wolves. I'm playing wolf. I'm marking out my territory, challenging that guy down there."

"By pissing on him?" Garth asked incredulously.

"It's a beginning. In order to work with large, dangerous animals, you have to understand a few things. The first and most important thing you have to understand is that they're not people, as cute, friendly, or otherwise human as they may seem.

You can never get them to do anything by trying to make friends with them, because they can't be your friend—at least not in the way we think of friends. One way or another, the animal must be dominated; it must be made to know that you're the boss, and that the shit's going to hit the fan if it doesn't do what you want it to do. There are a number of ways of accomplishing that end. The best way is to combine certain training techniques with lots of affection and respect. Or you can simply instill fear—beat the shit out of the animal, and hope you don't break its spirit."

"Like you do with Mabel?"

"No," I said, shaking my head. "I can't hurt Mabel. I told you. She only *thinks* I'm beating the shit out of her, and that's usually enough."

"I thought you were kidding me."

"No. Mabel's a special case. Some animals—African elephants among them—are almost never successfully trained or domesticated. Zebras are another good example. But with any animal, if you can establish close contact with it from the moment it's born, it becomes an enormous advantage. There's a phenomenon called imprinting. I didn't have Mabel when she was born, but I did get her when she was desperately sick, close to death. She was helpless, which is almost as good from a trainer's standpoint. I nursed her back to health, and she came to see me as care giver, provider of food, and so on. No matter how big she got after that, she would never really perceive me as small, as a dwarf. I was always her master—as much of a master as African elephants ever have. There are researchers who would even claim that she thinks I'm her mother."

"*Now* you're kidding me."

"The fact that you keep thinking I'm kidding you when I tell you how animals think and behave is the reason I can piss on this part of Nebraska and you can't. Luther has already imprinted this lobox and any others he may have around. Even though we don't know that much about loboxes, I think it's safe to assume I'd never be able to break into that brain circuiting—say, to try for affection—and so there's no sense in wasting time we don't have. If I'm going to wrest control of the lobox away from Luther, I have to break into another circuit in the animal's brain, in a manner of speaking. Luther dominates it on Luther's terms; the only chance I have is to dominate it on lobox terms. In short, I have to convince it that I'm leader of the pack, which is why I've been using my urine to mark off my territory. That's why I don't want *you* pissing out there, okay? I've been serving notice that he'd better watch his hairy ass if he keeps trying to mess with me."

"No more Mr. Nice Guy?"

"No more Mr. Nice Guy."

"You're crazy, Mongo. You plan to just keep pissing at him?"

"Nope. Like I said, that's just the first step. I think there are some factors in our favor. First, it's very smart, so it shouldn't take too long to discover whether or not I'm wasting my time. It actually seems to be able to comprehend its own existence and the possibility of death, so it can be intimidated—I think—if I can find the right buttons to push. I shot it; it knows I shot it, and that's good."

Garth slowly shook his head. "You don't have a gun now; it probably knows you don't have a gun now, and that's bad."

"I think it's safe to assume that I'm the first victim it's been primed for that it hasn't succeeded in killing. The lobox that ran with it was primed for Harper, didn't succeed in killing her, and was killed itself, by Harper. It will assume Harper is my mate—and only the leader of the pack could have such a powerful mate. Are you following all this?"

Garth grunted, laid a hand on my shoulder, and squeezed it affectionately. "I'm not the audience you have to convince, Mongo."

I was again getting an urgent call from nature. I stepped back to the edge of the vent, looked down. The lobox was still there, in the same position. I took the hickory trapeze bar, which I carried everywhere with me, rapped it hard a few times against the side of the silo, then shook it at the lobox. The lobox seemed singularly unimpressed. I rested the bar against the wall, again reached for my fly.

Garth continued, "What are you planning to do after you mark off your territory?"

I looked back over my shoulder at my brother, grinned. "Why, then I'm going to beat the shit out of it, naturally."

Garth the handyman had done a good job, and now that I had decided what had to be done, I was anxious to get on with it. I felt we were as prepared as we were ever going to be.

Using the tools and materials strewn around the complex, Garth had, among other things, transformed my trapeze bar into *nunchaku* sticks by sawing the hickory length in half and joining the two pieces with a six-inch length of chain secured to one end of each separate stick by a wood screw. It had been a long time since I'd practiced with *nunchakus,* and I hoped my martial arts skills weren't as rusted as the chain that held them together. Assuming I could use the sticks and chain properly, the speed and striking power of the weapon I now held in my hands was greater by at least a factor of five than the unaltered trapeze bar alone.

In my pocket was a padlock I had found in a dusty corner and picked up when Garth and Harper had been looking the other way. The lock was broken, rusted open, but I thought it was sufficient to do the job for which I needed it. I hadn't been totally candid with Garth and Harper as to why I wanted my trapeze bar transformed into *nunchakus,* since the argument that would have ensued would only have wasted time, and I was trusting to the padlock to prevent any arguments or wasted time in the future.

All during the preparations, we had taken turns standing at the vents, watching the sky, the surrounding landscape, the horizon. We had seen crop-dusting planes and trucks speeding on a highway far in the distance, but that was all. Most of the time the skies and surrounding countryside remained empty, and the lack of any kind of pursuit on the part of Luther Zelezian and his backers was becoming quite a mystery.

Not that it really made much difference, since the job ahead of us was more than enough to command our full attention.

Finally, we were ready. Garth and Harper stepped back into the tunnel that connected the first and second silos, positioned themselves on either side of the doorway. I walked across the silo to Mabel, who was standing near the double doors, using her vacuum cleaner of a trunk to idly pick through the grain on the floor. I stroked her trunk, then gently tapped her left tusk with one of my sticks. "Back, baby. Get back. I don't want you to intimidate our guest. Come on, now. Be a good girl."

Mabel dutifully backed away to the opposite wall of the silo. I went to the double doors, loosened the chain holding them closed, opened one a crack, and peered out. The lobox was lying on a patch of grass perhaps twenty-five yards away, off to the right. As always alert to my comings and goings, it immediately got to its feet, pricked up its ears, and stared intently at the small opening between the doors.

"Robby, please be careful!" Harper called after me.

Garth said, "Careful, Mongo."

Making as little noise as I could, I unwrapped the length of chain from the wooden pegs on each door. Then I took a deep breath and yanked the door on the right open at the same time as I spun around and sprinted toward the doorway on the opposite side of the silo. I wasn't about to break stride to look back over my shoulder, but I could imagine the lobox's virtually instantaneous reaction as it sprang forward, its legs churning, its body flattening out as it bounded after its elusive prey. As I ran, arms and legs pumping, I could hear it behind me. Then it screamed, the sound piercing in the closed confines of the silo, and I knew it was about to spring.

I reached the doorway and dove through it not a moment too soon. The lobox's killing scream was in my ears, and its saliva spotted the back of my neck as I left my feet. However, Garth and Harper's timing was perfect, and the animal's scream changed to a roar of surprise as the old, rotting net we had patched together out of rope and burlap bags dropped down from the top of the doorway and caught it.

I hit the ground on my right shoulder, rolled, and came up on my feet. I whirled around in time to see the lobox, its muscular body churning in a paroxysm of blind fury, tearing at the improvised net with its fangs and claws. But it was too late, as Garth closed the door firmly on the animal's neck, then leaned against it with all his weight. Harper hurried around to Garth's side and placed a measured length of two-by-four between the floor and the doorknob, wedging the door shut.

"He's all yours, Mongo," Garth said tersely as he stepped back from the door. The front of his shirt was covered with foam. "Show the furry fucker who's boss."

I paused to give Harper, who was white-faced and trembling, a quick hug, then stepped forward until I was only inches from the writhing lobox's fangs. I stared hard into the golden eyes, which were clouded now with shock and fear, as well as fury. I whacked it hard on the side of the skull with one stick, then followed that up with another hard whack on the opposite side. It yelped in pain, then began to thrash with renewed enthusiasm. The door and wedge both began to show signs of giving, and Garth leaned hard against the wood. I hit the animal a third time, on top of the skull; as it cringed and closed its eyes, I shoved a stick between its jaws to wedge them open, used both hands on the stick to shove its head back, then quickly leaned forward and bit hard into the fleshy center of its hot, foam-coated nose, drawing blood. Then I pulled the stick from between its jaws, stepped back, and waited.

The lobox, blood running from the wound in its nose where I had bitten it, stared at me, pain and fear swimming in its eyes, which had suddenly grown bloodshot. I decided that I'd certainly succeeded in getting its attention. Froth coated its fangs and flecked its lips, and its struggles were growing weaker as it became exhausted. I cracked the sticks together, and it cringed. It was the effect I wanted. Luther had his revolver, but—short of actually killing the animal—there was nothing he could do with it except cock the hammer. The weapon I used to produce sharp sounds could also inflict pain, which I had demonstrated to the creature. That circuit, I thought, might well be overridden.

It was time for the next step.

"Harper, love, turn around, will you?"

"Why, Robby?" Harper asked, puzzled.

"Modesty precludes me from allowing you to watch the next phase of my animal-training act."

"What are you going to do, Robby?"

"Oh, *that*," Garth said, and stepped in front of Harper.

I unzipped my fly, loosed a stream of urine over the beast's face and head. The lobox closed its eyes, tried unsuccessfully to turn its head away. When I had emptied my bladder, I zipped up my fly, brought the *nunchaku* sticks very close to the animal's eyes, and banged them together. Again, the animal cringed. A low whine escaped from its throat.

"All right," I said to Garth over my shoulder, "let it go."

Garth didn't move. He glanced at Harper, who seemed just as puzzled as he was, then back at me. "Say what?"

"Let it go."

"That doesn't make any sense at all, brother," Garth said quietly.

"Who's in charge of the animal training around here?"

"You are—but it looks to me like you've accomplished what you set out to do. You've got the damn thing under control."

"No. I've got it trapped, helpless, hurt, humiliated, and temporarily cowed. There's a difference. It isn't enough."

"It looks good enough to me. Why let it go when we had to go to so much trouble to trap it? How the hell do you know what it's going to do?"

"I don't know what it's going to do; I do know that it's going to do us no good the way it is. We have to find a way of getting it out of here. That cheesecloth net certainly won't hold it. Even if we could manage to hogtie it, we wouldn't be able to keep it up on Mabel's back. We have to take the next step."

Garth shook his head. "It's too risky, brother. Kill it. A dead lobox is just as useful to us as a live one, and a lot safer." He turned to the woman. "Harper, find me a rock or a wrench or something, will you? I'm going to beat its brains out."

"I don't want to kill it," I replied as I abruptly kicked the wedge out from under the doorknob.

The lobox seemed momentarily confused by the sudden easing of the pressure on its neck. I nudged the door open even further, then knocked the sticks together in front of its bleeding nose. The creature started, then wheeled around, its claws tearing free of the improvised net, and raced beneath the menacing tusks of the trumpeting Mabel, out of the silo.

"That was stupid, Mongo," Garth said in the same soft, even tone.

"It's basically after me. It was my call."

"And it was a stupid one. We should have killed it when we had the chance. I know how you feel about animals, and I appreciate that it's only following its instincts and training, but I can't believe you could be so sentimental about an animal that's determined to kill you."

"It's not sentiment. I say a live lobox *is* more valuable than a dead one. If Luther gets away with the others and they end up as assassination weapons, it might help if the good guys had a live lobox to learn from."

"Well, you shouldn't have let the damn thing get away. All you did was beat the shit out of it, and now it's going to run right back to Luther."

Harper moved closer to me, and I put my arm around her. "I don't think so, Garth," she said. "Robby hasn't wiped out its training program or its instincts. He hasn't created a cowardly lobox, just a very confused one. It won't go very far."

"Right," I said. "It won't go back to Luther unless it kills me—or chooses to believe that it can't, or shouldn't."

Garth looked back and forth between Harper and me. "So what happens now?"

"What happens now is that I want the two of you to go up to the cheap seats by the vents and watch my next trick," I said, and stepped out through the doorway.

"Mongo?! What the hell—?!"

"You said I should make it mine," I said, waggling one end of a *nunchaku* stick at my startled brother. I took the broken padlock out of my pocket, glanced at it, then tossed it away. There was no sense in trying to lock up my brother, because he would be through the door just about in time to distract me from what I had to do. And probably get himself killed. "Well, I don't have time to explain to you how I propose to do that, or why it has to be done this way. But I have to go *now*. I'll be all right. You wait here. If you want to watch, you take Harper with you and go up to the vent at the front."

Without waiting for a reply, I wheeled around and started walking across the silo floor, pausing to pat a very skittish Mabel on the trunk. I edged carefully up to the slightly open door and could feel Mabel moving up behind me. Standing just at the edge of a wedge of sunlight that streamed in through the opening, I took a series of deep breaths, trying to relax and steady my nerves.

If the lobox was waiting for me just on the other side of the silo wall, I was a dead man. Yet I had no choice but to go out and face it. I sucked in one last deep breath, slowly exhaled, then stepped out of the silo into the bright sunlight.

So far, so good.

The lobox was lying on the patch of grass about twenty yards away, to my right. It sprang to its feet when it saw me, but remained where it was. I spun my *nunchaku* sticks, first one and then the other, then gripped them and smacked them together. The hide of the lobox began to quiver, its ruff suddenly expanded, and it charged.

It might have been wishful thinking, but in the second or two I had to evaluate distance, speed, and angles as the lobox rushed at me, it seemed to me that the animal was not moving with its former speed. Since I had not really hurt anything but its pride, I had to assume that its relative slowness represented a newfound uncertainty and lack of confidence on its part. It was a beginning, I thought as I leaped to my left at the same instant as the creature screamed, left its feet, and came flying through the air at my head. For one terrifying second I thought I had misjudged, and that its claws would tear off my right arm, but it missed—and I swung my sticks-on-a-chain, caught the lobox on its right flank. It yelped in pain, landed, screamed, and spun around to face me.

I smacked the sticks together again, took two quick steps toward the animal, stopped and crouched, ready. The lobox backed away a few feet, then abruptly stopped and stared at me.

"Come on, furball," I said, banging the sticks together. "Want to try again?"

It most certainly did want to try again. The creature suddenly sprang forward, its claws slipping in the dirt at its feet. It seemed even slower now—or I was gaining confidence. This time I was easily able to sidestep the animal's leap, and as it passed me in the air I swung a stick down hard on the top of its skull, then managed to whip the stick around again and catch it on a hind leg. The lobox yelped loudly. This time it stumbled when it landed. It went down, rolled over, got up.

But now its ruff was down.

"Come on," I said, furiously clicking the sticks together. "Come on!"

I inched forward, to within a yard, again crouched and waited. Suddenly the beast seemed to collapse—or the front end of it seemed to collapse. It dropped the top of its head to the ground, pushed with its hind legs. Its rear end went up, and for a moment it balanced on its head, before toppling over on its side. It got up, once more appeared to try to stand on its head, toppled over. This time it didn't get up. It rolled over on its back, thrust all four legs stiffly into the air, and extended its head back, exposing its throat.

It was the damnedest thing I ever saw.

And then I remembered that I had seen it once before—or a depiction of a lobox trying to stand on its head, in the photograph Nate Button had shown me of one of the Lascaux paintings. Button had said that the painting had been done by a poor artist who had been unable to capture the terror Cro-Magnon felt before the lobox. Button had been wrong.

The Cro-Magnon artist had painted a lobox displaying a posture of submission.

Well, well, well.

I suppressed a nervous, near-hysterical giggle and backed off a few steps to ponder the meaning of it all. Behind and above me, from the direction of the silo, I heard the sound of clapping. I turned in that direction, using my peripheral vision to keep track of the supine lobox, looked up, and saw Harper standing at the edge of the vent halfway up the side of the silo.

"My hero!" Harper called.

"You did good, Mongo," Garth said in a low voice that nevertheless carried clearly to me. I lowered my gaze, saw that Garth was standing next to Mabel just outside the open silo doors. "You did real good."

I waved my *nunchaku* sticks in their direction, resisting the impulse to make an elaborate bow. In fact, I knew that the real test of just what I had actually accomplished was yet to come, and I saw no sense in further delaying it. Without giving myself any more time to think about it, I unhesitatingly strode over to the lobox, which was still lying on its back with its legs thrust stiffly into the air, looked down into its golden eyes, which now seemed curiously veiled, clouded.

"Be careful, Mongo," Garth continued in the same low tone. "Don't press your luck."

Very carefully, and also very gently, I touched the animal's rib cage with the end of one of my sticks. "Up," I said. I waited a few moments, then applied slightly more pressure. "Up."

Damned if it didn't get up, and stand with its great head slightly bowed. Up close, with things temporarily at a standstill, I was reminded of just how big this creature was; its shoulders were at a level with my head. Now, a single, even half-hearted swing of its great maw with its saber teeth would have stripped my face, and probably my head, away. And yet, suddenly, I was no longer afraid. I sensed what it sensed, that I was in control.

I gently applied pressure with the end of the stick to its hindquarters. "Uh . . . sit?"

Damned if it didn't sit.

"Bravo, Robby!" Harper shouted from her perch, clapping furiously. "You've done it! He's yours!"

"Garth!" I shouted over my shoulder. "Bring me a rope, will you?! Make it a long one!"

"No need to shout, Mongo. I'm right behind you."

His voice was so close that it startled me. "You've got balls, brother," I mumbled.

"Not as big as yours, brother."

I tentatively reached out, laid my hand on the lobox's flank. It didn't move.

"I was about to tell you to throw me the rope, so that you wouldn't have to get too close. What the hell do you think you're doing? This thing and I are just getting to know each other."

"Oh, it looks to me like you've got the situation well in hand," Garth said casually. "With Mongo the Magnificent on its case, what chance did this poor, dumb beast ever really have? I just wanted to get a close-up view of the fruits of your labors."

"Yeah, well, I don't want you to get lazy on me now. I still need you to bring me a rope."

"Why? There's no need to tie it up."

"I don't plan to tie it up. The rope is to use as a leash."

"I'll be right back," Garth said, and started walking toward the silo.

As Garth, with Mabel patting him on the back with her trunk, disappeared inside the silo, Harper suddenly cried out in alarm.

"Robby, there's somebody coming! It looks like one of those big circus trucks!"

CHAPTER TWELVE

It turned out to be one of the huge circus semis. It took it a while to wend its way through the grain elevator complex, but it certainly wasn't difficult to follow Mabel's and the lobox's tracks in the dirt and dust to the triple silo site. The semi came around a building, turned toward us, and then made another tight turn, finally coming to a stop seventy-five yards away with a squeal and hiss of air brakes. I was surprised to see the semi; I had expected cars or jeeps, with perhaps a spotter plane leading the way, and a small army of men with guns.

The door of the dusty cab opened, and Luther, dressed in brown leather pants and boots, and a leather jacket with long fringes, got out. He looked like Buffalo Bill with a shaved head, and he appeared to be alone—which was my second surprise. I had hoped to bluff my potential killers into simply taking me captive, but Luther didn't look in the mood to take prisoners. There was an air of desperation about him. He was wearing his Magnum in a holster strapped to his side, and he carried a Smith & Wesson 30-06 pump action rifle with a ten-round clip. He'd obviously come loaded for elephant as well as dwarf.

Luther slowly walked toward me, then stopped when he was about twenty yards away from where I sat perched cross-legged on top of Mabel's head, in front of the open double doors to the silo. He glanced to his right, toward the lobox, which was back lying on its patch of grass perhaps fifteen yards away, with its red tongue lolling out between its saber teeth, looking thoroughly inscrutable. Having no reason not to believe that the lobox was still patiently waiting for a chance to tear me up into bite-size morsels, Luther simply rested his hand on the holstered Magnum, but did not draw it. Then he turned his attention back to me.

"I wish I had agreed to sell you the circus, Frederickson," he said evenly.

I reached out and scratched Mabel's head. "You and me both, Luther. If you had, Nate Button would still be alive."

"As would my father. Being crushed under the feet of an elephant is not a pleasant way to die."

"If you and your father hadn't decided to field-test your assassination weapon on humans, a number of people would still be alive. Being torn apart by one of these fellows you people brought back from extinction can't be any picnic either."

The animal trainer nodded slightly. "We stayed too long. I had argued for some time that the animal had been sufficiently tested. My father wanted more."

"You're not only a murderer, Luther, but you're full of shit. Are you going to blame it on your father? For Christ's sake, how many people had to die before you'd proved to yourself that a lobox was a viable assassination weapon? I think you were just getting off on it, Luther. You were so proud of yourself that you just wanted to keep on playing with the toy you'd created. It must have given you an enormous sense of power. Maybe you were even amused by all the werewolf stories; you liked reading about your pets in the newspapers."

It was probably at least partially true, and he didn't like me saying it. "There were problems, Frederickson. You don't know the whole story. You don't understand."

"Poor you."

"You've jeopardized years of work and millions of dollars."

"Jeopardized? I'll be damn sorry if I haven't wiped it out—but

I think that's what's happened. I'm curious as to why you're so short-handed, Luther. Last night, back at the circus, you certainly had plenty of hired help. Or was it loaned? Those men were provided to you by the same people, government or private industry, who helped you set up in this country, weren't they? Where are they now? And what the hell are you doing traipsing all over the countryside in a truck that size?"

Luther glanced at the lobox, then back at the truck. "I have everything I need," he said in a somewhat cryptic tone that was barely audible.

So he *was* alone, I thought. On his own. I pondered what could have happened, then thought I had come up with the answer. "It was my last performance that did it. Right, Luther? That, and the death of your father. There was no way the local and state authorities could fail to hear about that; there were too many citizens. The cops' phones must have been ringing off the hooks. The people sponsoring you knew there were going to be too many questions, too much heat. They knew the game was up, and they closed you down, didn't they? They didn't care about you, or the lobox, or anything else except making sure they covered their tracks. They expected you to leave the country with all the rest of the performers, but you obviously had your own notions. You thought that if you could get this missing lobox, and kill the three of us, then everything might still work out. It won't. You've lost your sponsors, Luther, and at the moment I'll bet they're a hell of a lot more worried about *you* being a loose cannon than they are about me. *You're* lucky you're still alive."

"You're not exactly in a position to gloat, Frederickson."

"I'm not gloating," I replied, noting that he had virtually confirmed my speculation. "I'm just telling you the facts of life, as interpreted by me. I'm stating the obvious. So, why did you bring the semi? Couldn't you find anything smaller?"

He didn't answer—and then I knew. I felt a chill, and I swallowed hard. My mouth had suddenly gone dry. "You've got the entire lobox breeding stock in there, haven't you? Christ, you still think there's a chance you can get them all back to Switzerland, keep breeding them, start selling them."

"I believe you're sitting on my property."

"What a startling change of subject, Luther. Why don't you come up here and join me, and we'll talk about it."

It had been the wrong thing to say. He abruptly snapped the Smith & Wesson's bolt into place, put his finger on the trigger. "I won't challenge Mabel's loyalty to you, Frederickson. You know how I feel about animals, but I am prepared to kill her if you try to get her to move against me."

"I have no doubt of it. Relax, Luther. As you can see, Mabel and I are just kind of hanging out here, waiting for somebody to come around so I could surrender. However, now that the situation becomes clearer, I'm thinking that maybe you should surrender to me."

"Don't be absurd, Frederickson. Why are you still here?"

"I just told you. That fanged fiend over there makes it imperative that I stay where I am, and it's tough being on the run when you have to run around on an elephant. You should try it."

"Where are your brother and your girlfriend?"

"Garth and Harper? Oh, they split."

"Split?"

"They left. *Vamoose*. *Adiós*. Who wants to hang around this dreary place? Besides, they don't like elephants as much as I do."

"I don't believe they'd leave you."

"They didn't *leave* me, Luther; they went for help. As soon as we figured out just how single-minded a lobox is—in this case, single-minded about getting me—they split. Hell, there was no sense in all of us waiting around here for you or your people to come and get us. By now, they're probably sitting comfortably in some state police office telling their story."

"I don't think I believe you," Luther said after a long pause.

"You believe what you want, pal. The fact of the matter is that there are only us chickens here now, but that won't be the case for very long. Help is on the way—help for me, that is. Authorities your people don't control will know the story by now. Killing me won't do you any good, unless it will make you feel better. The best deal you can make is to put that lobox down there in the truck and then turn your guns over to me. You're a potential embarrassment to some very powerful people in this country, and you're probably in a hell of a lot of trouble for detouring from your established escape route. I know people who can guarantee your safety. You'll go to prison, sure, but prison is better than dead. You can spend your time trying to tame some of our wilder inmates."

Luther wasn't amused. He stared at me. He continued to stare for some time, then abruptly spun around and walked quickly back to the truck. He went to the right side of the semi, where there were three sets of double doors. He opened the middle doors and quickly stepped back. Two loboxes—females that were smaller than the males by almost a half, grayer in color, and lacking the distinctive black markings on their backs—jumped from the truck to the ground and streaked toward the open doors behind Mabel and me. They disappeared inside the first silo without so much as a glance at the male lobox, or me.

"Your brother and the woman don't appear to have gotten as far as you thought," Luther said as he walked back toward Mabel and looked up at me. His glacial blue eyes glinted in the bright sunlight.

There was no sound from inside the silo, and I imagined the two loboxes crouched somewhere in the semidarkness, lying in wait for their prey.

"Tough luck, Luther," I said, glancing behind me toward the silo, then looking back at Luther. "Garth and Harper *were* in there; we all were. But they took off out a door at the back of the third silo while I sat out here to make sure this lobox remained preoccupied with me. Those two females are on an old scent."

"We'll see," Luther said. His voice was even, but he looked slightly uncertain.

"Why are you running females now, Luther?" I asked, watching him carefully. "And they look to be pretty puny females at that—maybe lobox-wolf hybrids. Considering all the years you and your father have spent breeding these things, I'd have thought you had a sufficient supply of males, but I guess not. Reverse breeding with a wolf and a kuvasz to get a lobox must be even more difficult than I thought. It looks to me like you're running low on stock."

Luther said nothing, but the muscles in his jaw and face tightened revealingly. I wondered just how many loboxes were in the truck, and why he would run females after Garth and Harper now. Harper had killed one male . . .

I wondered if the lobox crouching on the ground could be the only adult male Luther had left.

Finally, Luther said, "If your brother and the woman are in the silo, and I believe they are, the females will be sufficient to find and kill them."

Not unless Luther had trained them to climb vertical steel ladders. "I told you they're gone, and the authorities are probably on their way here now. Maybe that's your good fortune, considering the other people who may be after you. After you've thought about it a while longer, you'll see that it's in your best interests to surrender to me. In the meantime, let's talk about that whole story you said I didn't know. Maybe it will explain why you stuck around so long, and why so many innocent people had to die. There's something wrong with the lobox breeding program, isn't there? Tell me how you and your father failed—"

"My father didn't fail!" Luther snapped, and his blue eyes glinted with anger. "The flaw was within the species, not with my father! The same thing happened to the lobox as is happening now with the cheetah! Their gene pool became too limited! The DNA of each lobox is virtually the same! You have birth defects! They are largely . . ."

His voice trailed off, but I finished for him. "Sterile," I said. "Maybe that's why they became extinct."

"The problem can be corrected, with enough time. I must produce more hybrids in order to—"

"It's over, Luther. You've run out of time. Garth and Harper are gone, and the story is out. Even if you do kill me, you'll never make it out of the country. Although it may not look like it at the moment, I'm in a position to help you. Let's talk about how we can get you and your stock to people who will protect you. How about it?"

Luther took the Magnum from his holster. "Get down, Frederickson."

I glanced over at the lobox. "Thanks, but I'd prefer to stay where I am."

Luther raised the Magnum and pointed it at me. "I think you'd better come down anyway. I don't believe your brother and Miss Rhys-Whitney left you. They're somewhere in the silos, and the loboxes will eventually get to them. Nobody is coming to help you, but my sponsors will again agree to help me when they find out I still have the means to develop what they're looking for."

"If I come down, your pet will tear me apart."

"If you don't come down, I will shoot you."

"I wonder. It seems important for you to keep up appearances. If you wanted to shoot me, I'd be on the ground right now with a bullet in my head. You'd like the police to keep speculating about 'werewolf killings,' and if I'm found with a bullet in me, people may start to wonder why a werewolf would carry a Magnum. If that's what you've got in mind, forget it. It's all unraveled, Luther, and there's no way you're going to weave it together again. If you're going to shoot me, shoot me; neatness just doesn't count anymore."

Luther reholstered the Magnum, gripped the Smith & Wesson with both hands, swung the barrel around. "I would hate to kill Mabel, Frederickson, but I certainly will if that's what it takes to get you down on the ground. You'll have to decide whether it's worth sacrificing this magnificent animal's life just so that you may enjoy, at most, a few more seconds of your own."

Crunch time.

Luther, of course, had no way of knowing what had been going on between his last, presumably virile male lobox and me—but then, I had no way of knowing if the lobox's previous submission to me was going to make any difference now that his master, with his Magnum, was back in the picture. Now seemed as good a time as any to find out just what the creature would do.

I reached behind me for the *nunchaku* sticks lying on Mabel's back, draped them by their chain around my neck, abruptly stood up. Luther said nothing about them; if he knew what *nunchaku* sticks were, he obviously didn't consider them a threat. Considering his perception of the situation, which might very well be the correct one, I couldn't fault him.

Mabel, sensing that I wanted to get off, obediently curled her trunk upward. I stepped into the cradle of muscle and leathery hide, and Mabel slowly lowered me to the ground. I stepped off the trunk, then slowly turned and positioned myself so that Luther was on my left and the lobox on the right; man and beast were about twenty yards away from me, in opposite directions.

It wasn't taking Luther long to catch on to the fact that

something was wrong, for he was staring with intense curiosity at the lobox, which had raised its head but had not gotten to its feet. It was certainly not the reaction the animal trainer had expected.

Luther bent down and laid the Smith & Wesson on the ground—very slowly, obviously wary, keeping his eyes on the lobox. Then he straightened up, drew the Magnum from his holster, cocked it. The sound of the hammer clicking back seemed to me almost as loud as a gunshot.

"Kill!" he commanded.

Now the lobox sprang to its feet and stood stiff-legged, its hide quivering. But its ruff did not expand, and it did not move. It looked at me, lowered its head, and began to shake. This was one conflicted lobox.

I took the *nunchaku* sticks from around my neck, clicked them together.

Luther went pale, and his jaw dropped open slightly. He stared for a few moments at the reluctant lobox, then pulled the trigger of his gun, firing a bullet into the ground. Dirt kicked up at his feet, and the sound of the gunshot echoed in the surrounding forest of grain silos.

"Kill, damn you! Kill!"

The lobox's reaction was to spin around and race full bore around behind the silo.

There wasn't any moss growing on that lobox, I thought. In attempting to resolve its dilemma of choosing between dying from a bullet—and I no longer doubted that it could conceive of its own death—and killing, or at least attacking, its new "leader," the lobox had opted to simply depart the premises, at least for a while. I considered it an excellent choice, and I wished I could join it. Since I couldn't, I instead took advantage of Luther's momentary distraction to dart around behind the formidable shield of Mabel's left front leg. I doubted he was ready yet to kill Mabel; he would do that only as a last resort, or if she attacked him. First, I hoped, he would try to angle around to try to get a clear shot at me.

If he did that, and if he wandered too close to the silo, I would have the opportunity of seeing how much moss was growing on Garth.

However, Luther didn't seem to be in any hurry—for the moment, at least—to flush me out. He still seemed stunned by the lobox's behavior. For almost a minute he simply stood and stared at the corner of the silo where the creature had disappeared. Then he slowly turned toward where I was peering out from behind Mabel's leg.

"This is somehow your doing, Frederickson," he said in a low, tense voice, his Swiss-German accent suddenly more pronounced, giving his tone a guttural sound. "I can't conceive of how you managed it. You are a most remarkable man."

What I did next was dangerous, but I considered it worth the risk. Discovering that Luther had brought along two fresh loboxes primed for Garth and Harper had been a nasty surprise, but the unpleasantness had been tempered considerably by the fact that they had, of course, immediately run into a cul-de-sac in pursuit of their prey. I wanted to make sure they stayed put, and I took advantage of Luther's continuing dyspepsia and distraction to back up, and then move quickly over the five yards or so to the silo. I closed the double doors, secured them with the chain I had left hanging on one of the inside pegs, then scurried back behind my elephant barricade.

Luther hadn't moved. He didn't appear to have even noticed that I had temporarily exposed myself to his gun—or he didn't care.

"Flattery will get you nowhere, Luther. Are you ready to surrender?"

"How did you do it, Frederickson? How is it possible?"

"Throw your guns over here and back away, and I'll tell you all about it. Obviously, I know things about loboxes you don't. Give it up."

"I can't, Frederickson," he said in an odd—almost plaintive—tone of voice. "I couldn't . . . survive in prison. I'm only happy when I'm with animals. To spend the rest of my life caged like a beast myself . . . no. I would much prefer to die."

I believed him, but it didn't answer the question of why he hadn't yet made any attempt to move on me. I was resigned to the fact that he would eventually shoot Mabel, thinking that would be the end of it for me too; but if he did, he would soon find out just how formidable an obstacle the corpse of an African elephant can be. He was going to have to stalk a dwarf over and around a mountain of tons of dead flesh. I had no doubt that I was quicker than he was; if he made just one mistake, and he would, he was going to find out how quick I was and how deadly a pair of *nunchaku* sticks can be.

"Hey, Luther," I said quietly. "Was I right before, about most of the loboxes being sterile? Is that lobox that ran off the last male you have?"

At first I didn't think he was going to respond. Then, after some time, he slowly nodded. "The only one that is so close to a full-blooded lobox—the actual, separate breed. It would take many breeding generations to produce another like him."

"Too bad. I guess that one animal is even more valuable than I thought."

Luther apparently didn't feel like chatting any longer, for he abruptly wheeled around and stalked back to the semi. I didn't like the feel of the the situation, and I liked it even less when he stopped next to the tractor-trailer, yanked a second set of double doors open, and quickly stepped back.

Even before the grayish-brown shape shot from the opening, hit the ground, and came sprinting toward me, I guessed why Luther had been in no hurry to play hide-and-seek with me between and around Mabel's massive legs. He'd hedged his bets with me, as well as with Garth and Harper, and before setting out had primed another lobox to kill me.

The small female was covering the ground between us in great bounds, and I had only milliseconds to make a decision: try to keep dodging around behind Mabel's leg, where freedom to swing my *nunchakus* was severely limited and I could only poke at it, or move away and try to kill it with a lucky hit before it opened my arteries with its teeth or claws.

As Mabel lifted her trunk and trumpeted, I sprang away from her great bulk, crouched down in the lobox's path, and began to swing the sticks.

I knew I was in trouble. With the male, as big as it was, I'd had time to work on its mind, to hurt it, to at least make it hesitate in its dealings with me. The female coming at me, although smaller, was even more deadly. To her, I was just a piece of meat to be torn apart, and nothing short of a crippling blow to break one of her legs, or a killing blow to her head, was going to stop her; she might be able to make any number of passes at me, but if I failed just once to steer clear of her fangs and claws, I was dead.

I was awash in an ocean of sound as Mabel continued to trumpet her distress, stomp her feet, and move her great bulk dangerously close to me. The lobox was still fifteen yards away when it suddenly screamed and prepared to spring. I whipped my sticks around and was just about to jump to my left when an enormous, tawny shape flew past my head, so close to my right ear that I could feel the wind of its passing against my cheek.

The male collided with the female in midair, virtually in front of my face. The male's weight straightened the female up, knocked her backward. When they landed, he was on top of her, growling, his fangs poised over her throat, one hind leg raised, extended claws hovering over her exposed belly.

The female's reaction was instantaneous. She immediately arched her head back, exposing her throat, and all four of her legs were raised, stiff, in the air.

Submission.

It was all over in a matter of seconds. The male accepted the female's submission, backed off her as it growled and bared its fangs. I turned around and ran back to Mabel, who had quieted down somewhat, and again took up my refuge behind her left front leg. When I looked back, I was alarmed to see Luther taking aim with his Smith & Wesson at the male lobox. The male cringed, flattening its ears against its head, and turned away—but stood its ground, certainly knowing that it now faced its own death.

"Shoot it and the lobox becomes extinct again!" I shouted, wondering why I seemed to care so much. "That's your last fertile male! Kill it, and everything you and your father have done will be for nothing!"

Luther hesitated, then swung the 30-06 in my direction. His face had gone white. "You interfering little bastard! You've ruined everything! I'll see you dead!"

He set the rifle on the ground, drew the Magnum. Holding it with both hands, he moved toward Mabel, who moved back a step, almost knocking me off balance. Luther then began to circle to his right in an effort to get a shot at me. It was precisely what I'd been hoping for, because his route took him close to the silo. Garth and Harper were ready. As Luther moved beneath the vent, they cast the rope and burlap net we had constructed to trap the lobox. The net floated down through the air, fell over Luther's head and shoulders.

Luther clawed at the net with the barrel of the Magnum and his free hand, but I was already sprinting toward him, *nunchaku* sticks swinging.

The female lobox beat me to him. Primed to kill, her bloodlust fanned by her failure to kill me, frustrated by the male's dominance, she now sensed her master's helplessness, and her instinct told her to kill. Unrestrained now by the male, she leaped at the hapless figure struggling in the netting; her jaws were open, her hind legs curled up beneath her, claws extended to disembowel. Luther's scream was cut off, abbreviated by death, as the creature's jaws closed over his throat and the claws tore into him, opening him up, spilling the contents of his stomach onto the ground.

Above me, Harper screamed at the sight of the female lobox shoving her maw into Luther's body, tearing at his flesh. I certainly no longer cared to go in that direction, and I came to a screeching halt. The Magnum had fallen next to Luther's body, and I wasn't going to contest the lobox for it; I retreated, slung the *nunchaku* sticks around my neck, stooped down and picked up the Smith & Wesson off the ground. I smacked the clip to make sure it was in place, then swung the rifle around and leveled it on the female. My finger tightened on the trigger, but I didn't fire.

Although I was clearly aiming at the female, who had stopped chomping on Luther and was now standing stiff-legged and staring at me, the male lobox was also reacting strongly to the sight of me with a gun in my hands. There was a look in its eyes that was almost—accusatory. In fact, I didn't really want to kill the female—and I wondered what would happen to my relationship with the male if I did.

Animals aren't people, I reminded myself. Indeed, people were probably the lobox's natural prey, which made it the most dangerous creature—next to people—on the face of the planet.

The female was primed to kill *me*, and I couldn't afford to play games with her. And yet . . .

"Shoot them, Robby!" Harper called in a high-pitched voice laced with tension and fear. "Shoot them both while you can! Don't take any chances!"

What the hell, I thought as I slowly lowered the heavy rifle and backed away, keeping my gaze on the female, my main concern. In for a penny, in for a pound. Killing things was easy. Although the female was a hybrid, there was no telling how many generations of wolf-kuvasz breeding she represented. She too was a precious thing on a world that was exterminating species of living things at the rate of hundreds a year.

I kept backing away, moving toward the truck. When I was fifty yards away, I rested the rifle in the crook of my left arm, took my *nunchaku* sticks from around my neck.

The female started to move toward me, but the male immediately blocked her way, bared its fangs, and growled.

"That's good," I said evenly, talking directly to the male, struggling to keep my voice steady. I slowly bent down, laid aside the Smith & Wesson. "If you want your girlfriend to live, you're going to need all your smarts, and then some. It's up to you."

"Hey, Mongo!" Garth called. "What the hell do you think you're doing? Stop farting around! Pick up the fucking gun and shoot them!"

I clicked the *nunchaku* sticks together, and the male's ears pricked up. I signaled with the sticks, pointing them toward the open doors at the rear of the truck.

"Here," I continued, rapping the side of one of the open doors with a stick. "Pay attention. If you want her to live, put her in here."

I rapped the door again, harder, then moved away from the truck.

It wasn't until I was better than ten yards away that I realized I had neglected to bring the rifle along with me. This did not escape the female's attention. She had no reason whatsoever to fear me or the *nunchaku* sticks, and she abruptly leaped forward to attack. I crouched and readied my sticks, but it wasn't necessary. The male surged forward, easily overtook her, headed her off. She veered off and spun around, snarled, and he bit her hard on the left flank. She screamed in pain, her bloodlust instantly dampened, then immediately tried to stand on her head before rolling over and adopting the now-familiar posture of a submitting lobox. The male nudged her from behind, got her to her feet, and started moving her forward, gently nipping her from behind—heading her toward the truck, almost as if he had understood my every word. She veered away; he again headed her off, turned her around, headed her toward the truck.

I draped my sticks around my neck and watched in amazement as the male, working the female as if he were a champion sheepdog, kept herding her toward the semi. He kept at it, nipping her first on one flank and then the other, moving her closer and closer. One last good nip on the hindquarters sent her hurtling through the air, through the open doors, into her cage in the truck.

I sprinted to the truck, virtually shoving the huge male out of my way, and slammed the doors shut, locked them in place. Gasping for breath, winded as much from tension as from physical exertion, I scowled at the creature whose face was now only inches from mine.

"Sit."

It sat. Then, without really giving a lot of thought to what I was doing, I reached out and patted it on the head, then began to scratch it under its chin.

"Good b—"

The lobox's reaction was instantaneous. It uttered a sound from somewhere deep in its chest, something between a bark and a growl, then abruptly surged forward, butting me in the chest with its head and knocking me down onto my back. It was instantly on me, its huge forelegs straddling my shoulders, its barrel chest bearing down on my chest and pinning me helplessly to the ground. Its golden eyes stared into mine, and I tensed, waiting for the surge of a clawed hind foot that would tear away the lower half of my body, or the snap of jaws that would remove my face and throat.

It made a soft growling sound, then proceeded to lick my face with a long, red washcloth of a tongue that was at once slimy and rough, like a cow's.

I had offered it a sign of affection, and now the damn thing wanted to play.

Well, this just wasn't the time for the leader of the pack to play, but the problem was finding a way of communicating this fact to the huge creature that was pressing down on my chest.

The first trick was to pull my right arm free from where it was pinned next to my body by one of the lobox's legs. My *nunchaku* sticks were within reach, but I didn't want to hurt the animal now—just get its attention, get it off me, and then get it to do the next thing I wanted it to do. I made what I hoped was an appropriately menacing growling noise, then whacked it across its wide, wet muzzle with the flat of my hand.

"Get the fuck off me!" I snapped, and whacked it again. "Work now, play later."

The lobox whined, then backed off me and stood at my feet with its head bowed, looking amazingly reproached.

I stood up, wiped saliva off my face, then picked up the *nunchaku* sticks and clicked them together. "School's not out yet, pal. Pay attention."

At once, the animal raised its head, pricked up its ears. I walked over to the open doors in the center of the side of the truck. I beat a tattoo on the inside of one with my sticks, then started walking toward the silo. The lobox dutifully trotted along beside me, its tongue lolling out. We reached the silo and I looked up at the vent, where Garth and Harper were standing at the edge, staring down at me. Garth was grinning and shaking his head as if in disbelief. He gave me a thumbs-up sign, which I returned. Then I loosened the chain holding the doors shut, pushed one open slightly, motioned the lobox in.

From inside the silo came a cacophony of sound—barks, yelps, roars, lobox screams, and generalized bustling about. About a minute later the two females came scampering out of the silo, virtually under the startled Mabel's trunk, with the male right on their heels. There was much chasing around, with the male doing his sheepdog number, nipping at the females' flanks, and once the three of them disappeared around the other end of the silo. But then they were back, with the male herding them. I walked back to the truck, waited. It took the male another five minutes but he finally managed to get them both to leap, almost simultaneously, into the truck. I grunted with satisfaction, slammed the doors shut behind them.

"Now sit," I said to the lobox, pointing with a stick toward its flank. It sat. I unhesitatingly put my hand on its head, scratched it behind the ears. "The Road Runner's very proud of you, Coyote."

I looked up in time to see Garth and Harper emerge from the silo. Garth, ambling along with his hands in his pockets, was still grinning and shaking his head. Harper broke into a run. She came up to me, brushing right past the sitting lobox, threw her arms around my neck, and hugged me.

"Robby," she breathed in her huskiest, sexiest voice, "that's the most incredible thing I've ever seen. I *love* you!"

"Not too trashy a show, Mongo," Garth said to me as he came up and laid his thick right arm across my shoulder. "I'd have actually paid to see that."

"Thanks, brother. I realize that's your highest compliment."

Garth grunted. "That truck has a CB antenna, so it must have a radio. Let me see if I can't rustle up some help."

I said, "Tell whoever you get hold of to bring food. I don't know about you people, but I'm hungry."

Garth climbed up into the cab of the truck, closed the door. Harper and I simply held each other, gazed into each other's eyes, and I knew I was most definitely, hopelessly, in love.

"Help's on the way," Garth announced, climbing back down from the cab. "And food. Heroes and coffee for us, a hundred pounds of horsemeat and a ton of hay for our entourage."

I nodded. "That sounds like about the right take-out order to me."

"I charged it all to your personal Amex card, brother," Garth said with a grin.

"Thanks a lot, Garth. What's the going rate for horsemeat and hay?"

"Beats me. I expect it's the handling and transportation charges that are going to be expensive. I thought it would be a good lesson to you. Just because you keep getting yourself involved in strange business like this, there's no reason why the company should have to pay for it. This way, it will save us the trouble of trying to explain expenses for hay and horsemeat to our accountants and the IRS."

"Oh, yeah. Good thinking, Garth."

Harper nodded toward Mabel, who was off to one side of the silo nuzzling her trunk in a patch of grass, then placed her hand next to mine on the lobox's head. "Now we really need a circus."

Garth said, "I don't think it's going to be all that difficult to find one for sale."

EPILOGUE

Ah, yes. The usual congressional committees had announced the usual hearings, and they were all planning to round up and grill the usual suspect: the CIA. The thinking was that this time that venerable agency, indomitable defender of individual liberties, might even have been collaborating with the KGB—or some Eastern bloc country whose leaders were now more worried about insane mullahs, renegade Arabs, and Israelis than they were about the traditional ideological conflicts of East versus West. Such were the fruits of *glasnost* and *perestroika,* as harvested by the ever-fumbling intelligence communities. Three committee chairmen had even had the remarkable good sense to inquire about the possibility of having Frederickson and Frederickson assist in their investigation. Garth and I had told them we'd think about it. Personally, I didn't think they were going to get very far.

"I always said you had a mystical way with animals," Harper said as she wrapped her arms around my waist and kissed my neck—to the hearty applause of the huge crowd jammed inside the Big Top of the Statler Brothers Circus.

I flushed, thoroughly embarrassed, and raised my arms to

acknowledge the cheers of the crowd—as if being kissed on the neck by a beautiful woman while riding on the back of a monstrous elephant was an astonishing trick.

"There was nothing mystical about it, my dear," I replied, leaning back slightly so that she could hear me above the roar of the crowd. "Loboxes are smart. They learn quickly. But they aren't people; they interpret things in an animal way. I've explained it all to you. Their first attack on us was a failure—"

"Thanks to you," Harper said, and I felt her shudder. "If you hadn't pulled me back, it would only have been half a failure."

"Whatever. It couldn't get us, I shot it, you killed his buddy, I challenged him for territory, and then made it stick by whacking him around. Also, it could see that I controlled Mabel, an animal that was much bigger and more powerful than he was. He probably also thought I controlled you, which is a howler. Anyway, lobox logic dictated that it should stop screwing around with me. That was all there was to it."

Harper giggled. "Then it certainly doesn't appreciate the full range of your many talents. I love to screw around with you."

"Harper, this isn't the time or place to talk dirty."

"Like I said, Robby," Harper persisted in her husky voice, "you have a mystical way with animals. And it's not only with Mabel and Coyote. You make me feel like an animal . . . and there's no question that you put me in heat."

"Now you've done it. You've given me a hard-on in front of a few thousand people."

"I'll tend to it later."

Mabel had reached the enlarged VIP box and was going into one of her patented, dainty pachyderm pirouettes. Below us, the occupants of the box cheered, grinned, and clapped wildly. Phil Statler, stockholder and managing director for life of the circus that once again bore his name, looked at least fifteen years younger than when I had seen him lying close to death in Bellevue Medical Center. Garth and Mary sat on either side of him, and in the rows behind them sat the dozen or so freaks who, with Garth, Harper, and me, were also shareholders in the circus. Everyone looked most pleased on the occasion of this, the grand reopening of Statler Brothers Circus.

And well they might. There had originally been a matinee and an evening performance scheduled for the opening day. Then the state troopers had called at eleven o'clock in the morning to tell us the roads were jammed with cars and that people were coming from all over the region to see us. Phil had hastily scheduled an extra late afternoon performance and was even thinking about adding a midnight show to accommodate the tens of thousands of people parked in cars, vans, and campers all over the local county fairgrounds.

Garth had been promised that he could ride the elephant in the midnight show.

But, of course, it wasn't the elephant, or the circus, the people were coming to see. They were coming to see the "werewolf"— or, as Phil's ads put it, the EIGHTH WONDER OF THE WORLD, BROUGHT BACK THROUGH THE CLOUDY MISTS OF PREHISTORIC TIME BY MAD SCIENTISTS.

Now, *that* was a draw. Already, the big indoor arenas from coast to coast, and in Europe, were offering exorbitant financial guarantees if the Statler Brothers Circus, with its strange creature, could be booked sometime before the close of the century. Everyone, it seemed, wanted to see a lobox.

For a time there had been considerable pressure from some quarters, understandably, to kill Coyote—the name Harper and I had decided on for the lobox, for no other reason than the fact that it made us smile—and all the female hybrids and younger breeding stock, to destroy them all as killers and menaces, but cooler heads had prevailed. It had been patiently pointed out that a lobox could not be held responsible for its natural instincts, any more than a leopard, tiger, or other wild beast. The evil existed in the men who had exploited those instincts to murder other men. Loboxes were killers, yes, but they weren't murderers. In any case, there was a very real chance that the lobox would once again become extinct if Coyote died before a solution could be found to the genetic problem that had doomed it to extinction in the first place. Somehow, Coyote had to keep making babies with the hybrids, and a way had to be found to diversify the gene pool of the offspring.

When it was decided that the creatures would not be destroyed, and when no individual, organization, or corporation had rushed forward to claim rights to the lobox, ownership to Coyote and the animals in the van had gone by default to the Statler Brothers Circus, through me, and it was further decided—at my insistence—that I would be "nature conservator" on behalf of the animals. I'd arranged for them to spend the off-season, half a year, in a special compound in the Bronx Zoo—named, again at my insistence, the Nate Button Crypto-zoological Research Center—where experimenters would study them and work to keep the species alive. There was speculation that loboxes, properly trained, could become the greatest "Seeing Eye dogs" ever, and much talk about all the other uses the animal could be put to.

I didn't much care, as long as the military—ours or anyone else's—didn't get hold of them. Or the CIA. Or anyone else who would use them to kill.

"We're going to be married, of course, aren't we, Robby?"

Suddenly I felt light-headed, short of breath. "Say what?"

"You heard me. I just offered you a proposal of marriage."

"No, Harper, we're not going to be married."

"I'm serious, Robby. I love you, and I know you love me."

"I certainly do love you, Harper," I said, glancing around me at all the thousands of pairs of eyes following our progress. "But I can't marry you."

"Why not?"

"Wild things should stay wild."

"Are you talking about you or me?"

Suddenly I felt a lump in my throat. Not trusting myself to speak, I simply shook my head. I was, I realized, very happy—even if I couldn't marry Harper. She loved me, and I considered that a great gift.

Then Harper's arms tightened even more around my waist, and I could feel her lips against my right ear. She continued, "It's because you're a dwarf, isn't it?"

"Maybe," I said tightly, after a long pause.

"Oh, really, Robby," she said in an exasperated tone. "With all the remarkable things you've accomplished in your life, don't you think it's past time you stopped worrying about being a dwarf?"

"But I am a dwarf, Harper. It's not something you grow out of, if you'll pardon the expression."

"It's not what I meant, and you know it."

Suddenly I recalled the innumerable times Garth had joked—half seriously—about my constant need to overcompensate. He was right, of course. Certainly, if Robert Frederickson had not been born a dwarf, he would never have become Mongo the Magnificent. And the chances are that he would never have become a Ph.D. criminologist and college professor, earned a black belt in karate, or become a private investigator. Still, loving and being loved by a woman like Harper Rhys-Whitney in marriage was not an adventure I was ready for. I did not have the courage for that kind of undertaking and wondered if I ever would. But I did have the courage to give Harper—and myself—honesty.

"I'm afraid of you, Harper," I said evenly. "I'm more afraid of you than I ever was of Coyote and the other loboxes. A lobox might take my life, but you could take my soul. You wouldn't mean to, but it could happen. It would be something I might do to myself through insecurity and self-doubt. Precisely because you are so beautiful and so desirable, and because I love you so very much, I'm afraid of marrying you. It would make me even more vulnerable than I am. If I marry you, the first thought I'll have every morning when I wake up is that I'm a dwarf. I just don't have the courage it takes to *accept* love, Harper, and maybe I never will."

I thought—maybe hoped—she would argue with me. Instead, she squeezed me hard, said, "I think I understand."

"Thank you."

"Do you think that someday you might have the courage and good sense to make me happy by marrying me?"

"Maybe someday," I said carefully.

"So maybe I'll just hang around and wait. Hell, it's not much of a commute between Florida and New York, especially when you have your own plane, and I like the city almost as much as you do. Do you think you can handle it if we spend a lot of time together?"

I swallowed hard, managed to say, "That would . . . be just fine with me, Harper."

"Good," she said. Then she pulled my head back, leaned over my shoulder, and kissed me hard on the mouth. Mabel pivoted, and the crowd roared.